The Highlande Secret Princess

CW00523621

Loved by a Highlander
Book 1

by Debra Chapoton

ISBN: 9798376548691
Imprint: Independently published

Books by Debra Chapoton

The Highlander's Secret Princess
The Highlander's English Maiden
The Highlander's Hidden Castle
The Highlander's Heart of Stone
The Highlander's Forbidden Love

Christian Fiction:
Love Contained
Sheltered
The Guardian's Diary
Exodia
Out of Exodia
Spell of the Shadow Dragon
Curse of the Winter Dragon
 Second Chance Teacher Romance series:
  Aaron After School
  Sonia's Secret Someone
  Melanie's Match
  School's Out
  Summer School
  The Spanish Tutor
  A Novel Thing
 Unbridled Hearts clean sweet cowboy romance:
  Tangled in Fate's Reins
  Rodeo Romance
  A Cowboy's Promise
  Heartstrings and Horseshoes
  Kisses at Sundown
  Montana Heaven
  Montana Moments
  Tamed Heart
  Wrangler's Embrace
  Moonlight and Spurs
  Whispers on the Range

Young Adult Novels:
A Soul's Kiss
Edge of Escape
Exodia
Out of Exodia
Here Without A Trace
Sheltered
Spell of the Shadow Dragon

Curse of the Winter Dragon
The Girl in the Time Machine
The Guardian's Diary
The Time Bender
The Time Ender
The Time Pacer
The Time Stopper
To Die Upon a Kiss
A Fault of Graves

Children's Books:
The Secret in the Hidden Cave
Mystery's Grave
Bullies and Bears
A Tick in Time
Bigfoot Day, Ninja Night
Nick Bazebahl and Forbidden Tunnels
Nick Bazebahl and the Cartoon Tunnels
Nick Bazebahl and the Fake Witch Tunnels
Nick Bazebahl and the Mining Tunnels
Nick Bazebahl and the Red Tunnels
Nick Bazebahl and the Wormhole Tunnels
Inspirational Bible Verse Coloring Book
ABC Learn to Read Coloring Book
ABC Learn to Read Spanish Coloring Book
Stained Glass Window Coloring Book
Naughty Cat Dotted Grid Notebook
Cute Puppy Graph Paper Notebook
Easy Sudoku for Kids
101 Mandalas Coloring Book
150 Mandalas Coloring Book
Grandma's 5-Minute Bedtime Stories

Non-Fiction:
Brain Power Puzzles (11 volumes)
Building a Log Home in Under a Year
200 Creative Writing Prompts
400 Creative Writing Prompts
Advanced Creative Writing Prompts
Beyond Creative Writing Prompts
300 Plus Teacher Hacks and Tips
How to Blend Families
How to Help Your Child Succeed in School
How to Teach a Foreign Language

Christian Non-fiction:
Guided Prayer Journal for Women
Crossing the Scriptures
35 Lessons from the Book of Psalms
Prayer Journal and Bible Study
Teens in the Bible
Moms in the Bible
Animals in the Bible
Old Testament Lessons in the Bible
New Testament Lessons in the Bible

Chapter 1

E LEANOR LIFTED HER long skirt and moved the toe of her
brand-new boot toward the steaming manure. And giggled.
"El! Don't you dare," her companion called after her.

Eleanor smiled slyly at the young maid, her best and only friend,
Hannah, who'd been her constant shadow for as long as she could
remember. "Lady Beth will have these thrown away if they stink and I
want her to throw them away. They hurt my feet. I wish I could wear
my old ones." She crinkled her nose. "And the boy's clothes, too. I hate
dresses."

Hannah nodded in agreement. "Yes, it was easier pretending to be
boys than ladies. We fought like the Chaddertons and got as dirty as the
Miller twins."

"I know." Eleanor held her toe over the fresh horse dropping a
moment more, "I wonder what those boys would think of us now if they
could see how we've changed." She stepped back without soiling her
slipper, let her skirts sway, and sighed. "I don't much like learning to
sew and paint and play that horrible pianoforte, but I don't want to be
an insignificant servant with a meaningless life either." She caught the
look on Hannah's face and was instantly sorry she made that comment.

Eleanor, since she was a little girl, had been allowed to run free,
dressed in a stable boy's uniform of baggy but belted pants and a coarse-
woven shirt that billowed when she cantered through the meadows,
risking another beating for a moment's freedom. Her upbringing at
Ingledew castle had been secretive. Lady Beth had kept her existence

1

hidden from all who called at Ingledew by disguising Eleanor as a boy. It was easy when she was little, but as she changed into a young woman, she'd had to layer vestments to hide her bosom. Hannah, too, had been trained to disappear with Eleanor, whom she'd had to call El and never Eleanor. The sounds of visitors' carriages and the clip-clop of hooves would send the pair into the stables or the forest or, if they were in the castle, down into the cellars. Hiding, always hiding. Fearing Lord Edgeworth's whip or the butler's cruel hand, and as always, the stablemaster's thrashings.

"I rather like the pianoforte," Hannah said. "And I like being called Hannah and not by my last name."

"Hannah Pascoe of Feock, Cornwall. You must never forget where you came from. I wish I had such memories. My mother is a vague wisp of a dream and Lady Beth won't tell me much. I don't know who I am."

"I've heard Cook call you the Hanover heir. Perhaps you're a cousin of King George's."

"More likely the unwanted child of a scoundrel." She waved a delicate hand in the air. "An embarrassment. And so I've been punished for my parents' sins. That would explain the cruelties, but why are they suddenly grooming us?"

They continued walking around the side of the stable. Eleanor changed the subject. "I do miss riding."

"Lady Beth said you could use her side-saddle." Hannah stroked the long braid she'd pinned on this morning. It would be several more months before either of them would have hair long enough to style in the latest fashion.

"Ew," Eleanor groaned when she noticed what Hannah was doing, "how can you touch that thing? Cameron cut it from his dead mother's head not six weeks ago."

"And lucky for us he did. Your aunt paid him a week's wages for it. Not a single grey hair." She fingered the end and brought it up to tickle her nose. "You're going to have to wear the other one tomorrow when we leave Ingledew. Oh, I'm so excited. To leave here at last. I can't imagine. Our lives have gone from mud to stardust."

Eleanor snorted her amusement at Hannah's glee as they entered the stable, the warm fustiness enveloping them in the scents of hay and mildew and horseflesh. "Those honey-blonde locks may work on you, but I need something darker. I have a plan." She withdrew from her skirt pocket a pair of shears with wide, looped handles. Hannah frowned and Eleanor explained, "Old Brownie won't miss half his tail."

At the sound of their voices several horses nickered.

2

"I'm more than a little sorry that we have to leave before May-Day Eve," Hannah sighed as she held Brownie's tail out.

"As am I." Eleanor clipped and clipped. "I shall miss the fires and our mischief night." She made a final cut and watched as Hannah smoothed the strands. "Though I don't suppose we'd have as much fun encumbered by these skirts."

"And we'd never catch the fairies."

Eleanor startled Brownie with her laugh. "You still believe in fairies?"

"Of course. And there will be plenty of them to dance with when we get to Scotland."

"Scotland? I thought …"

"Oh, El, I shouldn't have spoken. Lady Beth told me it would be a surprise, but she hinted of the Highlands."

"I … hmm. Well, she'll certainly tell us more tonight."

"Hasn't it been odd … how nice Lord Edgeworth is to us now?"

Eleanor bobbled her head in a noncommittal answer then tucked the shears back into her pocket. She leaned toward Hannah to sniff at the horse hairs. "We'll have to braid it and then soak it in rose water."

Outside there came the sound of hooves and squeaking carriage wheels, the shout of a driver, the whinny of a horse and here, beside the girls, the answering neigh of old Brownie.

"Oh, no. They can't have come to fetch us a day early, can they have?"

***

KEIR MCKELVEY CHUCKLED as his nephew, barely seven, struggled to lift the claymore.

"Aye," Keir said, his voice gentle yet resonant, "ye be too wee a lad to heft the *claidheamh mòr* me own great-grandfather swung in battle. 'Tis a great sword she is. To be handled with both hands." Under his breath he added, *but gently as ye'd touch a woman.*

The boy, Huey Beldorney, repeated the Gaelic words and copied the wide-legged stance his uncle modeled for him. He gripped the handle and hoisted the blade a few inches off the flat rock. Keir's shadow moved over him as he dropped the weighty metal. The clang of steel on stone echoed down the hill.

"Try the axe, will ye? 'Tis lighter."

Huey turned to the stump where the battle axe had been thrown. He grabbed the handle with both hands and tried to wiggle it free from the wood. No luck. For his second try he pressed his foot against the stump for leverage. When he at last succeeded, the force of his pull with the weight of the axe sent him falling on his backside. Keir's quick hand

3

swiped the weapon up and away from the boy's face before the blade could halve him.

His sister's maternal voice cut through the air from the cabin doorway. "Ye'll nay be teachin' me son yer tricks, Keir McKelvey. Ye'll have him killt of his own hand afore he's old enough to grow a whisker."

"The lad's got nary a scratch," Keir assured her. "He needs fatherin' and learnin' of such things. I'm happy to take it upon myself while his father is away." His grin, which made all the maidens in the nearby village gasp, had no effect on his sister.

She shook her head at him. "The fields need a plough and I'll thank ye to let that be yer favor to me husband." She waggled a finger at Huey. "Come inside, lad."

Keir glanced across the fields toward the mountains. A small green loch at their base reflected their majesty in the early morning light. Farming wasn't his first choice, but he was pleased with his work, and he'd do anything to help his sister. He'd planted the broad beans, peas, and cabbage for her last week. Now he'd do the kale and radish. His gaze fell to the untouched soil. The earth had the scent of spring, warming its outer layer.

This was the murkiest morning of the spring, though, but it promised to brighten and make him grow hot behind the plough. He sloughed off his shirt and tightened his kilt. He tilted the felt hat he wore so its feather leaned forward to provide a small degree of shade across a nose prone to burn. An hour later his chest glistened and his biceps rippled as he guided the heavy wooden implement through the soil. His thoughts were on the news he'd received, a letter from England, coded with double meanings. It hadn't taken him long to figure it out. King George was teetering on the brink of insanity. Again. Trouble was brewing. His secret connections to factions unnamed would send his sister into paroxysms of fear. *If* she found out. But she would never find out. She'd chosen this simpler life, without intrigue; her husband was a good man, equally as settled though he had some patriotic ambitions. As soon as he returned, Keir would have to leave for Castle Caladh.

He worked until the sun was high. Huey brought him water twice and once a hunk of cheese. Grateful Keir was for the relief it gave him.

"I've drawn ye a bath for yer efforts," his sister said when he finished. "And thank ye for all yer work. I've baked yer favorite pie so once ye've bathed, come inside."

Keir nodded and glanced toward the side of the stone hut where the barrel tub was steaming. His sister must have been boiling water and

4

lugging pots for an hour. Upon a rope strung between trees hung his second set of clothes, clean and dry.

"Thank ye, Fenella. Ye're a good sister." It was hard to look too long at her; like his other two sisters she resembled their mother, lightly freckled and fair of skin, red of hair.

This time she returned the grin before closing the door to give him a small measure of privacy. Bathing in the open air was something he'd done all his life, usually in the loch, but also in the pond at Castle Caladh though not so often in the cold weather. He scratched his fingers through the short beard that had grown during his stay here.

The birds chirped as he dunked himself into the small tub, water splashing over the side and onto flat stones. Keir remembered how he'd helped his brother-in-law lay those stones years ago so Fenella wouldn't be dismayed by mud. Thoughts like that made him think of how much he envied their marriage. Fenella, the oldest of his three sisters, had eschewed her dowry—much to his father's delight—and married for love. He longed to do the same. He could have chosen any girl or woman in Scotland, but none had stirred his soul. Yet.

He rose from the water and dried himself with his old shirt, then plunged it into the water and swirled it around a few times. Clean enough, he thought. He twisted and rung it out, stepped naked toward the rope line and hung it on the end. The evening air moved the sable brown hairs on his body. He shivered, quickly redressed, and slipped his feet back into his deerskins. His stomach rumbled; he was more than ready for that pie. Already his mouth was watering at the thought of minced mutton and onions and that double crust.

***

"ARE WE HAVING a banquet?" Eleanor asked the cook as she and Hannah entered the kitchen. There seemed to be a flurry of activity for this early in the afternoon. She gave the cook a warm hug and gestured to Hannah to hide the horse's tail in her apron pocket.

The tables were laden with copper pots and pewter plates. Two footmen and the scullery maid were shadowing the kitchen maid, holding trays. The aroma of roasting chickens flavored the air.

Cook finished draining some grease and responded, "A banquet indeed. And in your honor." She put a finger to her lips. "But you're not to know that. Captain Luxbury believes he's the one deserving of this honor. Lady Beth purchased his commission for him. He is indebted to the Lord and Lady of Ingledew and thus ..." she squinted at her helpers to determine their interest and lowered her voice further "... he will be your escort on your journey. You must be careful."

5

Eleanor swung her head toward Hannah and whispered, "Perhaps this is a test of our manners."

Hannah giggled in a falsetto voice. "I know a fork from a spade, m'lady, but conversing with a captain? These new servants undoubtedly know more than I. We will surely fail."

Eleanor entwined her arm with Hannah's and, in a volume to match the clatter of an empty tray slipping to the stone floor, said, "Come along, Hannah, we best get changed for dinner." She looked back at Cook, who knew all the castle's secrets including how recently these two women had transformed. The others, though, would have thought magic or the devil was involved in changing the pair into attractive young ladies, had they seen them before. There were whisperings, however, amongst these hires, that Eleanor and Hannah must be addled-brained heirs or ill-bred wards, for all the mistakes in manners they seemed to make. The gossip didn't bother them; they were just happy the stablemaster and the old butler were gone.

Hannah squeezed back Eleanor's grip as they climbed the dank steps upward to the main hall. "I shouldn't be here except as a maid. Lady Beth reminds me often of my good fortune in being placed as your companion. I wish we could have learned the proper ways sooner."

"In truth, the good fortune is all mine in that you're my friend." She graced Hannah with a smile and added, "Or rather, my sister." She loosened her grip. "And haven't we had more than a little fun pretending to be lads? Now, I'll race you up the last ten steps."

It was Lady Beth's stern face that stopped their race and their giggles as they reached the landing.

"Ladies, you are well past the age of running." She harrumphed her disapproval, her high-coiffed curls wavering as she spoke. "Captain Luxbury is in the library; he might hear you. Go change your clothes. I've had the upstairs maid pack your trunks." She paused to eye their dirty hems. "I have last minute instructions for you. After you play some simple tunes for the captain, he and Lord Edgeworth will retire to the study and I'll accompany you to your rooms. I have much to explain."

Eleanor nodded, afraid to speak, but happy to know she might finally get some answers. Where exactly were they going? Why now and why in such a rush? What would be expected of her? Was Lady Beth marrying her off without a warning? She certainly hoped not, but she'd been suspicious of this 'week away' that had suddenly come up.

She and Hannah both curtsied as Lady Beth dismissed them. They walked as elegantly and unhurriedly as they could down the stone hallways and up another set of stairs to their adjoining rooms.

Hannah pulled the strands of Brownie's tail out of her apron. "I'll soak this now. Perhaps I can dry it and make your braid before dinner. It wouldn't do to have this captain see you with light hair now and dark tomorrow."

"The lace cap will hide the ends. No one will know."

Hannah tightened her lips, nodded, then excused herself to her room for a moment. She returned carrying a lovely silver gown, laid it next to Eleanor's, and said, "There. Brownie's braid is soaking in my basin."

They washed their hands and faces in Eleanor's porcelain bowl and helped each other get dressed. When Hannah had trouble with her hair, Eleanor had an idea. "We'll use the candle wax to secure the braids. You can wear both of Cameron's mother's braids tonight."

Hannah blushed. "I promised to send them back when my own hair grows out." She sat in the chair before the dressing table and folded her hands in her lap as Eleanor tipped the candle over her head. "Be careful."

She was. Not a single drip of hot wax fell anywhere other than the precise spots Eleanor deemed necessary. She curled her nose in distaste as she touched the dead woman's strands. She'd seen Cameron's mother a handful of times in the past year. And Cameron twice as often. She wasn't sure how she felt about that. About leaving right when her interest in the opposite sex was blooming. Same for Hannah. Undoubtedly Hannah was thinking of the handsome young man in the same way as Eleanor was. But of course, he was beneath Eleanor's sudden new station. Perhaps she should ask her aunt if Hannah might be betrothed when they returned. It wasn't out of the ordinary to let a house servant marry a farm hand.

She pressed her fingers against the warm wax and proclaimed the hair style finished. Hannah picked up a hand mirror and turned her head from side to side. Satisfied, she rose and stood before the cheval glass to admire herself from head to toe.

"Oh," Hannah exclaimed as she saw Eleanor's reflection behind her. She turned and assessed her friend. "The waist line is higher. A new fashion."

Eleanor touched the tucked stitches beneath her bosom. "I'm thankful the hoop petticoats are out of style."

"Cook says they're still worn at court. How do you think she knows such a thing?"

"Perhaps from the new staff."

"Of course. Lady Beth brought them back with her from her last visit to court. Cook told me Lady Beth spoke twice to Queen Charlotte who complimented her on her jewelry."

Eleanor half-smiled at this bit of gossip. "My dear Pascoe … I mean Hannah … are you hinting at wearing jewels tonight?"

"I think we should. Pearls, the teardrop earrings, and a brooch would look nice on you."

"And the same for you?"

"Yes, and perhaps a tiara to help hold the wax in place."

Eleanor nodded. "You're so clever, Hannah. A tiara for you and a bonnet for me."

***

CAPTAIN BERNARD LUXBURY sat stiffly as Lord Clive Edgeworth stroked his chin and chatted amiably with him about his commission. Luxbury was beholden to the Lord and Lady for his current political and military standing. They could never know, of course, that he'd manipulated his way into their good graces, earned their favor, and taken advantage of them, however it was all for a worthy cause. He knew this in his heart. He'd researched the rumors and followed the tittle-tattle. He'd confronted Lord Edgeworth two months ago and offered a solution. Now, at last, he'd see if it was all for naught.

When Lady Beth entered the room, he jumped to his feet, grabbed the bottom edge of his red coat to yank any wrinkle out of existence, and bowed. Edgeworth was slower.

"My dear Bernard," Lady Beth crooned, offering him her hand, "it's so good of you to do us this favor." She turned toward the door. "Come in, ladies. Allow me to introduce you to Miss Eleanor, er uh, Beldorney, my niece. And our ward, Miss Hannah Pascoe."

Luxbury's reaction was instant. He picked up his tricorne hat that had sat on the end table and brought it to his chest as he bowed again, keeping his bloodshot eyes fixed on their faces and not their bodices. Both women were comely, but the flash in Eleanor's blue eyes, the sparkle, drew him in, whereas Hannah, the completely unimportant one, lowered her gaze to the carpet.

"Ladies, it is a great pleasure to meet you." He took a step forward to gently take each gloved hand in turn and hold it briefly. His eyes remained on Eleanor.

He was sure he held up his end of the conversation as they moved to the dining hall. As they had the soup course. As they enjoyed the fish and chicken. As they relaxed with an assortment of Cook's best sweets and Lord Edgeworth's finest wine. But in truth Bernard Luxbury tripped over his tongue as often as he stared at Eleanor.

When they reconvened in the music room, he sat barely breathing as Eleanor played a simple tune on the pianoforte. He'd heard better in other households, but nothing as captivating. It wasn't her faulty playing as much as her boyish snorts when she made a mistake and the unabashed grin she'd toss his way.

The performance was over too soon and the ladies were whisked out of the room by Lady Beth.

"I am smitten with your niece … and your ward. Such charming ladies," he said to Edgeworth once he and Edgeworth retired to the study. "'Tis certainly a vexatious and lamentable circumstance that you have hired me to spirit them away to hide forever in Scotland."

"Not forever." Lord Edgeworth winked at Bernard. "Bring her back once you've found the parchments." He lowered his voice. "I've had word her mother may be near Kilmahew. The documents will achieve our success. Get them."

***

Eleanor pressed her fingers against her aunt's elbow as she helped her up the stairs. "Beldorney? You introduced me as Eleanor Beldorney. My last name is Beldorney?"

"Shush," her aunt warned. "No, it is not. I'll explain in the privacy of your room."

Once into the suite Hannah held the chair for Lady Beth and then both girls settled themselves on the edge of Eleanor's bed, a simple four-poster with a single pillow.

Reluctantly Lady Beth began, "No, your pedigree is not Scottish, but the captain himself chose that name for you. He has Scottish relations and he will install you into their care." She blinked several times. "Eleanor … you are a Hanover … a cousin of King George's."

"A cousin?" Both girls whispered the word together.

"Is she an heir to the throne?" Hannah dared to ask. Her surprise grew as she fingered the lace that fringed the top of her bodice.

"No … well, maybe … she is a princess, it would seem. But … there's a plan. Captain Luxbury has warned us. Queen Charlotte will, unfortunately, die by her own hand … or at least it will be arranged to appear so. King George will have to remarry." She took a deeper breath. "And … it would be best … if it were … you."

The silence was complete. At first Eleanor thought she meant Hannah and that she was speaking to her. Then her aunt's eyes found Eleanor's and she understood.

"Me? Marry the King?" Every horrible thing she'd ever heard about the regent raced past through her head. *He was crazy. He was cruel. He was a disgusting old man.* The tingling up her spine and down her arms felt icier than goose bumps. She flashed on the footman, the carriage driver, the huntsman, even the young farmer, Cameron. She'd be less disgusted to wed any one of them. But the King? No. Never.

9

"Did you hear her, El?" Hannah shook her arm again. She was barely aware that more had been said. "Lady Beth says it's all to prevent a palace revolution. The King will be poisoned after you marry and then you will be Queen. You will save the country."

"But first," Lady Beth hurried to say, "we must get you to Scotland. You'll have not only a week away, but several months of tutelage. I've been remiss in your education. The Beldorney clan will see to teaching you what you need to know."

"But ... really? I'm a Hanover? Who ... is my mother? My father? I thought ... I thought you were my aunt."

Lady Beth wrung her hands. "It's a long story, but I may never get another chance to tell you." Her eyes flitted about the room. "Your mother stayed here when she visited. She had some standing at court and her family was rich. She eloped with the third son of King George the Second and Caroline, the one they never speak of. A rogue. A scalawag." She shook her head violently. "Poor Mary—that was your mother's name—she believed his lies. But the King claimed the documents were forgeries, the priest a fake, the marriage a sham. She was utterly undone." Lady Beth began to tear up. "You were born here, Eleanor. Secretly. She stayed with us for three years. Lord Edgeworth allowed it. She was going to take you to the colonies. But the royals desired to further cover up the scandal."

Eleanor let her breath out. "What happened?"

"Your father insisted the marriage was real and he visited once a month though the King and Queen forbade it. Then he died suddenly, suspiciously, but he'd left money and instructions to send Mary and you to Scotland and then on to Boston." She withdrew a handkerchief from her sleeve and dabbed at her lashes. "Mary went on ahead to secure arrangements, but I've never had a single letter from her all these years. I fear she must have died."

Hannah put an arm around Eleanor's shoulders as Eleanor choked back a sob.

"And yes, I am your aunt. Your mother was my half-sister, though we lived in separate households. A quiet scandal, it was." A longer sob broke loose. "I had news ... that you were to be found and ... disposed of. You were in my care then. That's when I started dressing you as a boy. The rumors finally stopped circulating and Lord Edgeworth and I were accepted at court after King George the Third took the throne." Lady Beth started weeping loudly at that point and Eleanor rose to comfort her.

"It's all right, Auntie. You saved me."

"You were my responsibility. I had to keep you safe. It was my husband's idea to keep you hidden. And now … there are new rumors. I must say I don't approve of this plot to dethrone the King, to murder poor Charlotte, but my husband is a part of it all. Still … it is divinely fortunate that we have you. In the end … you can pardon us."

Eleanor, kneeling by the chair, continued to hug Lady Beth. "I don't want to be queen or princess or anything. Send me to Scotland if you must, but I shan't be a part of this. What of the King's sons? Ernst or Frederick or Edward or George?"

"They're too young. The country needs a ruler who can think for himself. Or herself." Lady Beth took Eleanor's hands in her own. "I've watched you grow. You are smart and kind and honest. Good qualities for a woman. But you are also like a man. Decisive. Passionate. Fiery. Perhaps that is why Clive, er, Lord Edgeworth was so hard on you." She peered intently at Eleanor. "And you have what a king should have … the wisdom of Solomon, the patience of Job, and the courage of David."

Eleanor stifled a laugh and lost her balance, plopping onto her backside, her skirts crumpling in a circle, but her aunt still claimed her hands. She rose and drew Eleanor to her feet and into a deep embrace. She whispered in her ear, "Go because Clive commands it. But I will understand if you rebel and find a way to refuse to go along with this absurdity. Trust no one. If you must, look for your mother and hide with her or find passage to the colonies. Clive vowed to have your mother killed if she returns. She has important documents; destroy them if you can." She squeezed once more, harder, a warning in her touch.

Eleanor looked over her shoulder at Hannah. "Give us a moment, please."

Hannah scooted through the adjoining door and closed it completely.

"Auntie Beth, how will I find her? I don't know what she looks like. And what name might she go by?"

Lady Beth raised a hand toward the painting by the bed. "There she is. You've seen her all your life. She'll have aged fifteen years, but she'll be wearing that brooch. You have its match. Wear it always and Mary Ainsworth Fletcher may find you," she touched above Eleanor's heart, "if she yet lives."

Chapter 2

TWO COACHMEN AND a footman took their spots on top and behind the carriage after Eleanor and Hannah were seated and Captain Luxbury settled himself opposite them.

Two slightly damp braids looped beside Eleanor's temples, the ends of which were hidden beneath her bonnet. She thought of Brownie and suddenly wanted to leave the carriage, race to the stable and cry into the old gelding's neck. She'd taken her life here for granted for so long, but she was afraid she'd never see Lady Beth or Cook or anyone here ever again. She glanced out of the window and saw the Lord and Lady of Ingledew looking lost. They'd been the closest thing to parents she'd known. Lady Beth's duplicitous instructions required that Eleanor either betray the King to follow the plan or betray Lord Edgeworth and escape. Lady Beth's final hug included a whispered hint that she'd hidden money in Eleanor's trunk. What was she to do?

She gazed at them again and pleaded with her eyes for them to take her back. Lady Beth looked away; Lord Edgeworth looked down. Behind them she spotted a plump hand raised in farewell. Cook. Sadly, she realized she'd never known the woman's real name. She loved Cook and she knew that Cook loved her, too. In that instant, she determined which path she would choose: the path that led to her own real name.

"Princess Eleanor ... may I call you that?" Luxbury's voice and question startled her out of her thoughts. "I mean, in private, of course.

Your secret identity is safe with me." He nodded with some hesitation at Hannah. "With us."

"Captain Luxbury, please ..." The words stuck in her throat as the carriage jerked forward to start the journey. She swallowed her complaint and tucked down her chin. She swayed with the coach, her hands clasped in her lap, her knuckles white.

Hannah spoke up. "I'm sure she'd prefer to be called Mistress Eleanor, if you don't mind."

Eleanor had noticed the subtle change in Hannah's behavior toward her. They'd been such close friends, but last night and this morning Hannah acted subservient as well as defensive.

"Of course, of course." He angled himself so his knees and the tip of his sword would not touch them. "But please, both of you, call me Bernard." His greatcoat lay rolled beside him and he rested an elbow on it.

The ladies nodded. The carriage rattled on as the horses began to trot. Hannah spread the throw she'd brought over Eleanor's lap. The morning was chilly and the ride was rough on the road through Lancaster and then Cumberland, close to the Irish Sea. The captain assured them the carriage portion of the journey would be over when they reached the port and then they'd sail the final leg. He bored them with the names of sea vessels that patrolled the coast and then he blathered on about military things that held no interest for them. Still, each in turn nodded and Hannah even made a face of rapt attention until, after more than three hours on the journey, the ladies began to squirm.

At last, the captain noticed his companions' discomfort. He knocked thrice on the carriage roof with the butt end of his pistol and hollered to the driver that it was time, *ahem*, to give the horses a rest.

As the coach slowed and then came to a complete stop, Luxbury scanned the landscape through the window. "Looks safe enough. There are some ... uh ... bushes over there ... for privacy. The men and I shall keep to the other side of the carriage."

"Thank you, Captain ... Bernard," Eleanor smiled and waited for him to descend first. She started to get out, but Hannah nudged her and whispered to let the captain take her hand.

Once they were a goodly distance from the eyes of the men and shielded by some foliage, they lifted their skirts.

"He's quite the bore, isn't he?" Eleanor said a few moments later.

"I must disagree," Hannah finished and stepped away, "I think he's rather handsome."

"More handsome than Cameron?"

13

Hannah blushed. "You've found me out. But a captain or any officer is beyond my station, surely. And quite beneath yours ... *princess*."

"Don't you call me that. I'm not sure I believe Lady Beth's story. And are we really talking about marriage? I liked things better when we pretended to be boys." Eleanor smoothed her skirts, then felt her braids and let loose an exasperated sigh. "Are these necessary? And these petticoats? And gloves? We should abandon it all and run away."

"You torment me." Hannah started to walk then heard a rustling in the bushes and stopped. "What's that?"

"Dinner, perhaps." Eleanor picked up a long stick and moved softly toward the noise. She saw what was moving and stabbed once. She held her victim up for Hannah to see.

"You've skewered a snake. Hide it at once. They mustn't know of your bravery. 'Tis not a lady's way."

The look on Hannah's face humored Eleanor too much. She jiggled the snake a bit and thrust it toward Hannah's face as any young lad might do, then laughed and dropped the unfortunate adder.

"I am not going to marry King George. We will escape tonight or ..." She left the thought incomplete as the captain's voice called a warning.

"Mistress Eleanor! Mistress Hannah! Conceal yourselves!"

They were still screened by shrubbery and trees, but the captain's shout caused them to shrink behind some bushes and listen hard.

"I hear more horses," Hannah said.

"It sounds like a coach and six," Eleanor agreed. "We've seen so little traffic. We must be near a city."

Eleanor moved some branches to peek through. She was wrong. It wasn't a coach, but a wagon, pulled by two grey mares. It stopped and she could see the captain arguing with three men.

"Brigands?" Hannah asked. "I remember my journey from Cornwall to Ingledew and we were afraid of robbers."

"Shh. I can just make out their words."

The two stayed still as rabbits and perked their ears. Bits of the conversation carried on the spring breeze.

" ... two hundred more or else ..."

"No ... as agreed ... put up your pistols ..."

"... stop! What are you doing?"

Eleanor lifted her head in time to see the fighting. The captain drew his sword, one of the strangers slashed the footman with a knife while the driver used his whip indiscriminately. Then the shooting began.

14

Eleanor let loose a curse. Hannah's grasp on Eleanor's arm equaled the grip she had on the nearest branch. They both shook, overcome with trepidation.

The guard lay in a pool of blood; one of the strangers fell upon him. Eleanor willed him not to be so still. Then her attention went to Luxbury; he was an accomplished swordsman, but it was his pistol that had killed the robber. Luxbury stood there fussing with the weapon, unaware that another brigand was coming up behind him. A warning shout was all she needed to do, but she froze. The enemy smashed the captain's head with the end of his musket.

She leaned into Hannah and whispered, "I think they've killed Luxbury. Remember when we fought the Chadderton boys?"

Hannah's brown eyes went wide.

***

KEIR MCKELVEY PACED the uneven floor of the great hall in Castle Caladh. Two servants scurried along close to the walls, one retrieving bits and pieces of the vases and bowls Keir had shattered, the other gathering the contents that splattered: mostly wet clumps of marsh marigolds. Both kept their eyes on him in case he elected to break something else. An arm. A neck. Everyone had heard the argument that only ended because Keir's father, Laird McKelvey, stormed out.

The candles in the chandelier made dancing shadows as it still swayed from its contact with the last bowl. Keir nearly slipped in the puddle of water it had made. He swore an oath at the top of his voice and scared an approaching maid into retreat. In the three weeks he'd been away helping Fenella, his father had secured a match between Keir and the eldest daughter of Bram MacLeod, leader of the MacLeod clan.

He knew the girl, Anabel, a fractious grump of a lass with red hair and freckles. Beautiful, yes. Pleasant ... hardly. Keir's father claimed she'd calmed and blossomed this month past, but actually what had changed was her dowry, which now included lands Keir's father coveted.

His temper abated suddenly. "No," he said to no one, "I'll not have her." Escape sprang to mind and he charged out of the castle, tricorne hat in hand, and headed for the stable where his gelding was no doubt still receiving a rub down from the stable lad.

He was surprised to find the stable empty. No lads. No horses. Ha! His father had such foresight, coming here and sending them away while Keir broke pots and jugs in the great hall. Keir hissed air through his nose. "I'll not have her. Ye hear?" He clenched his fists.

Exactly as he had surmised, his father was near. He strode forth from the side of the stable. "I hear ye, lad. When ye've settled yerself a wee bit more, we'll drink to yer health and toast forthcoming rites. The date is set for six weeks hence."

Keir stared at the scar on his father's forehead. Fuming again.

"'Tis done and settled." The old man swung his arm and pointed up the hill. "Off ye go now, lad. Hide yerself in yer secret place 'til ye make yer peace wit' yer fate."

Keir unclenched his fists, but stood rigidly glaring at Laird McKelvey, an older mirror image of himself. Tall. Broad-shouldered. Dark hair and passionate green eyes. Keir would sooner die than be bound to any lass, let alone one so disagreeable as Anabel MacLeod.

His father looked away first, then turned his back and started for the castle. Over his shoulder he added, "Ye'll not sup with us t'night. Let the fairies tend ye."

Keir snorted and watched till his father was out of sight. He muttered, "Fairies, indeed. I'll feast, ole man, and sleep on a softer bed than any ye have."

He considered the stable. His father most likely instructed the servants not to bring the horses back till the morrow. He could sleep in a stall, but he had a better place in mind. A secret place. His father thought it was up the hill, but it was not. Keir turned away from the hill and strode past the paddock and toward the woods. It was a bit of a walk, but worth the hike. No one, as far as he knew, not his brothers or his sisters, had ever found the hidden hollow.

He'd left his claymore with the horse, but he had his *biodag*, a long dirk, in its sheath at his waist, along with a fork and flint, of course. His sporran held a few coins and a handful of oats for his horse. He could eat those himself. He would make a fire, catch a fish or a hare, and sleep under the stars, or, if it got too cold, in the tree well. That was preferable to sitting with his younger brothers and one remaining unwed sister and enduring his father's remarks. His mother, God rest her soul, would have stood up for him.

Twenty minutes later he found the hollow looking the same as he'd left it the last time he'd been here, many months past. The stones he'd set, a miniature cairn a third the size of the one he'd laid at his mother's grave, still marked the entrance. He took a final glance at the sky. The wide expanse was bejeweled with stars, and the westering moon glowed with the promise of tomorrow's light.

He bent low to duck into the space. He'd always thought of the spot as a soft cave, an evergreen shelter grown of boughs that curved to the ground and kept most of the sunlight out. He'd camped here many nights, but tonight he'd be without a blanket. No matter, his kilt would serve. He ducked back out and went about gathering sticks.

Anabel MacLeod.

Never.

***

BERNARD LUXBURY HEARD groans, but he couldn't get his eyes to open. A moment later he realized the sounds could possibly be his own. Slowly he raised his head, felt dizzy, touched the back of his head and then stared at the sticky red stuff that smeared his palm.

A horse neighed.

Bernard still looked at his hand. He couldn't make sense of it. He sat up and closed his eyes again. What had happened?

He'd been in a carriage, hadn't he? Or had he been riding in formation? He squeezed his lids harder, tried to think.

The horse neighed again and stomped its foot. Something wasn't right. Bernard took a longer breath, opened his eyes, and gasped at what he saw. A man, dead beside a wagon. Two more men, one atop the other. Dead. The footman, sprawled across the ground. He appeared dead as well.

Bits of memory returned.

His carriage. Where was his carriage? He didn't see the driver's body. Could he have raced away?

His heart lurched when he remembered Eleanor and the young lady with her. He rose to his feet, wobbled a bit, and groaned.

There were answering groans on the other side of the wagon. He staggered forward, used the wooden sides for support and came around. There, tied to the wagon wheels with strips of cloth, were the other two brigands, moaning. Blood dripped down their faces from gashes on their heads.

Enough sense returned to the captain for him to realize these men, though thieves or worse, would be in perilous danger should the horses decide to bolt.

"Easy, there," he crooned as he moved ahead. The mare on the right gave him a wide-eyed whinny, but he grasped the reins in time. "Easy, girl." He calmed them both, wondering if the smell of blood and sulfur had set them off. He checked that the wagon brake was set, but unhitched the team anyway and led them to a tree, tying them as well as he could.

Where were the women? Had the driver overpowered the thieves, tied them to the wagon, and left the women?

He looked to the field where he'd sent them and called out their names.

Silence.

Good. They must have made it to the carriage. The driver was a good man. He'd see them safely to the port.

One of the thieves spoke up then, a string of filthy invectives followed by, "Witches they were! Clubbed us and tied us up with their own petticoats. Heard them order the carriage driver to hurry on. Meetin' the devil, they be."

Luxbury's face went flush with relief.

"Ay, cap'n, untie us, will ye? We've done ye no harm."

Luxbury eyed the two. "No harm? Which one of you whacked me?"

The thief who spoke glanced at his mate and raised a brow. "Nah, sir, 'twas the bigger one. That she-devil bashed you and came after us. Wild, they were. Uncivilized. Like those Scottish highlanders. Untie us."

Luxbury took a step closer. They were lying. He could see it in their faces. And of course a woman couldn't have taken him down. He turned toward the horses without a word. There'd be passersby within a day. The men would survive. He'd even leave them one of the horses. But the other he'd ride bareback and follow after the carriage. He didn't know how long a head start they had, but surely he'd catch up to them before night fell. The driver would still head to the port, finish the arrangement, get them on a ship, and collect his pay from Luxbury's contact there.

He felt terrible leaving the other man and the footman here, but he had nothing to use to bury them. He could at least get them off the ground, put them in the wagon, speak a prayer over them.

***

THERE WERE NO giggles or nervous laughter in the carriage. Serious reflection and quiet fear filled the small space. Eleanor was proud of herself for suggesting they fight like boys, but Hannah's hesitation had curbed the idea. Instead, they had sneaked up as close as they dared. She shuddered as she thought back to those terrifying moments. The captain's pistol lay near his knee. Two filthy highwaymen stood shoulder to shoulder next to the carriage. One aimed a musket at the driver, the other had caught the end of the whip and was in a tug of war with the driver up in his seat. Between their shouting, the horses' neighing, and the driver's curses neither had heard the women. Eleanor retrieved the captain's pistol and Hannah lifted the heavy rifle that had dropped behind the carriage when the footman fell off.

The driver saw them first and gave a surprised shout with a single added curse word, but the thieves didn't look behind them.

"We'll not fall for yer tricks," one robber said, a second before he felt the end of a rifle jammed in his back. He dropped his weapon.

18

The driver let go of his whip and the one holding the other end fell back, tumbling into Eleanor's skirts. Without a second thought, she swung the entire pistol at his head and knocked him cold. The driver jumped down, punched the second man hard in the face, causing him to twist as he fell. Hannah kept the rifle aimed at his head as he stared up at her. The driver picked up the musket and bludgeoned him senseless.

"Safe ye be." The driver reached for Hannah's rifle.

Eleanor clutched the pistol and kept it close to her bosom. "The captain's dead."

"Are ye sure?" The driver glanced at the bodies strewn around the area. He didn't wait for her response. "A pity these boys ain't. We'll tie these ruffians to the wagon wheels. Have ye anything we could use?"

Eleanor focused on his words and glanced at their trunks. Nothing came to mind. She lifted her top skirt and started ripping strips from her undergarments.

Now, sitting in the carriage as they bumped down the road, she pinched the hem of her skirt and felt the coins sewn in there. The captain's pistol rattled on the seat next to her alongside his great coat. She looked across at Hannah.

"Are you all right?"

"I touched that vulgar swain when we tied them. He woke. He saw us."

"You've nothing to fear."

"But the captain … the others … their bodies. Just left there."

"Driver said 'twas expedient to be on our way." Eleanor let out a sigh. "Yes, the captain. That was most unfortunate, but the driver said he'd see us to our destination. We'll be safe. And then he'll go back to bury them."

"I shan't ever forget his face." Hannah dropped her eyes to her lap and started to weep.

***

KEIR WAS UNSUCCESSFUL in catching a fish or trapping an animal. As his fire burned down to coals, he realized his hunger was amplified by the fact he hadn't eaten the oat cakes Fenella had given him for the journey.

"Och. The stable boy's made off wi' me supper."

He wasn't so proud that he couldn't walk home, raid the kitchen larder, and sleep in his own bed. He watched the last embers go out and then, by the light of a half-moon, made his way back to Castle Caladh.

He contemplated not his newly arranged marriage, but rather the intriguing coded letter, long since destroyed, that tantalized his Scottish thirst for adventure.

His decision was easily made. He'd go to the appointed rendezvous and take charge of the secret offspring of the long deceased and unrecognized son of George II. Keir had heard the tales of the battle of Culloden since he was a young lad. There was no war with England now, but traces of hate remained. George III was in trouble.

His feet made soft crunching sounds as he made a new path returning. It had always been his habit to vary his way. The secret place had finally lost its charm; perhaps he'd never go back there.

One of Fenella's tunes looped in his head and even though he was close to the castle he began to softly sing the verses. As he passed the stable his horse gave an answering nicker to the song he'd heard his master sing for most of the journey home.

Keir was surprised. He hadn't expected his father to allow the stable lad to bring them back so soon. He pulled open the stable door and entered. "Aha, ye've learnt me song, have ye?" Faint light was all he had to find his way to the stall. He was careful where he stepped. Soft nickers, like purrs, hummed through the stable as the other horses recognized his voice, too. "Och, I've na enough for ye all." He fed a handful of oats to his own horse and continued to speak in a soft calm tone.

He noticed another sound then, the gentle snoring of a tired lad. Keir shook his head. Was there no one on sentry duty? A MacNeil or a Campbell or a Galbraith might take advantage of an unguarded castle.

He'd no sooner had the thought than the lad awoke and scrambled to his feet.

"Sire, I have yer claymore. The Laird set me on watch to give ye it as soon as ye returned." The young boy held out the weapon. "Yer anger has abated?"

"Aye, but not me hunger. Can ye fetch me some bread and cheese from the kitchen?"

"Right away, sire." The lad started off, then turned and asked, "Are ye leavin', sire? Dae ye want it in a sack?"

Keir nodded and held a finger to his lips. "Tell no one."

Chapter 3

THE SOUNDS AND sights outside their window made Eleanor and Hannah forget they were hungry and tired. At last the carriage stopped its incessant bumping as it rolled onto the smoother lanes of the port town.

"Look," Hannah exclaimed, "have you ever seen such things?" They passed mansions that would rival Ingledew, and then buildings connected to each other, three stories tall with turrets and chimneys and six-paned windows. A church with huge pillars framing the front had them craning their necks to view its spirals. Their jaws dropped in awe. But the biggest surprise was the busy wharf. They had a view of the port as the carriage stopped to let several carriages and wagons pass. The ships in the harbor were packed in with scant room for the jolly boats to row between them, ferrying goods and sailors to shore. Most of the frigates and schooners had their sails rolled up, but topsails flapped on a few farther out.

"I'm scared," Hannah answered. "There are so many people. Men everywhere. And look at the ladies' bonnets."

Eleanor absently touched hers as she stared at the many women on the arms of men in knee breeches and long waist coats, walking close to the buildings.

"Lovely," Eleanor said, "but ..." she shook her head "we won't be staying here. I'm sure Lady Beth had our trunks filled with things more

21

… useful … for where we're going." She thought of her desire to escape, to look for her mother, to ruin the plan to be a political puppet … a queen. An undeserving queen. How could she be a queen when she didn't know who she was down deep?

She leaned across the space between them and took Hannah's hand. "Will you come with me if I should suddenly flee? And stay with me? No matter what?"

Hannah frowned. "Of course."

"Good." Eleanor's voice wavered as the carriage suddenly lurched forward and began rolling down the drop toward the wharf.

The driver called out curses on the passing traffic, screamed at his horses, and gave a single thump on the roof to warn the ladies to hang onto something or brace themselves. For several minutes Eleanor and Hannah shrieked and groaned as they were tossed about the interior. At last, the carriage stopped and someone pulled the door open almost before they could catch their breath.

"Captain!" Hannah squealed when she saw who it was. "You're alive."

"I am." He kept his eyes on Eleanor, though, and reached for his greatcoat which he'd left on the coach, and grabbed the pistol too, then he held a hand out to help them disembark. "I galloped the whole way and reached the docks these few minutes past. Just in time."

Eleanor was first out. She stepped down, heedless of the puddles that might seep up the hems of her skirt. She spied one of the brigands' grey mares, heaving and sweating nearby. "You must be quite the horseman to have ridden so far and so fast without a saddle." She feared her own panting might match the mare's. She moved toward the horse as Hannah descended. "You must walk the poor thing for a quarter hour at least."

"Ug," he coughed a sort of laugh, "'tis a robber's nag. Let someone steal the awful thing. It has served its purpose." There was a suggestion of rancor in his voice that made her inspect his face and find a humorless smirk marring his calm expression.

Both women fought to hide their disgust at his brutal opinion so openly stated.

The driver dropped down. "Cap'n, have ye whistled fer yer mate?"

Luxbury lifted his gaze to the dock and gave a wave to a soldier there. "Here he comes. He'll help you with the trunks and pay you. Don't forget my bag. I'll take the ladies and procure two jollies." He held both elbows out. "Ladies?"

Hannah started to take his arm, but Eleanor hesitated. "But the horse. You need … I'd be most grateful if you'd hire one of those lads to walk him about." She indicated a gathering of scruffy-looking boys, beggars probably, or wharf bullies. She wasn't sure her command would be taken seriously, but no harm trying out her newly learnt feminine wiles.

"As you wish, princess." He saw the ire rise in Eleanor's face. "Oh, I beg your pardon. 'Tis a common term of flattery, Mistress Eleanor. I'll not use it again." He turned on his heel and hollered at a lad, tossed him a coin, and told him to walk the mare to the nearest livery and leave her there.

Only then did both women latch onto the proffered elbows and walk gingerly toward the docks, not venturing to look right or left at the bedraggled dock workers shouting filthy curses, the shifty-eyed merchants hawking their wares, or the stinking fishermen leaving slimy footprints.

"A quick glance left, m'lady, and you'll see real pirates."

Eleanor dared to do so and saw two men hobbling along in silver-buckled high heels with tricorne hats under their arms. They were clad in combinations of colorfully-hued and mismatched garments of embroidered silks and satins. Eleanor thought it ludicrous that they would wear velvet and lace as well. One wore a powdered wig and had even powdered his stubbled face like the London dandy who had once visited Ingledew.

She took the liberty of a longer gaze, trusting her steps to the captain's lead, and deduced that pirates must love garish jewelry including elaborate ear pendants, heavy gold chains, and emerald crosses, no doubt stolen from Catholic ships.

She turned her eyes back to the dock and caught her breath at the sight of the small jolly boat she'd have to climb into.

***

KEIR LED HIS horse, Copper, saddled and packed with sacks of food and oats, out between the stone pillars of Castle Caladh. The gelding deserved a longer rest after the trip from Fenella's, but once Keir's mind was made up, he wasn't going to change it. He could, however, save the horse from having to carry his weight. They'd both rest on the morrow.

He wasn't in the mood to sing, but humming seemed to calm Copper, especially after they'd both stumbled down a rocky slope. Keir checked the horse's legs, running his hands down over the knees, cannons, and pasterns. All good. On they went, and as the sky brightened before dawn, he did start to sing, matching the volume of the early morning birds. His voice was deep and husky; he wasn't afraid to let loose. Surprised to hear an echo of the last word when he finished, he stopped leading Copper and scanned the trail behind him.

"Hey-oh," he called.

"Hey-oh-oh," came the reply.

Keir snorted and waited. Copper dropped his head low and began nibbling the new spring growth along the trail, unconcerned by the approach of another horse and rider. Keir huffed out a couple of sighs, resigning himself to the fact his younger brother would be tagging along. Logan, at nineteen, was a good three years younger than Keir, and much closer in age and temperament to their youngest brother, eighteen-year-old Jack. But shadowing Keir had been Logan's custom since he was three, a habit encouraged by their mother. Where Keir was cautious and restrained, Logan was impulsive and reckless. Logan had a good heart, though, and he tried to emulate his older brother.

Those traits were slowly rubbing off on Logan. But whenever Keir was away, Logan would get into mischief with Jack.

"Saw you leavin'," Logan said, looking down on Keir's head from his seat on a horse Keir didn't recognize.

Keir reached to pat the mare's neck. "Who's this?"

"Won her a week ago from the McDoons. Racin'."

Keir voiced a disgusted grunt. "She got a name?"

"I dinnae learn it."

Another huff. "Get yerself down and walk beside me. I'll not be ridin' till Copper's had a proper rest."

Logan jumped down and faced his brother. They were the same height, tall for highlanders. The sons had all taken after their father in coloring and physique.

"So ye've been racin' again. What had ye put up as yer stake?" Keir pulled Copper's head up and they began their trek again.

"I bet the young McDoon a look beneath our sister's skirts." He quickly added, "They was hanging out to dry after Rory'd washed'em. I didna tell'im that."

Keir laughed. They chatted as the sun rose, catching up on castle news. When they reached a meadow, Keir hobbled both horses and let them graze. He didn't share his food with Logan as Logan had his own bulky sack of pantry goods he'd grabbed after the stable boy tipped him off to Keir's journey.

"Ye haven't told me our mission. I wonder … 'tis more of that quagmire of English lunacy? Are ye hopin' to quell an insurrection?" Logan opened his sack.

"Somethin' like that. There's a plan to murder the king and replace him with someone more sympathetic to Scottish sensibilities."

Logan spoke with food in his mouth. "Mm … I've nay heard a fair word … mm … spoken in favor of King George." He swallowed. "Are ye plannin' to ride clear to London?"

24

"Aye."

"And go to …" he took another large bite of roast mutton "mmm … Kew Palace?"

"They say the king has a room for star-gazin' at the top of Kew Palace, somethin' I'd be pleased to see … but, nay, he doesna live there now. He bought Queen Charlotte a new home, Buckingham House it's called, and there they'll be."

"And there he'll die?" Logan dug through his bag for something else.

"We shall see, lad, we shall see." Keir leaned closer to Logan's ear. "I've been commissioned to see it doesna happen. 'Twould be bad for Scotland, Ireland, too, and we've a better plan to bring the King to our way o' thinkin'."

Logan furrowed his brow. "'Tis said he weeps for losin' the colonies. And that he's mad."

"Aye. And French doctors dinnae do him good. His opponents be emboldened by his failures. There be revolutionary stirrings bubblin' here, as well as in France. Ole George finds it hard to move from castle to house when mobs break the royal coach's windows." Keir paused and studied the concern on his brother's face. "'Twill be all right. And … I'm pleased ye've come along. That'll split our father's ire between us when we return."

Keir sat down on the grass then and nibbled on his breakfast, explaining bit by bit the intricacies of a plan that needed to tip-toe around two other factions—one that wanted the king to reign and one that wanted to replace him with a royal impostor.

Neither spoke of the elder brother's nuptials that loomed six weeks off.

***

CAPTAIN LUXBURY HANDED Eleanor a handkerchief to wipe the salt water from her face. They'd all been splashed several times by an oarsman who offered no apologies. And then the most unexpected thing happened—the captain warned them to avert their eyes as two naked young men were pushed over the side of the ship. They splashed the jolly as well when their flailing arms hit the sea. *Stowaways*, the captain apprised them. Eleanor passed the kerchief to Hannah to wipe the splatter away as she watched the poor lads inexpertly frog-kick their way to shore.

The captain helped the ladies board the small frigate then ushered them toward the sea captain's cabin.

"This is not a passenger ship. I'm most sorry, m'lady, but the journey won't be long. A matter of hours is all. I've paid for you to sit in the captain's cabin where you'll be out of the way of ropes and sails and crew hands."

Eleanor felt much safer out of the jolly and onto the wooden planks of the larger frigate. There was little sway and her stomach settled as they walked to the stern. A sudden thump drew her attention back and she saw their trunks landing on the boards. Beyond the rails she saw the next ship, its figurehead of a naked women holding her attention a moment more. She'd heard of the wooden sculptures and knew she should exhibit some feminine mortification at the sight, but she did not. She smirked and redirected her attention to the way before her.

"Here we are." Luxbury held the door.

"Thank you … Bernard." The working and living space of the cabin was rather large, with the windows along the stern, two long tables laden with loaves of bread and pitchers of beer, a dozen chairs, and a desk. From the ceiling hung lanterns, but none was lit. Eleanor turned back to Luxbury to say, "Won't you sit with us a while? You must be exhausted … and … are you hurt?"

"He is! Oh, captain, your head." Hannah, who stood behind him, could see the wound. "We must tend to your injury."

As if given permission to sink into an arm chair, he did just that. "There, that door leads to the washroom, the other to the sleeping cabin."

Hannah, still holding Luxbury's handkerchief, scurried through the door and returned at once with it rinsed and ready to dab away the dried blood.

"Perhaps you should lie down," Eleanor said.

The ship's captain strode in then and snorted a gruff greeting. He waved the women aside and stopped in front of Luxbury, leaned into his face, and growled. "Where's me pay, mate, and as there's two o' dem, it be doubled."

Luxbury withdrew his money purse and counted out the coins without an argument. The skipper pocketed the payment, raised an eyebrow at the women, and left. Luxbury looked sheepishly at Eleanor.

She knew why. "Bernard … I thought you said you'd paid already."

"I … uh … that was my understanding. Lord Edgeworth's last words to me were that the payments had been made. No matter though. The Lord and Lady of Ingledew are honest people. They will reimburse me." He coughed and glanced toward the sleeping room.

Eleanor read his mind. "You should lie down. We'll be fine in these chairs."

"I think I shall, but wake me when the bells ring eight times. That's when the shift ends and half the crew may barge in ready to eat whatever else the cook brings here."

Hannah clutched her hands against her bodice. "Here?"

"Where else?" Luxbury rose and forced a smile toward Eleanor, then ambled to the door and closed it behind himself.

"We'll be at those wretched sailors' mercy alone here." Hannah gripped the back of the chair Luxbury had vacated. "I saw some breeches, linen shirts, and grey jackets in the washroom. We could transform ourselves. Remove our braids and hide our clothes, stuff our mouths with bread. They'll think we're lads."

"Be Pascoe and Eldridge again?" Eleanor shook her head. "I think we should trust the captain. He rode all that way after us and got us safely on the ship."

"I don't know …"

"Have your feelings for him ebbed?"

"Feelings? He's clearly in love with you, El, er … Mistress Eleanor." She gave a half-hearted curtsy and walked toward the windows. She set the captain's kerchief on the desk and studied the ocean view. "I should be nervous. Would a lady faint at the sight of it?" She chuckled. "But I feel a striking amount of exhilaration. The sea, El, it's so vast."

Eleanor crossed the room to stand beside her. "It is. I thought we might escape to the United Colonies, but I doubt we've enough coins in my hem to book such a passage."

"But we could work, could we not? Aboard a bigger ship that makes that voyage? In disguises, of course."

Eleanor let her breath out. "It's a thought."

***

BOTH WOMEN WATCHED the careful maneuvering of their ship and four other vessels that pulled up anchor at the same time and floated out with the tide. Sails were unfurled and expert rudder work kept their frigate from colliding with a larger schooner. Then they caught the wind and passed, moving faster and farther out to sea. The wharf grew smaller in their sight and then the land seemed to suddenly and completely disappear as they sailed on. With nothing much to do then, they sat at one end of the long table and began recounting various parts of the journey.

"I can hear the captain snoring." Hannah giggled. She'd grown accustomed to the pitch and roll of the ship. "It's almost musical." She put a hand through a slit in her skirt to access one of her pockets. With a bit of two-handed magic, she managed to pull out the pocket—a nicely embroidered bag she'd had to untie from her waist. "I have some candied figs Cook gave me." She held out two for Eleanor.

They enjoyed the sweets in silence for a few moments before Eleanor said, "I am conflicted. We've had so little time to accept our circumstances … my circumstances … I think you could return to Ingledew or perhaps find employment in Scotland, if you wish. I shall share the coins with you." She interpreted Hannah's expression and knew what she was thinking. "All right, I see your obstinance. We shall stay together."

"Of course, we shall. And I may be better able to learn of your mother's whereabouts if I am employed as your maid instead of your companion. You know how much servants gossip." Hannah busied herself tucking her bag back where it belonged. Should the captain or a crew member enter and see it, there'd be much embarrassment all around as such an item was considered an undergarment.

No sooner had she straightened her skirts than the main cabin door opened and a large man, obviously the ship's cook, entered carrying a tray of victuals. He stopped immediately and went wide-eyed.

"Women!" He made it sound like a curse. He shook his head. "No, no, no, no. 'Tis bad luck." He scooted sideways and moved along the table, keeping his murky eyes on them, until he reached the far end and could set the tray down. He made several hand gestures and mumbled superstitious phrases.

Eleanor looked to the sleeping room for help and when the door didn't open, she said, "'Twill be all right. Ye need not worry. We are passengers."

He backed himself to the doorway he'd entered and said, "Nay, the seas'll be angry. They be takin' their revenge on ships what carry women." He glared at them, face red and angry, then he relaxed and a smirk crossed his countenance. "Only if ye take yer clothes off will we be safe. Have ye not seen the lady on the prow? She calms the sea for us."

Eleanor's recollection of the figurehead sprang to mind. And so did something she learned from someone important to her: Ingledew's cook. She rose and spoke in her best imitation of the hearty woman, "Off with you. Be gone this instant or I'll curse you."

The door slammed shut. The next instant Luxbury came out of the sleeping room.

"My dear Mistress Eleanor, what goes on here?" He spied the food on the table and before Eleanor could answer he said, "I … the cook's been here. Let us indulge before the gang arrives." He moved to fill a plate with meat and bread. "Have I been asleep long?"

Eleanor reseated herself. "Three hours at most. How do you feel?"

"I ... I shall live. Hmm, three hours, you say? We should be close to our destination." He walked toward them and set the plate in front of Eleanor. "The same for you, Mistress Hannah? I should be happy to serve you as well."

She nodded and he returned with a plate for her and another for himself. Before he sat, he walked to the stern windows and leaned close. "Ah, yes, I can get a glimpse of trees. And islands. We'll sail through the channels and make land well before dark."

He came back and sat next to Eleanor. Before he took a bite of anything he asked, "I heard you speaking to someone, the cook I assume. Is it your custom, Mistress Eleanor, to curse those beneath you? Am I in any danger of eliciting such wrath?"

"I'm sorry, Captain. It was vulgar of me." She sighed.

Hannah came to her defense. "The cook was rude. She was right to order him away. He suggested that ... well, he made a most lewd suggestion."

"I was remiss in leaving you unattended. My sincerest apologies." He gave Eleanor an expression that made her think of a puppy she'd once had, a sweet thing she'd scolded for barking and nearly giving away their hidey-hole in the cellar.

"It's quite all right, Bernard. We all make mistakes. I expect to make quite a few if I'm to go through with this ... uh, royal ruse."

"If?" The captain pushed his plate aside.

Eleanor tried to read his face. There was something akin to caution in his eyes. He darted them between the women, pressing his lips tightly while the tip of his nose seemed to scrunch down of its own accord.

"Yes ... if." Eleanor matched his gaze and said, "I am here of my own free will, am I not?"

There was barely any hesitation before he answered, yet Eleanor felt a chill go up her spine.

"Of course, of course. Lady Beth and Lord Edgeworth were most eager to give you over to my professional care. My job is to see you safely to the Beldorney estate. But ..." He gave Hannah a cursory look. "'Tis a shame you aren't more of the same ... coloring. There are some risks in what we plan ... down the road, when you leave the Beldorneys. Perhaps we should introduce you, Mistress Hannah, as the future queen. And Eleanor, you switch identities with her and act as the maid ... for your safety."

Eleanor's lips parted in astonishment. Inside her chest her heart flickered against her ribs like a trapped bird.

29

Chapter 4

E VEN LUXBURY WAS shocked by the heavy-handed authority of the supervising port inspector who demanded he and the ladies remain in the cabin until a thorough search of the ship was finished.

"I've not heard of such nonsense," he fumed aloud after the door closed, though in reality, he'd only been on a frigate once before. The ways of the sea and seamen were as new and confusing to him as to the women, though he'd never admit it.

"M'ladies, please remain in your seats. I'll see to your trunks."

He opened the door with false bravado, stepped through and scanned the deck. Several ship inspectors were lifting lids, opening barrels, and prying apart boxes that had been lined up for the stevedores to unload. He easily spotted the Ingledew trunks; they'd been opened, with dresses and various other items strewn about around them.

"I say!" Luxbury shouted, striding toward the man who was digging into the second trunk. "What do you think you're doing? Those things belong to ... to my guests, two young ladies ... courtiers ... friends of King George."

"Aye, this here's Scotland ye be in. Delivered from the power of yer English aristocracy ..." he flung a dress sideways "and its oppression." He lowered his voice. "We be lookin' fer smuggled goods ... and people."

30

"People?" Luxbury shivered. Could his plan be thwarted before they got to shore?

"Aye. We've word the Brits be sendin' lads to worry us." He thrust his hand to the bottom of the trunk and poked around. "None be here." He gave a hearty laugh. "Nay. Ye may repack yer ladies' fine things, cap'n."

The inspector moved on. Luxbury grunted in disgust, but he gathered the clothing and hoped he got each piece in the right trunk.

***

HANNAH JUMPED FIRST when the door opened and an inspector entered. His tight shirt concealed tough and stringy muscles. He eyed them with suspicion and Hannah began to twist the middle of one braid that peeked from the right side of her bonnet.

Eleanor rose, smoothed her skirts, and spoke. "Yes? Can we help you?"

The inspector wobbled his head and scratched at his chin. His odor reached Eleanor and she crinkled her nose.

"Mayhaps." He walked closer, keeping his beady eyes steady on Hannah as she sank back into her chair. "What do ye ken of smugglers and stowaways?" He was rough-edged and spoke in a distinct growl.

"Nothing, nothing," they both said. Eleanor also lowered herself into her seat, mostly to put some distance between herself and the man with his grey whiskers and unhemmed pants.

"Ye look young … young as the lads we be asearchin' fer." He leaned in close and sniffed at them. His nostrils flared and the long hairs that protruded wiggled. "Washed up, have ye?" He glanced up at the doors to the washroom and the sleeping room. "Keep yer arses in yer seats." His eyes narrowed and his mouth curled into a chilling smile.

Neither woman reacted to the vulgarity. The inspector narrowed his gaze further. "Hmm." He glanced into the sleeping room, then moved to the washroom. "Aha! Ye've been caught! A lady woulda gasped at me comments. I dinnae ken where ye got yer frills, but ye didna hide yer breeches well enough."

Startled, Hannah twisted her braid and it came free. The bedraggled man took two quick steps to her and pulled out the other braid, yanked off her cap, and ran his fingers through her short hair. "Ye be one. And this here must be yer partner. Eh?" He pulled off Eleanor's bonnet, freed her horse hair braids, and laughed. Both girls began to whimper and protest in a manner that confused the truth. For all the times that they'd practice denying their female traits and lying to outsiders that they were orphans allowed to work the stables and gardens of Ingledew, no reasonable protestation escaped their lips now.

31

Hannah resorted to weeping.

"Don't think ye can fool me more with such sounds. And no need to. I'm on yer side, ye miserable Sassenachs. I'll get ye off the ship and to safety. Up ye go. Get in yonder room and change into yer rightful things. Now." He withdrew a weapon from his pants and brandished it at them. He wrenched Hannah from her seat with his other hand. Eleanor rose too and pushed Hannah ahead of her without a word. Once inside the small washroom, they whispered back and forth.

"Can you bar the door?" Eleanor asked.

"No. Oh, where is Bernard? What's keeping him?"

"We should do as that dreadful man says and change into these things."

"These rags belong to those stowaways. The boys that man is looking for were stripped and pushed overboard. Are we to take their places?"

"We may not have a choice. We have to abandon our fine lady disguises. I've been uncomfortable in petticoats and gloves. I say we become the lads who wore these breeches and coats and go with this unpleasant Scotsman. We can find Bernard later."

Hannah stared at Eleanor. "And if they jail us? With men?"

Eleanor gathered up the hem of her skirt and ripped the seam. She extracted all the coins, one by one. "We can pay a fine and be on our way. Here, let me help you out of that dress."

The inspector pounded on the door. "Make haste now. I can get ye past the captain and on to the meetin' place. The McKelvey boys'll be awaitin' on ye."

Half-undressed, they gave each other a puzzled look. Eleanor called back in a conspiratorial whisper, trying to mimic the inspector's accent, "Ah, the McKelveys … we'll be sore glad to see'em ag'in." She finished pulling on the breeches, tussled Hannah's hair, then stuck her fingers in the bowl of water and slicked her own short locks behind her ears.

"Here." Hannah tied a second, relatively plain, linen pocket around her waist and held the pouch open. "Put the coins here."

The door handle jiggled.

***

LUXBURY COMPLAINED TO the ship's captain, but all he got in return was a threat to throw him in the brig with some scalawags who wouldn't do their share of work. He went back to the cabin, opened the door, and was stunned to see the room vacant, except for an inspector working the handle of the washroom door.

"Sir, sir, I beg you, leave the ladies be. This is most distressing." He strode toward the inspector, his hand on his pistol, his thoughts on Eleanor.

"Ladies, ye say? There be no ladies here. Check the gangway. The skipper likely hauled them off the ship. Women be bad luck on the sea."

Luxbury backed up a foot when the inspector aimed his pistol at his knees. "'Tis only some deck hands in there. Stowaways. I'll oust them off for the skipper."

Luxbury frowned, but as the door came open and he saw two lads start to slip out, he turned away and raced off to begin his search for his charges. He gulped down the rising bile. This plan had been going to shite since he'd stopped the carriage this morning. His head ached still, his bottom was sore from riding, his anger at the girls' disobedience vexed him, and now the abrupt appearance of inspectors and the delay in disembarking had him flustered. He glanced back before he left the cabin and saw too wincing lads, one on either side of the repulsive inspector who had a firm grip on each boy's ear. Their hair fell over their eyes, but he bet there were tears there. Stowaways, they'd get what punishment they deserved. No doubt the skipper would have them scrubbing decks and mopping latrines if he wasn't in the mood to throw another pair overboard.

Luxbury laughed as he exited, then shut his mouth and moved out of the way as a dozen or more hungry crew pushed their way past him.

***

CLIMBING DOWN THE ropes after Hannah felt natural to Eleanor. She even smiled to herself once the pain in her ear diminished. They dropped into a jolly boat, followed by the gruff man who believed they were lads and not lassies. She pictured Lady Beth's face and imagined it devolving into a horrified expression. Well, the woman—her aunt if she really was—had inadvertently prepared them for this escape. It was easy for them to slip into old ways, swing their arms, take longer strides, grunt and huff and even burp or fart as the need arose.

This port wasn't nearly as busy as the one they'd come from. The sun had set and there was barely enough light left to determine much from the silhouettes on shore. The inspector rowed with strong arms, the muscles in his back rippling under his shirt, and his face grimacing. Eleanor pressed her own arms against her chest. She'd hastily bound her bosom; luckily the shirt was large and bulky on her anyway. She and Hannah could hunch their shoulders and hide their figures. Men were easy to fool.

"Och, grab that wee post, tie the front," the phony inspector hollered at Hannah. He stowed the oars and grabbed a second rope to secure the jolly boat to the flimsy dock. The boat tilted as Eleanor stood. She lurched toward the edge and caught her hand on the splintery dock. She gritted her teeth and kept her composure.

"Hey," the man yelled at a lad onshore, "bring the wagon."

The girls leaped onto the dock and their kidnapper followed. He gave them both a slap on their backs. "Mighty fine actin' back there. Had that cap'n fooled, did ye? I dinnae ken how ye had the cheek to hide yerselves in women's things. We shan't speak aboot it with the McKelveys. They be hearty warrior types, ye ken."

Eleanor tried to grunt a response, but coughed instead. The smaller wharf area was deserted except for the young lad, but the sound of splashing oars behind them signaled the return of the real inspectors. The cargo and their trunks would follow. Eleanor wondered how long the trunks would sit unattended and whether Captain Luxbury would look after them. She supposed not, but he'd given her too many bad feelings for her to hope he wouldn't try to rescue them. *Did she even want to be rescued?* Her sixth sense filled her with foreboding and now, with this competing scheme unfolding before them, curiosity filled her.

"Do ye know, er, do ye ken our names?" she glanced at the man.

"I only ken how's a man named Sylvan sent ye, though Sylvan mayn't be his real name. Ye can call me Tavish. Who be ye?" Sweat gathered on his forehead; invisible quivering was detectable through his grip on her arm.

He gave Hannah a rough cuffing on the shoulder and she answered, "Pascoe. And that's Eldridge. I call'im El."

"Pascoe and El. Easy 'nough. And that there's me son, Malcolm."

A small wagon rattled toward them. The lad held the halter of the single horse and led him forward, stopping when his father waved a hand.

"Hop up, lads. 'Tis a wee bit of a jaunt to Killearn. The McKelveys arrived at the Buchanan farm this fornuin. They'll be pleased to meet ye."

He put a finger to his lips and warned his son to keep watch and follow on his pony if he had sight of any fancy Sassenachs. The boy went back to the dock and Tavish said, "Thought for half a second one o' ye might be the verra gentlewoman the Earl of Bute had in mind to bring to Scotland. McKelvey'll stop that scheme, he will."

The ladies settled themselves in the small bed of the wagon. Wisps of straw littered the bottom, but there was nothing smelly or disagreeable, no lumps of clay or other unspeakable irritants. They sat with legs crossed and listened to Tavish prattle on about people and secrets and governments and kings. Eleanor deduced the meanings of several words she'd never heard before.

The 'wee bit of a jaunt' turned into an hour, the stars came out, but the trail the wagon was on seemed well-known to the horse and to Tavish and the scant light was enough to see their way. At last, a lantern threw some light out on the dirt several feet before the porch of a wood frame farmhouse. Tavish stopped the horse a few feet away. The thatched roof was barely visible, but nevertheless intriguing. It was nothing like anything either girl had ever seen before. To the right there was a small oddly-shaped barn and a corral as well. The night air felt crisp, but Eleanor didn't notice she was getting cold, not when she saw two broad-shouldered men in kilts step out of the barn and approach the wagon.

***

KEIR WOKE HIS brother when he heard Tavish and the wagon coming up the trail. They'd been sleeping on the hay pretty much the whole day since they'd arrived before noon. The Buchanan clan was no longer in residence except for the cross-eyed son, Thomas Buchanan, who'd stayed to tend the scraggly sheep and barren fields. Thomas had fed the pair and listened to the men outline the scheme when Tavish arrived with his son. Keir had meant to use Tavish's wagon, but he and Logan needed sleep. So it was Tavish who was tasked with bringing in the lads who they hoped would be on the English frigate due in that very afternoon. The coded letter indicated there'd soon be the arrival of a Hanover relation, ready to be groomed for the plot against the throne. Keir was secretly commissioned with adding two English lads as extra guards for the Hanover heir, though they'd be bought and paid for as infiltrators. There was some disagreement and confusion about the heir's gender. Keir was certain the plan was for a secret prince, not a princess, to arrive, and he was still holding hope that he'd have to deal with a young man and not some unfortunate female.

"Get yer haid off the hay, ye lazy dog. We've company. Ole Tavish is returned." Keir pushed his brother further into the hay, then pulled him up and out. Their horses whinnied and Keir gave Copper a comforting stroke along its neck.

"Whaaht? Whot?" Logan adjusted his accent to sound more Brit than Scot. "Has Tavish brought the lit'l lads what'll be our English spies?"

"Aye. 'Tis too dark to see'em yet. Come along. And stop with yer play-actin'. Ye'll not be gettin' the part. Ye'd be recognized." He gave Copper another pat and pushed the barn door the rest of the way open. His brother came along and the two men walked shoulder to shoulder toward the lantern. Keir kept his eyes on the wagon, straining to see the lads.

"Hullo, Tavish. I see ye got'em both. Any trouble playing inspector?" He reached down for the lantern Thomas must have set out at dusk.

"Nay, nae trouble a'tall." He slithered down from his seat and ran his hand along the reins until he reached the horse's muzzle. "Thomas's old gelding kent the way back in the dark. 'Twas black as the Earl of Hell's waistcoat." He chuckled and pointed back at the wagon's inhabitants. "Lads, jump off. Give the future Laird of Castle Caladh a deep bow. 'Tis Keir McKelvey ... and his younger brother, Logan."

As they scrambled out of the wagon Tavish dug into his shirt and pulled out something he waved at Keir and Logan. The movement caught Keir's eye, but he was more interested in the way the boys were acting. Strange, he thought, that they were brave enough to risk the journey, but now seemed awkwardly fearful of him. He raised the lantern higher.

"See?" Tavish still waved the braids. "Ye mayn't see well 'nough, but these are ladies' braids. The lads were clever buggers to disguise themselves as maidens. They couldna fool me, o'course, but with bonnets and braids and fancy dresses they risked their lives ... on the verge of being thrown overboard, fer cursin' the ship, nae doubt."

Logan touched his capless head in a gesture of greeting, then elbowed Keir. "They're a wee bit scrawny." He looked to Tavish. "Did ye bring the dresses?" When Tavish finished answering in the negative along with a slur of self-deprecating curses, Logan said to Keir, "I ken 'tis yer plan, brother, that they be guards, but perhaps a change is warranted. One or both could be ... hmm ... hidden under petticoats."

Keir had yet to speak, spellbound he was by one of the lads. An emotion he hadn't felt since enduring the deep melancholy of losing his ma came over him. A vague scent tickled his nose. He couldn't identify it, not flower, nor animal, nor food. What other thing elicited such a reaction to put him in this uneasy state?

"Keir? What think ye?" Logan nudged him again. "I can tell from how ye're starin' at the lads, that my plan'll make more sense."

"Aye," Keir finally managed to croak out a word.

"Maybe Thomas has some things of his mum's. Dress one of them as a maid, the other as a guard. Or send them both to the Beldorney castle as fine English ladies."

Keir took a step toward the wagon, lifting the lantern higher yet. Tavish started to lead the horse toward the barn and the sudden lurch of the wagon caused both of the creatures cowering before him to take a step forward. One stumbled and Keir grabbed for a flailing arm, yanking its owner upright.

He grunted. "Ye'll be the dress-wearer," he let go of the abnormally soft flesh, "seein' as how ye're less steady." He lowered the lantern and handed it off to Logan. "Yer name?"

"El."

"Ye'll have to learn some grace, El, if ye're to play the part of a lady's maid."

"Nay," Logan said, "ye mean a lady's companion, should the Hanover heir be a she. And the other one can be the guard … for either prince or princess."

Keir nodded. "And yer name?"

"Pascoe."

"A'right then. We'll look for clothes and such on the morrow. Ye'll sleep in the barn tonight."

"Have ye need of the jakes?" Logan gestured toward an outhouse. "Or will a tree do ye fine enough?"

Chapter 5

ELEANOR AND HANNAH were left alone in the stable, which was nothing more than a long shed partitioned into four compartments. They'd have to sleep on a pile of hay with two smelly horse blankets for warmth. It wasn't loathsome to them. Many were the nights when, by choice, they slept with the horses back at Ingledew.

They dared to whisper to each other. Their heads were close together and not even the closest horse was disturbed by their barely audible conversation.

"We've been kidnapped by the vilest of England's enemies," Hannah complained. "What do we do?"

"We pretend to be boys or girls or maidens or guards or whatever they expect."

"But they're taking us to the Beldorney estate. Isn't that where Captain Luxbury was taking you? Us?"

Eleanor grinned in the dark. "Perhaps our trunks will be there before us." She closed her eyes as there was no reason to keep them open. But as soon as she did, an image of the handsome future Laird of Castle Caladh bloomed on her retinas. He had touched her when she almost fell. His strong fingers may well have left a mark on her upper arm, but all she remembered was how every nerve in her body had responded.

"We have to run away," Hannah pleaded. She shifted her weight, rising to a sitting position. "We could steal the horses. There are three. We could ride two and lead the third so they'd have no way of coming after us."

Eleanor put a hand out where she thought Hannah's shoulder might be, connected with her neck, and gently pulled her back down to the hay. "No. We are in the middle of something extraordinarily important."

"El, I'll do whatever you say. You know that."

"Good." Eleanor rolled onto her back and closed her eyes again. "What did you think of them, Pascoe?"

"The young lairds of a castle?" There was a hesitation. "I thought them fairly handsome, even in those short skirts they call kilts." There was a yawn in her voice. "But I won't be distracted, not if I'm to play the guard."

"I rather like the position we're in. It's more exciting than the games we played with the Miller twins, when the Chaddertons pretended to be the colonists, revolting against whichever Miller twin was playing the King."

"It was William, he always played the Regent. Callum and I were nameless soldiers. And you, you were best at being General Howe."

Eleanor still whispered. "I was. And those childhood war games may serve us well. Who would expect two females to execute a military deception or two? I wonder ..."

Eleanor paused to form her racing thoughts into words. But Hannah's breathing grew steady and she didn't ask Eleanor to finish her sentence. To herself Eleanor continued to consider the situation: she pondered the difficulty of pretending to be a boy who was pretending to be a princess. How amusing. She yawned.

But it was also quite terrifying, for it was obvious to her that Lady Beth and Luxbury's plan to make her queen was known to these Scotsmen. They were equally set on subverting the plan. If they knew that not only wasn't she a lad, but she was the lass they were arranging to ... oh! Good heavens! ... was she to be a part of arranging her own demise?

Eleanor's sleepiness fled. These thoughts kept her mulling over their predicament for a lengthy while. She would have liked to talk it over with Hannah, but the sound of her gentle breathing dissuaded her. She listened to the other night sounds. The hoot of an owl? A rustling in the straw, perhaps a mouse? She wasn't frightened. It was Hannah's steady measured breathing that calmed her.

She considered how she might undermine both plans. Her loyalties should lie with the English ... and yet, if her mother were somewhere in Scotland, then it might be advantageous to burrow into the Highland life. *Hmm.* And that made her think about Keir McKelvey. At twelve and thirteen she'd had no romantic interest in the Chadderton boys or the Miller twins. At sixteen she'd gotten her monthlies and curiously that had awakened some sensibilities toward the male species. Cameron had held her interest for a while. And now, at nearly eighteen, she noticed dreadfully clearly how differently her mind and her body reacted to disagreeable men like the ship's cook or Tavish, as opposed to the genteel Luxbury or the fetching McKelvey men. *Mmm, the McKelvey man to be precise ... Keir ... future laird ...*

She nodded off finally, but woke when the horses made snuffling sounds.

"Who's there?" she called out, suddenly feeling vulnerable in the dark.

"'Tis only me, Malcolm, come wi' me pony. Me da told me to follow after ye. Remember?"

Eleanor felt Hannah move. "Pascoe, Malcolm is here."

"Malcolm?" She sounded groggy.

"Aye, 'tis me. Dae nae worry. I'll be asleep a'fore ye can say g'night." Eleanor felt him nestle down beside her. Then he lowered his voice and whispered, "G'night."

***

KEIR ENDURED HIS brother's questions with patience. He, along with Tavish and the cabin's owner, Thomas Buchanan, had taken turns fielding the what if's and but's and why not's of Logan's misgivings. They sat around a table in hand-made chairs that Thomas's father had crafted before he lost a hand in the battle of Culloden. Thomas hated the British and got up from the table several times to check that his shed had not yet been burned to the ground by the prissy English lads Keir had allowed to bed down there.

"Sit yer arse down, Thomas," Tavish scolded him again. "They be soundly sleeping. Ye've nay a ting to worry yerself over."

"But ..." Logan raised his brows yet again, "ye said yerself, they were more clever lads than ye'd met before. Could they nae be workin' fer the crown?"

"'Tis a thought," Tavish said.

Keir dropped his head and shook it slowly side to side. "Nay, brother. Nay." He'd twice before refuted that selfsame fear.

Thomas moved away from the window, threw another log in the fireplace, and lowered himself onto his chair. His face was long and hawkish, his salt-and-pepper hair worn long and styled back in a mane. He tapped his blackened fingertips on the tabletop.

Keir lifted his head. "The dress, Thomas? Could ye fetch it?"

Thomas nodded at Keir, one eye gazing on the black-haired Highlander, the other eye fixed on his own nose. The chair creaked as he rose again. The cabin had two adjoining rooms. Thomas took one of the candles from the mantel and lit his way to the bedroom. He grumbled loudly, but returned with a grey shift and a formless dress that needed mending.

"'Twas all there be in the trunk."

Keir recognized the shift as an undergarment. He averted his eyes immediately. His three older sisters had trained him early on to look away and though there was no woman in the room, he felt his skin go warm.

Tavish grunted, scratched at his whiskers, and laid his head on his arms.

"Looks proper enough to me," Logan laughed, "fer a scullery maid." He nudged Keir. "That town we skirted, could we nae fetch us somethin' better from a seamstress there?"

Tavish popped his head up. "Stealin' from a Sassenach 'twould be more to me delight. I saw a redcoat on the vessel, a'searchin' through a pile of lady things a real inspector tossed. Two trunks of dresses. I'll send me boy back in da mornin'. He'll sniff'em out. Swipe a couple."

Keir nearly upset the table. "A redcoat! With trunks of women's things?" He saw confusion on the other men's faces. "Were there women on the ship, truly?"

"I dinnae ken. 'Tis most unlikely that frigate would carry passengers."

"But there was a redcoat. Did ye notice, was he a captain or a general?"

"A captain, by me chin. I ken the difference."

"They let generals bring their wives, but a captain …" Keir thought a moment, "… a captain couldna bring his wife. Were there other soldiers?

"Nary a one to poke his nose in me business."

"No soldiers. That could mean this redcoat ye saw was secretly escortin' the verra woman of their scandalous plan. Two trunks. 'Tis a clue." Keir narrowed his eyes and thought.

Logan and Thomas watched Keir, while Tavish yawned and stretched.

"Ye got a new plan. I see it formin'," Logan said.

"Och, I do. The captain shan't arrive at Beldorney Hall with a lady and two trunks, nae before us. He'll be obliged to rent a wagon, stay the night at the Drovers Inn … mm … we'll need to use yer wagon agin,

Tavish." He opened the sporan at his waist and withdrew two coins. He slapped them on the table at Tavish's arm.

"Are ye plannin' on killin' the redcoat?" Thomas's eyes focused on Keir's face for an instant before one went askew. "'Cause if ye are, I've got it in me heid to make a wee bit of payback for me da's injuries. I'd slit a redcoat ear ta ear, if ye think it necessary."

Keir heaved out a breath. "It may well be, Thomas. Ye're welcome to come along."

***

ELEANOR CAME AWAKE to light streaming in through the open barn door and a face, a dirty one, staring at her, not six inches from her nose.

"Get back," she demanded in her best imitation of a Chadderton brat, "or I'll wallop you into the river."

"Ain't no river here." Malcolm scooted back though. "Why's yer face like that? Ye sleep like me little sister. Be ye dreamin' o' the fairies? They put angels' faces onto girls, ma says. Better watch out, I could see one a'formin'."

Eleanor sat up and took a longer look at the boy resting on his knees and knuckles, leaning in as familiar as a mother hen. She scrunched her face into a boyish, she hoped, scowl. "Malcolm, is it? You talk a lot. How old are you? Twelve?"

"Fourteen, this winter past. Tall as ye be, ye miserable Sassenach. I thought … och, never mind."

Eleanor looked over at Hannah who was wide awake. "Pascoe, did you know the fairies here could turn our faces into girl faces?" She smirked and a look passed between them.

Hannah pushed herself up to sit, ran her fingers through her hair to remove bits of straw and dirt, and spoke to Malcolm. "We may need your help in conjuring up some of these fairies, boy." She started to sneeze.

"Call me Malcolm. And ye be Pascoe, I heard this one called ye that, but," he looked at Eleanor, "what be yer name, Englishman?"

"Eldridge, but call me El, though I suspect the Lord may want me to be called by … mm, something befitting a lady's maid, as that is what I'm to pretend to be." She shot another look at Hannah who'd finished sneezing and was now moving onto her knees and rubbing at her crotch like they'd seen the stable hands do.

Hannah ended with a contented grunt then raised a fist and punched at the air. "I've got it. I know what you could be called. How about Eleanor? That's rather close and I won't spoil the ruse if I call you El." She nodded at Malcolm who began to nod in rhythm.

"We should practice callin'im her and she." Malcolm started his own scratching routine.

"Malcolm, that is a very good idea." Eleanor gave him a hearty slap on the back. "Now … my stomach is grumbling. We've manly appetites, no matter our size. Agreed?"

Malcolm flicked a booger away and nodded. "Me da, Tavish ye ken him as, will have somethin' tucked away for us. Follow me."

***

KEIR AND LOGAN hadn't needed much more sleep. The last hours of the long night were spent discussing possible hitches and glitches in their proposed plan as Thomas slept in his own bed and Tavish snored on the table.

"I ken there'll be complications, the first being how to explain a Hanover heir in a farm maid's dress, but …" Logan peered into the pantry cupboard that Thomas had promised held a bowl of eggs. "Brother, dae ye ken how to make these into our breakfast? I dinnae fancy eatin' raw yokes."

Keir snorted at his brother. "I dinnae believe ye've nivver seen cook boil an egg. Ye spent half yer life in the kitchen, nosin' the pots 'n pans."

"The sun's up," Logan ignored Keir's taunt, "so I'll try wakin' ole Thomas." He stepped to the door and knocked. When there was no answer, no sound even, from the other side, he nudged the door open and spied. "Nae sign of Thomas. He musta sneaked past when we all laid our heids on the table, like Tavish."

"Gone to the jakes, no doubt. Or checkin' on his sheep."

"Or collectin' more eggs, I hope."

Tavish woke then, as the outer door sprang open and Thomas returned using the front of his shirt as a basket.

"Got ye more eggs. When me family was here, me hens were used to layin' for seven hungry mouths."

"We'll pay ye for yer fine hospitality, Thomas. Did ye notice … were the lads awake?"

"Yup. Two turned into three. All headed for the jakes. Got an extra horse in the shed, too. Fair small."

Tavish stretched. "Me boy, Malcolm's pony."

"Ye can send him home, Tavish. We'll have nae need fer the lad." Keir adjusted his kilt, felt the need to go out and relieve himself, and headed for the door.

Outside he surveyed the farm and fields. The morning was crisp and clear, the heavens a cloudless blue; the sheep were far out in the pasture; a few chickens pecked at the ground around the house. He looked to a copse of trees he intended to make use of and saw Malcolm finishing his own morning ritual there. Keir looked in the other direction. At the jakes stood one of the English lads, the one he thought could play the guard. Then the second lad, the one who caused his brow to furrow, came out of the outhouse and looked to the sky and smiled. It was a curious act and more curious when his companion did the same. He didn't understand at first, but then he figured they were simply in awe of the fine Scottish morn, a treat for English men used to grey days.

Keir signaled them to come to the cabin. Their smiles were gone by the time they reached him. They came up slowly with some hesitation. He was well aware of the reason behind their reluctance to get too close. He knew he was an imposing figure, but perhaps with a more substantial Scottish diet than the gruel and soggy biscuits the English fared on, they'd fill out. "In ye go. I'll join ye to break our fasts as soon as I tend to a wee bit o' business."

Malcolm raced up, slapped both lads on their backs and scooted into the cabin in front of them. The screech one of them emitted made him think of Fenella. And that gave him another thought. They'd have to pass near enough to her place on their way to Beldorney Hall. Surely he could convince her to lend them a dress. Of course, it would have to be her best one to be presentable for his purposes. Well, she owed him, did she not?

He walked off to the trees thinking about that simple little sound. A feminine squeak, it was.

Chapter 6

THE SMALL ENTOURAGE rattled down the path. Malcolm's pony was harnessed to the wagon and Malcolm, sitting next to his father, held the reins. Eleanor and Hannah sat uncomfortably in the wagon with a frayed dress folded unevenly and resting on Eleanor's lap. Thomas, Keir, and Logan rode their respective horses, single file in front. Eleanor and Hannah resorted to lip-reading and gestures to communicate unless it was to comment on the Scottish scenery they passed. The sights and smells were new to them. The earth was briny and wet, the bogs gave off a dank tangy scent, but new spring growth peeped up through the soil.

Eleanor couldn't help but stare ahead at the backs of Tavish and Malcolm, because between their shoulders she'd get a glimpse of the riders. There'd been a short introduction of Thomas, who'd given them hard-boiled eggs for their breakfast and a cup of something she heard the younger McKelvey call watered-down whipkull. She didn't like it, but she drank it. The brothers had eaten standing up, staring at her and Hannah, who had been given the seats. She'd been terribly uncomfortable and had answered all questions with one-syllable responses, keeping the timbre of her voice low and husky.

Their plan seemed to be in flux, with an upcoming stop at a small farm along the way. Eleanor gleaned from the morning's conversation that the McKelvey brothers had a sister who married a Beldorney. They lived on a farm not far from the Beldorney estate or Hall as Keir had called it. She thought Luxbury had called it a castle. Perhaps Beldorney was a common name in Scotland. She wasn't sure if the Beldorney clan was high-born, but Lady Beth had intended for Eleanor to go by that name. She thought back a couple of nights to Lady Beth's admonitions. She said Luxbury had relatives in Scotland, of the Beldorney clan, and that the captain had chosen that name for her to use; the Beldorneys were English sympathizers and would teach her things she should know as a Hanover heir.

She felt her heart rate quicken. She was in the middle of something outlandish and her feelings and fears made amendments by the hour. She clutched at the hidden brooch and tried to remember her mother more clearly.

The pony pulled the wagon steadily and turned to follow the riders along a bumpier path. Then the path opened up onto a beautiful expanse of meadows and fields. It took her breath away. And she had a perfect view of the horsemen, now riding abreast. The McKelveys' kilts flapped against their horses' rumps, but the men themselves wore tartan trews, leather lined to protect them. Their hair, ribboned into hasty tails, bounced at their necks. She admired their posture, their shoulders … and then Keir twisted in the saddle to look back at the wagon. Their eyes met for a full two seconds before she remembered to breathe. She quickly looked down at the ratty dress in her lap.

Hannah nudged her. "Look, a farm."

She raised her gaze again and saw a small house on the hilltop. Keir was now galloping up the trail, his brother trotting after him. Thomas stayed nearer to the wagon and laughed when Tavish made a remark in Gaelic.

Hannah poked at Malcolm's back. "What was that your father said? We didn't understand a word."

Malcolm looked over his shoulder, a smirk on his face, and repeated the Gaelic phrase.

Hannah punched him harder. "In the King's English, please."

"Och, he said he hoped to see some teats."

Both Hannah and Eleanor nodded and laughed. They'd heard much worse and had been expert at making their own bawdy retorts in their capacities as young male stable hands, before Lady Beth took them in hand to transform them.

Hannah gave Eleanor an eye and said, "My friend El here could show you his, or rather, hers." That got a chuckle from Tavish and a disappointed groan from Malcolm. To Eleanor she said, "You'll need a couple rags or maybe stuff some pouches with wool to give yourself the look, El."

Eleanor clutched the dress up to her chest and made a face at Tavish's back. She let an uncouth rejoinder slip out of her mouth, followed by, "When you see me next, wearing this frock, you'll fall in love with me yourself, Pascoe."

The wagon picked up some speed as the pony tried to keep up with Thomas's gelding. The girls took a bad bounce and groaned, but they finally reached the cabin.

Tavish jumped down and told Malcolm to hold the pony at the halter, to keep his head up from nibbling the light green shoots sprouting up everywhere. The girls stayed in the wagon, awaiting instructions. At last they had a moment to speak privately while the McKelveys embraced their sister.

"I think I may have a problem," Hannah whispered, clutching her stomach. "I always get these painful stomach flutters a day or two before my monthly comes. How am I to hide it?"

Eleanor swung her head up, looked at the small woman smiling up at that handsome Highlander. "Perhaps we'll get a chance to confide in that woman."

Hannah looked over. "But she's their sister. She'll be on their side. We have to keep pretending we're English lads, pretending to be a guard and a lady. If I get my monthlies—"

"We'll figure something out. Shh, here they come."

Keir brought his sister to the wagon and immediately spoke to Eleanor. "Stand up, lad. Show me sister the dress."

Eleanor got to her feet and held the fabric a few inches in front of her body. Even with the height of the wagon she wasn't much above the Highlander.

"What think ye, Fenella?"

"Oh, it's long enough for him." She tittered and grasped Keir's elbow, still looking up. "But even as delicate and, er, graceful as this fella is, it'll take a miracle to pass him off as a lady in waiting or such like. Lad … if ye could be anywhere now, where would ye be?"

Without hesitation Eleanor responded, "America." She was pleased with how she'd lowered her voice, grateful it didn't quiver, though it was flat and lifeless.

"Aye," Fenella nodded, "America. A place fer new beginnin's."

Eleanor held her tongue, glanced back and forth between Fenella and Keir. Fenella would hold her stare, but Keir would not meet her eyes. He looked at Hannah.

47

Fenella nudged him. "Then the other one, perhaps? Stand up, Pascoe."

Hannah stumbled to her feet and crossed her arms. She lifted the left side of her upper lip to approximate a sneer. Then she snatched the dress from Eleanor and curtsied.

"Well," Fenella clapped her hands, "that was quite a change. He may be yer lady. I'll fetch ye a better dress. And me bonnets."

Keir looked at his sister. "Does it grieve ye to nae be called Lady, Fenella?"

"Not at all." She waved a hand at her house and fields. "Here be me own Beldorney estate, a piece of Scottish heaven all to ourselves. I'm Lady Beldorney here." She gently touched her hand to her belly then shielded her eyes with a palm and looked far off. "And there be me own prince. Hubert. And Huey by his side."

"Aye, a prince of a man is he. Little Huey'll take after him." Keir turned his body away from the wagon and began to lead his sister back toward the house. "Has Huey been practicin' wi' the hatchet?"

Hannah and Eleanor sank back into the wagon.

"So, we've switched roles again?" Hannah frowned at Eleanor. "I'm sorry."

Eleanor brushed off the concern. "No matter. The only thing that matters now is getting to that outhouse beyond the cabin. I'll go first."

"Take the dress. Change. Maybe we can both be ladies. Again."

***

"'TIS SETTLED," KEIR crossed his arms, towering over everyone as they circled around him by the sideyard bathing tub. "Thomas, ye'll be staying in the bothan on the edge of the heathers, a'waitin' for us." Then he said, "The lads'll bunk wi' me nephew in the loft and you two ..." he raised his voice and indicated Tavish and Malcolm who still stood off a ways with the pony, "... I thank ye much, but ye may ferry yerselves along home now."

"Ye have nae further use o' me wagon? How will ye get the lads ... er, lassies ... to the estate?" Tavish scratched at his beard.

"They'll ride wi' me and Logan and don the dresses a mile from the Beldorney gates. We'll say they were waylaid by highwaymen and we McKelveys came to their rescue. Thus they'll be without carriage, bag, or baggage. Just a lady and her servant." He looked at the women. "I shall decide which is which once Fenella pretties them up. Oh, and Tavish, have ye got the braids still?"

Tavish felt his pockets and withdrew the blond human hair braids and the darker horse hair braids. He came close and dropped them onto Keir's outstretched palm.

48

"Och." Keir frowned at the locks and touched the darker ones first. "Rather coarse they be. Me gelding, old Copper, mayhaps could donate from his mane. Though I'd nae expect a high-born lady to wear somethin' from a horse's arse." The men all laughed.

***

ELEANOR, STANDING BEHIND Hannah, moved forward and swiped a braid from his hand. In her lowest, most practiced male voice, she tried out a lie, "These were fine enough to fool the ship's purser and bribe our way onto the frigate."

Heads nodded, but Keir looked down at Eleanor. "Tell us, El, how did ye get on board? Ye were hired by ... well, can ye tell me the name of our English partner?"

Eleanor racked her brain for the name Tavish had mentioned last night. "Sullivan."

"He means Sylvan," Hannah interjected.

"Right. Sylvan." Eleanor stared at Keir.

***

KEIR'S TONGUE CAUGHT on his teeth. The lad was deceptive, he was certain, but Tavish was nodding. "And what," Keir got his mouth to move, "what was it ye were hired to do?"

He watched the lad suck in a breath. There was something pulling at Keir's inner being and he meant to figure out exactly why this small nothing of a person brought out such confusing feelings. "Well?"

Eleanor huffed, pounded one fist into her other palm, and answered, "There's a plot against King George and Queen Charlotte too. Some want them both dead. Her first. There's an illegitimate princess, born and raised in secret ... I daren't say where ... and we, me and Pascoe, are meant to spy when they move her to Scotland. And either kill her or bring her to reign ... we weren't told which."

Keir handed the braids to Fenella. "Well, the lad has a grasp on the main points ... and is as confused about the plot's end as this McKel-vey." He touched his chest and nodded at Eleanor.

"I think we need to study the topic a might bit more. Perhaps wi' the princess herself." He looked over their heads at the shapes of his brother-in-law and young son walking through the fields, making their way closer to the homestead. He resumed his attention on El and Pascoe. "Have ye any qualms if ye were to be asked to slip the fair maiden a poison?" Both of their faces gave away their answer. He put his hand up to stop them, if they were to lie. "Don't answer. I'll nae ask ye to do such a deed." He glanced at the other men. Thomas raised an eyebrow, but Tavish gave a gruff farewell and climbed onto the wagon with Malcolm.

They all watched the wagon roll off, then Keir looked to Fenella. "And I won't ask ye to feed five more mouths. Logan can come wi' me to hunt the wood pigeons I saw signs of in the fields we passed. Thomas, ye're welcome to come along."

Keir gave his sister a quick embrace and whispered a request. "Can ye see to it the lads get a proper bath?"

***

FENELLA WASN'T STUPID. She smiled warmly and drew her shawl tighter around her shoulders, inviting the two pitiable creatures into the cabin to help her with the fire, the potato peeling, and the water fetching. But as soon as they came in, she barred the door, leaned against it, and demanded, "Just what are ye lassies attemptin' to prove?" She clucked her tongue. "I'll nae suffer ye to pretend this nonsense aroun' me own lad. 'Twould be confusin' to Huey."

Eleanor looked at Hannah and Hannah shrugged her shoulders. Eleanor let out a long breath and lowered her head in a semi-bow. "We beg your pardon. How did you know?"

Fenella looked them up and down. "Ye've clipped yer hair, but long hair doesna make a lady a lady. Ye've mastered a few of the manly traits, I'll give ye that, but I saw ye touchin' hands walkin' from the outhouse. An' ye couldna hide yer blushin' when ye looked upon me brothers. Handsome men they be, and nary a lassie in the parish can look away when one or t'other passes."

"We didn't know what to do." Hannah crumbled into the nearest chair.

Eleanor touched her shoulder. "That's right. We were on the ship, in the skipper's cabin, when an inspector, well, we thought he was an inspector ... when Tavish came in and ordered us to take off our dresses and get into these grimy breeches and shirts."

"A mistake, then?" Fenella's scowl softened. "Ye musta been sore afraid. Dae ye ken what matter ye've gotten yerselves involved in?"

Eleanor nodded, tears gathering in her eyes. "We've been planning our escape, but ..." She dropped into the next chair.

"Aye, ye've been scairt inta submission and then drawn in further by me brothers' good looks an' charm. I dinnae blame ye. I ken what those emerald eyes can make a lass do. Still ..." she stopped leaning against the door and stood straighter, "ye've burrowed yerselves into a knot of conspiracy. I see all the nonsense the men are aboot. Me own husband, a Beldorney relation, ye ken, is privy to the plan. Me brothers aim to protect me from the truth, but I ken more than they think." She stared at Hannah until she dropped her eyes then turned her attention to

Eleanor. "But ye're English. I cannae make sense of it. An' wi' yer hair so short, an' braids cut off before Tavish found ye. I cannae guess why."

She folded her arms and waited.

Hannah spoke first. "We worked for Lady Beth and Lord Edgeworth at castle Ingledew. In the stables." She glanced at Eleanor who gave her the slightest nod. "It was by the Lady's mercy that we lived there, pretending to be lads until she thought it best to teach us to be proper ladies. I was brought from Cornwall, but El, er Eleanor, was born at Ingledew. Her mother ran away to Scotland, Lady Beth said, and we've," she took a breath, "we've determined to search her out."

Fenella dropped her rigid stance. "Ye poor lassies. And ye," she touched Eleanor's shoulder, "'twere but a wee bairn and abandoned by yer ma?" She tisked her tongue.

Eleanor lifted her head and wiped her eyes. She reached in her breeches and unpinned the brooch she'd hidden there. "Have you ever seen a woman wearing a brooch like this one? And calling herself Mary Ainsworth or Mary Fletcher?"

Fenella reached for the brooch. "There be nae ring to either name, but I've seen a pin like this holdin' fast to a young lad's kilt."

Eleanor's eyes went wide. She reached for Fenella's hand and gulped. "Can you tell us where?"

Fenella handed the brooch back. "'Twas at a fair, aye, a year or so past. Two days walk north. But the fair draws folks from all parts." She moved back to the door, unbolted it, and hung her shawl on a hook protruding from the center.

There was a silence in the small cabin then. Fenella threw another log in the fireplace. She kept her thoughts to herself a few moments more as she opened the potato bin and filled her apron with six large potatoes. She snapped off the sprouts that had begun to grow and tossed them on the fire.

"I'll keep yer secret," she said, setting the potatoes on the table and going back to a cupboard for a bowl and a knife. "An' I'll help ye on yer way ... after ye help me brothers wi' their politickin'."

Eleanor shifted her gaze and stared steadily at Fenella. Fenella took the knife and pared the first potato.

"Me husband, Hubert, had a fallin' out wi' the Beldorneys. A marriage was arranged between the Beldorney clan and the McDonough clan. He was to take his vows and marry Morag McDonough, but we'd already met ... an' Hubert had fallin' heelster gowdie in love wi' me... so he broke off the engagement and wedded me." She sighed. "Which brought such shame to the Beldorneys that they disowned him." She shook her head. "Though as soon our bairn was born, they gifted us this land."

She finished all six potatoes and threw the peelings out the back window.

"A word between women: marry fer love." She smiled at the girls and was encouraged to see a hint of a smile appear on Eleanor's face.

Fenella suddenly became serious. "I'll nae spend hours boiling water fer yer baths. Ye'll get as clean in cold water." She opened a trunk that sat along the outer wall and pulled out another dress and two bonnets. "Here ye go. The spring's a wee walk behind the house. There be rags to wash with dryin' on the bushes. We'll show the men what bonnie lasses ye can be."

"But ..." Eleanor stood, "I think I understand. You want us to help them and if all goes well, then perhaps your husband might be reunited with his family."

Fenella nodded slowly. "If ye please, could ye dae a wee bit of spying on me behalf? Soften up the Lady of the house, Hubert's mum? Ye'll get yer pay from Keir, and I'll add to it from me own stash, to help ye on yer search. I'll write ye a letter, too, a letter of introduction to me sister at Castle Caladh and me married sister further to the north. Ye'll have places to stay whilst ye search."

Fenella watched Eleanor release a full smile. *Och, me brothers both will be smitten should they learn her true sex.*

***

THE ICY WATER was shocking. They splashed themselves with handfuls of it and rubbed off two days' worth of dirt with the rags. The sun at least was helpful in drying them and they donned the dresses and bonnets as soon as they could. Hannah gathered the boys' clothes and dunked them in the spring and rung them out as well as she could. They both arranged them to dry on the bushes.

Eleanor grinned at Hannah. "You look beautiful, Pascoe. It must be the blue of the dress."

"You should have let me wear the old one. I don't want to be the lad pretending to be the lassie that's impersonating a lady's companion ... or the lady herself." She laughed at the complicated ruse. "But I understand. This way we'll keep your true identity better protected. I wonder if we'll run into Captain Luxbury."

"I hope not." Eleanor lifted the hem of her skirt as they stepped over rocks and then took the narrow path back to the cabin. "She seems to love her husband."

"Who?"

"Fenella. I wonder how she could leave Castle Caladh to live here."

Hannah shrugged. "Perhaps they call it a castle, but it's no bigger than the hut she has now." She looked at the cabin as they approached it. "I miss Ingledew. The cook. The horses. The warm baths." She laughed. "I even miss Lady Beth."

"As do I," Eleanor said. "I've had no other family. Just them and you."

"Eleanor," Hannah touched her arm and they both stopped walking, "I didn't say before, but I think it was wrong of Lord and Lady to try to send you off and make you into a princess … and to usurp the King's throne. It's treason, is it not? You could be hung or beheaded."

"It will all work out. It always does. Remember all the tricks we pulled? The thefts? The pranks? Even when we were caught, the punishments worked to our favor. And now, so recently, the attack of the highwaymen—where were we when that happened? Safe in the bushes. Then when we sneaked up, did they catch us? No. Safe again. Getting on board the ship where women are thrown off because of the sailors' superstitions?—safe again. Kidnapped by Tavish? Safe with the McKelveys. Everything works out for me, for us, Hannah. Don't worry."

They started walking again. "Oh, I see that now. And Fenella knows we're girls and she's not going to reveal our secret. Safe again." She went silent a moment. "Though I wouldn't mind if that younger brother of hers knew me as Hannah and not Pascoe, a lad."

"You like Logan?"

"Mm-hm. And don't deny you're attracted to Keir."

***

KEIR WALKED COPPER the last quarter mile, plucking feathers as he trailed after the others. Thomas had gone on to find the bothan, but Hubert and Huey had joined them on the hunt when they'd crossed paths in the far meadow. Now they rode double beside Logan, with four more naked birds tied and bouncing against their mounts' flanks.

When they reached the stone hut, Logan took Copper's reins and unsaddled his brother's horse for him. There was a small paddock for the horses and Fenella had already filled the troughs with water. Logan opened the gate and led them in.

"Where be ye, Fenella, me fine bonnie lass?" called out Hubert. His son echoed the call to the laughter of his uncles.

Fenella came around from the back of the small home carrying the now dry clothing that had been left near the creek.

Hubert dismounted and helped Huey down, then strode over to embrace his wife.

"What have ye there, me bride? Have ye stripped some poor beggar boys of their fancy garments? Teased some swain out of his livery?" Hubert kept Fenella squeezed in his arms as he pretended to look about for the lads Keir had told him of. "Yer brother says he left ye to do the work of fairies and make changelings of two poor lads." He laughed, looked at his wife, and gave her a quick kiss.

"Ye'll be surprised, ye will." Fenella struggled half-heartedly to free herself, the breeches and shirts stiff against her bosom. "There's some little things yet to be figured out, but if ye expect to see two lassies, then two lassies ye shall see. I've named them … Eleanor and … Hannah." She raised her voice, "Come out and show yerselves."

All eyes turned to the cabin door. Keir pulled the last feather out of the wood pigeon and looked up, his fingers still clinched on the feather. Hannah stepped out first, tying the strings to her bonnet. Keir snorted a laugh and dropped the feather.

The disguise seems quite good; it will fool anyone, he thought. He was pleased with his sister's skill and also thankful she'd never done this to him when they were young and she bossed him around.

Then the second lad appeared. All the air in his lungs fled. He made a convulsive effort to breathe as he stared at Eleanor, twirling on tiptoe, lifting and dropping her hem, fluttering her hands, and … and laughing, song-bird high and musical.

"Are ye fooled?" his sister's voice cut through the laughter. He glanced right and left at the other men who seemed equally stunned. Fenella cackled, "Aye, ye all looked fair blootered. 'Twill be easy to fool the Beldorney staff and intrude as ye wish."

Fenella handed the dry clothes to Hannah who made a face and said, "There is one problem. I held the braids too close to the candle, to warm the wax already on the ends, and now we have no braids at all."

"Ye burnt'em?" Fenella frowned.

Keir ripped his eyes from Eleanor, caught his racing breath, and pretended to be checking the pigeon for any bristles he missed. *'Tis not a she, but a he. 'Tis a boy, a lad, a verra young man, a male of me own sex.* He kept his eyes on the bird and berated himself for his ridiculous reaction. The voices of the men rose in strange praise of Fenella's handiwork. *Fenella is the only woman here,* he repeated to himself.

"Are ye nae pleased, brother?" Fenella came close to him whilst he scolded himself, and now freed the bird from his hand. He nodded at her, still unable to speak. Fenella chuckled. "Aye, I see that yer eyes believe what yer heid denies. But ye'll be sayin' *him* and *he* again as soon as I pack the frocks in a sack. And the bonnets. Ye cannae lose the

54

bonnets." She pointed to Eleanor. "Show them your hair, Mistress Eleanor."

Keir risked watching as the lad, he had to think of him that way, removed the bonnet and shook out a curly head of brown hair. When he'd first met the rascal who'd called himself El and who'd been ungraceful in jumping off the wagon, his hair was slicked tight against his skull, but now …

Keir looked away.

***

THE GIRLS SLEPT well in the loft, their stomachs full, and the blankets warm. The soft sounds that the child, Huey, made were comforting and lulled them both to sleep in a matter of minutes. But Eleanor woke before dawn and lay there thinking about Keir McKelvey. She knew he'd looked at her and seen her, the real her, and he must have known right then. Was he not kin to Fenella? Did he not have the same intuition she had?

But he kept his eyes averted through the fine supper Fenella served. He seemed intent on bringing in armload after armload of firewood. He and Logan spread horse blankets in front of the fireplace to make beds for themselves on the floor.

Once she and Hannah changed back into the shirts and breeches, she expected Keir to give them more instructions, but he still would not look her way. She didn't know how to act anymore. Should she be more girlish in the breeches or more masculine in the dresses?

She turned onto her side and watched the flickering light from the flames below dance along the wall. She raised herself enough to see over the edge. There he was, on the floor. She knew which clump of blankets covered Keir; Logan's face was visible, but Keir's was not. She looked past his shape to the fire. The flames were wiggling upward, sparking and popping to ignite a newly place log. One of the McKelvey brothers must have recently added new wood. Perhaps that was what had awakened her.

Eleanor leaned farther forward. Keir rolled over; his eyes opened. She knew if she moved to duck down, the little bit of motion would catch his attention. She didn't blink and kept as still as she could. A minute passed, then two. Beneath her the door from Fenella and Hubert's room creaked. She saw Keir's gaze dart that way. Fenella crept into the room and Keir raised himself to a sitting position.

"I jist added a log," he whispered.

"'Tis me habit, since Huey was a bairn, to wake twice a night, and e'en now that he sleeps through, I still wake."

Eleanor rolled back and listened. Their voices changed from whispers to low tones.

Fenella said to him, "Our brother told me the news. Ye had a rumpus with our father."

"Hmph, old MacLeod raised the dowry on Anabel and Father accepted. I threw a fit and broke a few things."

"She's a lovely lass ... but ye want somethin' more than a pretty girl to give ye bairns. Ye want a wife ye love, who loves ye back." She put a hand on his back. "Have ye any other lass in mind?"

Keir stayed silent.

"Perhaps," Fenella gave him a final tap, "after these secret doin's ye have yerself mixed into, ye'll find yerself a woman ye'd risk losing Castle Caladh fer, like Hubert did fer me." She glanced at the fire. "That should last till mornin'. Get some sleep."

The door creaked again and Eleanor heard Keir sigh. Men didn't cry, but it sounded as if he was grieving about something. She pondered the bit of information she gleaned from the quiet conversation. Keir was betrothed. How soon would he marry? And why did it bother her so much?

Chapter 7

L UXBURY HAD SEARCHED the ship and had questioned several crew members. One clever seaman coaxed a coin from him and told him he'd seen a large Scotsman hurry two peculiar passengers over the side and into a jolly boat. Luxbury then got himself and both trunks to shore, hired a wagon to send the trunks to Beldorney Hall and rented himself a saddle horse to go in search of the women.

Lord Edgeworth will have my commission rescinded should he find out of my ... misplacement ... of Eleanor, he thought to himself. He rode for half the night, searching, with no success. In the small town of Killearn he found a place to shelter the horse and himself. Early the next morning he asked for directions to Beldorney Hall. Surely, he prayed, the clever young women would continue to Beldorney. They had, after all, managed to get to the wharf when they thought he hadn't survived the attack of the highwaymen. Perhaps they believed he'd been incarcerated by the Scots, that the inspectors had discovered his duplicitous terms of passage: paying the skipper directly and not dealing with the purser as he should have.

That must be it. I'll find them at the castle. Safe and sound. He urged the lazy nag onward and considered what he might do and the lies he'd have to invent if he was wrong and the women were ... lost ... kidnapped ... or worse.

***

LITTLE HUEY CHATTERED through breakfast and his uncles devoted all their attention to the lad, while El and Pascoe, so called while they were wearing breeches, ate their mush without a word.

Fenella fluttered about the table, happy for the warmth of family and dreading the moment when she'd be alone with her son and her chores, for Hubert announced he would go along to guide them to a place closer to the castle gates.

"Och, we'll be off now," Keir suddenly announced. "Grab the sack with the dresses, lad," he motioned to Hannah, "and ye can ride wi' me."

Warm, honeyed sunlight beamed down on their heads as the men saddled up, but it was still chilly out. Fenella stood between Eleanor and Hannah and whispered last minute encouragement. When Keir was ready first, Fenella pushed Eleanor toward his horse.

"Ye'll be better weighted," she called out to Keir, "if ye ride with El and let Pascoe sit behind yer brother." She saw the flash of emotion cross Keir's face and read it for what it was, but she was enjoying her bit of matchmaking. She wished she could be there when they donned their dresses again. She'd love to see her brother squirm uncomfortably. How long before he'd figure out the truth?

***

ELEANOR APPROACHED THE horse's head and spoke softly to the gelding. She rubbed the spot between his eyes and said, "Hello, Copper, I won't add much burden to your back—"

"Talk to horses, dae ye?" Keir interrupted. He stuck a foot in the stirrup and mounted the horse.

Eleanor scrunched her face into a scowl. "I've worked in a stable since I was … as long as I can remember. Not talking to a new horse before jumping on its back is just plain stupid." She ran her hand down Copper's neck and moved next to Keir's left leg. He kicked his foot free of the stirrup so she could use it.

"Here, gi' me yer hand."

"I don't need your help."

"Not takin' me hand is …" he smirked, releasing a hidden dimple, "just plain stupid."

She put her foot into the stirrup, clasped his hand, and pushed off the ground. It was one smooth motion to come up and onto the horse's hindquarters. Keir let go of her hand without another retort. She kicked her foot free of the stirrup and put both hands on the saddle's cantle. She spoke to his back. "Thank you." She immediately wished she'd grunted the words as a stubborn boy would have, or not said anything at all. Her hand still tingled from his touch and now, with a mere two inches of space between them, she could feel his heat, smell him, sense his

58

masculinity. And here she was, legs spread out behind him, heart pounding, perspiration beading up. Her mouth went dry.

She glanced over at Hannah who was climbing up behind Logan a bit more slowly and awkwardly, one hand grappling with the clothing sack. No doubt Hannah was equally disturbed to sit in such an arousing manner behind a handsome young man.

Copper moved forward suddenly and though Eleanor had ridden bareback numerous times, she had a sudden fear of falling backwards. She clutched at Keir and gripped him around his chest.

"Hold tight, lad." Keir slapped the reins and they cantered off, Hubert next, then Logan with Hannah.

They rode fast and Eleanor relaxed into the rhythm and even rested her cheek against his back. The short ponytail she'd made of her hair beat against her neck. She watched the countryside bounce past, yellow wildflowers boldly jutting out of the soil between the road and the forest, and then, when she lifted her head to press the other cheek against Keir's back, she caught a glimpse of dramatic mountains to the north. A moment later they were slowing down to trot through the moorlands. They slowed even more when they came to a loch. Keir reined his horse in and allowed it to stretch its neck to the water and slurp a long drink. The others did the same.

Eleanor unwrapped her arms from the Highlander and made eye contact with Hannah.

Hubert spoke. "'Twas a nice bit of plantin' ye did fer us, Keir. If I didn't thank ye afore, I thank ye now."

"'Twas me pleasure to be of service. Did yer business go as ye'd hoped?"

"Aye. 'Twas most profitable. And … I assume ye got me message?"

"Aye, yer code was easily solved."

"And yet here ye are."

Eleanor felt Keir tense up despite the fact she was no longer touching him. The horse also reacted and backed away from the water.

"Aye, here I am."

"And wi' two English lads instead of the two Scots I paid fer."

Keir cleared his throat. He twisted in his saddle and peered down at Eleanor. "Who'd ye say sent ye, lad?"

"S-S-Sylvan."

Hubert frowned. "'Twas Horace Sylvan, indeed. I met the Scots and paid the price. I wonder what became of those lads."

"Perhaps jailed by the bloody English."

Hubert looked squarely at Eleanor. "Lad, dae ye ken the plan? Are ye brave enough to play the part and slit a throat if the need arises?"

***

KEIR HAD LOOKED down at the small hands clasped around his chest as he'd galloped away from Fenella's home. He was embarrassed by how he felt. There was pleasure in being held by this lad, but it was laden with guilt and a trace of revulsion. He knew what the matter was. He'd seen this creature in a dress and had been horribly deceived, as if some spell was cast and now he couldn't think clearly. These wretched English boys … and soon he'd have to face an equally wretched Englishwoman and pretend to install El and Pascoe as her steadfast, dependable servants. Female servants, at that. Was this an abomination? Had he forgotten his clan vows? Perhaps he should concentrate on Anabel MacLeod. She was beautiful, if not an agreeable or pleasant woman. He would beg his sisters to influence her, mold her into a more congenial companion.

The hands no longer grasped him. Copper had his head down, drinking his fill. Hubert was speaking to him. He answered. They went back and forth and Keir had to concentrate to keep his attention on what Hubert was suggesting. When Hubert asked the lad behind him a question, he felt the lad's body stiffen.

He twisted to ask El a question. The answer was correct.

"Sylvan," she said.

Hubert asked her another question and she outlined the plan as she had before. *She?* He was thinking of this lad in feminine terms. His mind was certainly muddled. Hubert asked about slitting throats and *the lad* answered with conviction. *He* was shifting position behind him. *He* was slipping back over Copper's rump to jump to the ground. No lassie would ever do something so impolite.

Keir breathed more normally once *the lad* was no longer so close.

Keir watched *him* and Pascoe walk off toward some trees, no doubt to relieve themselves. He patted Copper's neck and looked over at Hubert.

"What's got ye flummoxed, Keir? Are ye havin' second thoughts aboot helpin' in the cause?"

"Nay." He forced his focus on Hubert's question. "Ye ken I haven't killt a man, but Thomas is willin'. We'll leave it to him."

"'Twon't be a man, Keir. 'Tis a lass that they're sendin', a Hanover issue, certainly a bastard child."

"Child?"

"Woman, I mean, but nae doubt childish in her ways if she needs to be taught manners and skills at Beldorney."

"Aye." Keir cocked his head. "Ye'll nay be makin' amends wi' yer family, if they learn how ye're conspirin' wi' the English."

60

"Politics be a complicated subject, but killin' a usurper is preferable to killin' the king."

"I'm havin' second thoughts aboot any killin'. Perhaps a kidnappin' and passage to the colonies would be a better plan."

Hubert laughed. "And ye'd be the volunteer to take her, would ye? And miss yer weddin' to Anabel MacLeod? I ken all aboot that. Logan told me." He nodded toward the brother who'd dismounted and was splashing a handful of water on his face.

Keir perked his brows up. "I hadn't thought that far aheid, but I thank ye fer the solution. Anabel's humours are not in balance, ye ken. She's an irascible lass, one I'll nae be tied to. A long voyage could be in me future." He started to laugh, caught sight of the two English lads returning, and swallowed hard. He was unable to avoid noticing how graceful and smooth her, no *his*, short strides seemed.

***

"YOU'RE IN LOVE," Hannah hissed the whisper at Eleanor. She pulled up her breeches and grinned at Eleanor. "Your face … when we were riding down the hill … the look of ecstasy you had … you are most certainly enamored of the young laird."

"I am no more in love with a McKelvey than you are." Eleanor huffed, tightened the string in her ponytail and made sure her shirt was loose over her bound chest.

"Ah," Hannah teased, "so it's true then. Because I could keep my arms around Logan McKelvey's chest for the rest of my life, be it long or short."

"In love? You think you're in love?" Eleanor scoffed. "We haven't time for such nonsense. We must play our parts, deceive them, and then dissuade them of their plans to marry me off to the King and then borrow or steal enough money to go in search of my mother."

Hannah frowned. "So … you've been thinking through strategies … like your war game campaigns. And when you were clutching that Highlander with your face pressed against his strong, muscular back and your eyes firmly closed, a smile on your face and the glow of love rimming your features … you were devising solutions to our predicament? I don't believe you, El."

Eleanor brushed imaginary dirt from her clothing and peeked around the bushes. "We better get back."

They lengthened their strides and put scowls on their faces as the three men watched them walk back. Logan shouted something about male genitals that should have made them blush, but they'd heard worse around the stable and Hannah hollered back the expected bawdy reply.

61

Eleanor came up to Copper's head and stroked his face, felt the soft muzzle, and spoke a calming word. She relaxed the scowl, but forced its return when she looked up at Keir. He was watching her with a scowl of his own. She tapped his leg and held the stirrup. He slipped his foot out and she stuck her foot in, reached her hand up and they repeated the mounting with an even smoother action than before.

"We'll be walkin' the rest of the way, through the woods. Ye dinnae need to squeeze the life from me ribs." Keir stuck his foot back in the stirrup. "Are ye set, Englishman?"

Eleanor smiled at his back. "All set."

In love? Hmm. She thought about Cameron—she liked him—and the Chaddertons and the Miller boys—they were bearable—and then she thought about love. She loved her old horse, Brownie. She loved Hannah. She loved Cook. She loved a sunny day and she had great affection for Lady Beth. Lord Edgeworth was ... tolerable. She felt indifference toward Captain Luxbury.

But what were these feelings she had toward Keir? Logan and Hubert and Thomas, all strange, new male acquaintances, did not elicit the reaction she had whenever Keir was near, or when he spoke, or when she thought about him.

Her heart was pounding even now, those new fluttering tickles spreading through her chest and fanning outward to all her parts ... why? What was it about Keir McKelvey? He'd been kind, but aloof. He didn't seem to approve much of the English. He merely tolerated her. And yet ... there was something in the flash of his eyes when he did look at her. Something invisible.

Copper plodded on. The path narrowed and they had the lead. She decided to speak to Keir.

"How much farther?"

"Och, lad, are ye needin' to piss agin?"

"No, I thought ... I thought we needed to put on the dresses soon."

"Ye will as soon as we get to the bothan where Thomas is. Not much farther."

She had a sudden thought that made her shiver. They would be expected to disrobe and redress in front of the others. How would they hide their secret identities then? A bothan wasn't particularly large; she knew it was a small shelter for any traveler to use, unmolested. She had to think of a reason to keep the men out while they changed. What could she say?

Keir cleared his throat. "Ye'll surprise ole Thomas, ye will, when ye present yerselves in dresses and bonnets. We'll keep him outside the bothy till ye're ready. Might uncross his eyes." He laughed and Eleanor's heart caught up in her throat. She smiled at his back again.

***

"ZOUNDS!" THOMAS CRIED out when Eleanor and Hannah stepped out of the bothan. "What'd ye put in the front to give yerselves such womanly mounds?" His crossed eyes appeared to be gazing at both girls' chests at the same time. Left eye to the right and right to the left. He reached as if to pull down the front of Hannah's bodice. Hannah clutched her dress at her bosom and turned aside.

"You must treat us as the ladies we pretend to be. Would you touch a maiden so boldly? Oh … my!" She feigned the cry a trifle too dramatically and in doing so strengthened the notion that she was a male who was play-acting.

Eleanor was more emphatic and uncharacteristically coarse. She put both her hands on her breasts and jiggled them. "A bit of lamb's wool from Fenella is all, but keep your distance, *gentlemen*." She stressed the last word. "Remember, *she* is Mistress Hannah and *I* am Eleanor." She eyed Keir, who looked quickly down, and then she scanned the other three men, who were all smiles and Scottish grunts.

"Oh, Lady Eleanor," Hannah raised her voice to a falsetto, "whatever shall we do? Our trunks of clothing and jewels are gone. Our chaperone has left us to the mercy of strangers. If it wasn't for the charity of these fine Scottish Highlanders, I don't know where we'd be." She fluttered an imaginary fan at her throat.

Thomas cackled. "Ye'd be workin' in a hoor-hoose, ye would."

Eleanor couldn't control the red blush that warmed her neck and then her cheeks.

"All right," Keir stopped the folly, "we need to get them to the Hall. I was thinkin' we could lift them up onto the saddles, sideways a'course." He looked at Eleanor who was tucking a stray lock up under her bonnet. "Dae ye think ye can mount and twist yerself to sit so?"

"Step aside, Mr. McKelvey." Eleanor reached her left hand up to the saddle and lifted her skirts to allow her foot into the stirrup. With one quick push off the ground with her right foot, she pulled herself up onto the saddle, bringing her right leg through the space between saddle and left leg. "Will you be riding behind *me* this time, or walking?"

"'Twill be more appropriate to walk … as yer rescuers. I'll lead ole Copper." He took the reins and nodded at Hannah. "Yer turn, lad."

Hannah huffed and went through the same simple mounting quite expertly. She had readied Lady Beth's side saddle for her many times and had learned the trick.

"Well dain, lad," Logan praised her. Hannah leaned forward and stroked the horse's neck as Logan took the reins.

"Thomas," Keir said, "ye go ahead and watch for that redcoat. Hubert, dae ye think ye should be seen wi' us?"

"I'll keep back, once I show ye the short way to the gate."

Eleanor and Hannah gave each other secret smiles, comfortable atop the horses and almost as comfortable in dresses and bonnets. The small group was ready to start off. Thomas galloped ahead, but Hubert walked his horse, turning his head often to speak on family topics or to tease Logan and Keir.

The girls learned of Logan's race to win his horse, Keir's unselfish help on Hubert's farm, and Hubert's great pride in his son. Keir described how he'd tried to teach Huey about swords and hatchets. And Logan told Hubert about Keir's loss of temper when he found out their father had arranged for him to marry Anabel MacLeod.

"Wheesht. Ye'll not speak o' me temper as if I didn't deserve to express it." Keir made several gutteral sounds. A storm loomed on his brows, pushing warning wrinkles around his eyes, but he controlled his ire. "Ye ken I'm the rational one, not given to bouts o' anger."

"That ye are, brother," Logan agreed. "And I aim ta shadow ye and learn ta control me humours."

"The gate's right aheid," Hubert said, stopping his horse. "There's no guard. The lads can walk in." His horse turned in circles and he spoke while continually twisting his head to see the others. "We can give'em a while to beg for help ... for work. I'm sure me mum will employ them, especially if this Hanover heir ... or bastard ... has arrived."

Keir looked up at Eleanor. "Be sure to tell them it 'twere the McKelvey brothers what rescued ye, so we'll be received more readily when we come ta check on ye in a day or two."

"You're checking on us?" Eleanor kicked her foot free of the stirrup, intending to jump down, but then realizing her dress might tear in the effort.

Keir reached up and grabbed her around the waist. Their eyes met as she put her hands on his shoulders and he gently brought her down to stand before him. He was a tad slow in releasing her waist and she was equally hesitant to take her hands off him. Then both realized their mistakes. Keir coughed and Eleanor stuttered her thanks.

"Ye're welcome. And aye, we'll be visitin' the Beldorneys, perhaps wi' Hubert and Huey. He's been takin' the lad there for a year now. He doesna tell me sister. There's more patchwork ta do ta get her forgiveness. 'Tis a longer story." Keir wiped his brow.

"Will we meet secretly, do you think?" Eleanor used the moment to study his face, memorize the laugh lines around his bright green eyes, the straightness of his nose, and the shape of his lips. Oh … she needed a handkerchief to wipe her own brow. She wished … she wished she could tell him who she really was. Would he still want to kill the Hanover heir?

"Aye. If I can, I'll pass ye a note. There'll likely be a servant I can bribe."

"All right then." Eleanor hesitated, then gathered up her skirts to walk between Keir and Hannah. Logan followed and Hubert stayed back out of sight.

"Hullo!" Keir began calling as they passed the gate and neared the estate. This wasn't the main entrance and they were approaching the mansion from its garden side. The stone structure stood proudly under a dapple-grey sky, stalwart, catching the sun's rays, stones gleaming as if covered with flecks of diamond dust.

Eleanor assessed the size and manor of construction. It was nearly equal to Ingledew in height and stateliness, but the grounds were better kept, and the outbuildings numerous. She could smell the stables. A true lady would have thought they soiled the air with an unpleasant scent, but Eleanor breathed it in deeply. She noticed a servant girl leading a swaybacked nag to the watering trough and she wondered why the Beldorneys would keep such a worn-out mount.

"Take me arm," Keir said, interrupting her thoughts.

She slipped her hand through his, remembering her part as an unfortunate female attacked and bereft of clothing and valuables. She clutched unconsciously at his sleeve, wanting to blurt the truth, but afraid of how he might react.

Hannah, next to her, stopped to wait for Logan, and took hold of his arm as well. She heaved a little sigh that was almost undetectable.

"Shall we say we're late of some castle in the best lands of England? I know the names of three or four. Let's say we were sent from … oh, I don't know … perhaps Ingledew. Would the Beldorneys have heard of it?" Hannah asked.

Keir breathed out heavily. "Ye are ready wi' yer lies, I think. Och, say whatever needs be said. Only one o' ye do the talkin'."

Chapter 8

ELEANOR LOOKED TOWARD the stables and beyond them to where they'd tied the horses. Could she run in these skirts fast enough to reach that beautiful copper-colored gelding, jump on its back, and ride off? Would Hannah keep up? Or would these McKelvey men catch them?

Keir and Logan were deep in conversation with the butler, explaining the fictional predicament. The butler sent a footman to bring the housekeeper and after a few words with the McKelveys, she stepped out between them and assessed the looks of Hannah and Eleanor.

"We should curtsy," Eleanor nudged Hannah.

"Come, come along," the housekeeper made a hurry-up gesture and by her size alone—wide of girth and tall as well—her unspoken command for the McKelveys to step aside and let them through the small side door was obeyed. The girls followed the housekeeper into the castle and since they were not at the main entrance, they came first to a small foyer with pegs along the wall from which hung various cloaks and shawls.

"I'm Mrs. Perkins. I'll be assigning you your tasks." She looked them up and down and made a face. "The young lord says they rescued you." She clucked her tongue and reached out to push a short strand of hair back under Hannah's cap. "From I brothel, I suspect. Well, we won't speak of it. We'll get you cleaned up and into uniforms. Follow me."

Neither looked back, but they heard the door close and knew that Logan and Keir were on their way. The butler passed by them, looking down his nose and curling his lip in disgust, then went through another passageway and disappeared. They kept walking behind the house-keeper.

Eleanor tapped her on the shoulder. "Excuse me, Mrs. Perkins. We have something we need to tell you. And since I can deduce by your manner of speech that you're English too, I'm sure you'll understand."

The large housekeeper stopped and turned, raised both eyebrows, and folded her arms. "Yes?"

"I am Eleanor … Beldorney. I was meant to arrive with Captain Luxbury, but we were separated when the ship docked and—"

"Heavens!" Mrs. Perkins gasped. "My oh my. Oh, the Scotsmen who brought you …" she dropped her arms, "… they didn't know. Oh my, oh my." She stared at their bonnets, struggling to find the words. Finally she said, "The captain is in the study, just arrived. I'll inform him at once. Oh my." She wrung her hands. "Oh, I must apologize. I'm so sorry."

"It's all right," Eleanor soothed the woman's fears. "We had to hide our identities. We've had to conceal ourselves from highwaymen, sleep in a child's loft, beg for food even … but we are here now. Safe and sound."

"Oh yes, oh yes. Safe and sound. Oh, the captain will be most delighted to see you. I could tell he was not anxious to see Lord Beldorney. But thankfully the master is not yet home."

A maid came up behind them, the same one Eleanor had seen leading the nag to the stable. Mrs. Perkins clasped a large hand onto the girl's wrist. "Oh, Carla, you must take these ladies at once to the guest chambers, the ones we readied for Lord Beldorney's niece." To Eleanor she said, "You and your maid," she nodded toward Hannah, "will find everything you need. Everything."

***

"WELL, MY DOUBTS are quelled," Hannah said once the door was closed and they were alone in the bed chamber. "But when did we beg for food? That was the sole lie you told."

Eleanor looked about the room and shook her head at the opulence. The bed was large and had elaborate posts and a hand-carved hunting scene on the headboard. The bed itself was laden with embroidered bedclothes and pillows and sat under a ceiling as high as the ones at Ingledew, twice the height of an average man. There were two stuffed chairs at the foot of the bed and a large tub under a velvet-draped window. The walls, except for the fireplace, were paneled and covered with oil paintings of landscapes and horses.

"Yes, I lied ... for practice. I don't know what we shall tell Captain Luxbury." She walked to the table that held a lamp, quill pens, an inkwell, blotting paper and sand shakers. She picked up a pen then set it back down, and glanced at the door to the adjoining room where Hannah would sleep.

"Look," Hannah pulled the wardrobe doors all the way open, "here are all our things. The trunks must have been sent along."

Eleanor came closer, eyed the clothing, and looked up at the top shelf. "And there are wigs, hair switches, and wefts."

There was a shy knock at the door and then it opened. The maid, Carla, came in carrying a pitcher of water.

"I'm most sorry, m'ladies. I brung ye some water to wash the dirt of yer travels away. And I'll light the fire." Carla set the pitcher down next to the bowl on the dressing table and then knelt down on the hearth. Once she had the fire crackling, she bowed and backed her way out of the room as if they were both royalty.

"Do you think she knows?" Hannah asked. She untied her bonnet and shook her short hair out, then pulled a day frock from the wardrobe.

"Servants know everything." Eleanor sighed. "We'll have to get them on our side somehow. And we need to decide exactly what we tell the captain about how we got off the ship. I don't think we should tell him about the disguises." She lifted a dress out of the wardrobe. "This looks similar to what we were wearing when he last saw us. I think I'll change into this one.

Before she started to undress, she carefully removed the brooch she'd pinned inside the bodice of the dress Fenella had lent her. She'd felt the rounded edges of the brooch when she'd vulgarly grasped her bosom in front of Thomas and the others. She was vaguely mortified by her action then—who was she that she could be so ill-mannered?—but ... that was water under the bridge. Whatever the men, and Keir in particular, thought of her then, they weren't going to see that El again. She realized she'd unconsciously made the decision to be who she was meant to be: the Hanover heir. She intended to learn how to be a Lady and embrace her feminine side. No more being a lad. If she saw Keir again, she would make him fall in love with the real her.

"Are you deaf now?" Hannah raised her voice. "I've asked for your help three times. Where is your head?"

Eleanor looked over at Hannah, struggling with buttons and hooks, and apologized. "I was thinking ... that I want to learn all that the

68

Beldorneys can teach me … us … and then … perhaps the McKelveys will spirit us away to the Highlands."

"Didn't you hear?" Hannah snorted. "Keir is betrothed."

"I heard. And he did not sound enthused. I have six weeks to become … whatever it is he wants in a woman. I'll find out from Fenella."

"Fenella? There's another bit of conversation you must have missed: Lord and Lady Beldorney do not entertain their daughter-in-law at the family seat."

"Mm, I did hear that. We shall make it our mission to mend that fence."

She slipped the clean dress over Hannah's head then gave a disconcerting sigh as she discovered a tear in the seam. "Oh no."

Hannah looked down at the seam. "I saw a sewing kit on the night table. I can fix it."

***

BERNARD LUXBURY NEARLY had an apoplectic fit upon seeing Eleanor enter the study from the great hall. The room was bright enough, the drapes open and the windows tall and wide, with sunlight streaming in, but he couldn't believe his weary red eyes. His foot caught on a ripple in the Persian rug and he slid forward, catching his balance by grabbing a six-foot candle stand. He gripped the iron base, turning his knuckles white, and choked out two words, "You're here!"

He straightened himself, let go of the iron, and bowed. "I'm most happy to see you. Please, please forgive me. I did not mean to abandon you. I mean I did not abandon you. The ship's inspectors made a mess of your trunks. By the time I got things put back, you were gone. I … I … I sent them on and came searching for you."

Eleanor smiled, motioned Hannah to come stand next to her, and said, "We were wholly capable of finding our way here, Bernard. We shall not mention the trouble again."

"I was in a terrible state of alarm."

"Your trepidation was unwarranted." Eleanor made a slight curtsy to signal the subject was closed. To Hannah she said, "Shall we sit?"

They took the long settee and made themselves comfortable. Luxbury picked an armchair near the window and sat on the front edge of it, stiff and straight.

"My word. You look … most beautiful. What did Lady Beldorney say at your …" he stared at Eleanor, " … your arrival?"

"We've not seen the master or the mistress of the house. We thought it best if you introduced us, Bernard. We've just arrived this forenoon."

"Today?" A strange look fell over Luxbury's face; he relaxed and inched back into the chair.

"Of course, of course." He thrummed his fingers on his knees. "I'm sure that before you left Ingledew Lady Beth told you why you are to be called Eleanor Beldorney, did she not?"

"Indeed. She said you had Scottish relations … and since this is the Beldorney estate, I assume Lord Beldorney is your … uncle?"

"Not quite. He's a cousin of my father's; they would stay with us on visits to England. As a young lad I'd listen to their politics." Luxbury kept his focus on Eleanor. "They are most eager to help you."

"When do you suppose we will meet them?" Hannah asked.

Luxbury startled at her voice, looked at Hannah as if for the first time, and answered, "Yes, well, the butler has informed me that they left early this morning to visit their daughter. They had word of a new grandchild."

"How fortunate for them." Eleanor clasped her hands on her lap. "Is that their only grandchild?"

"Oh no. Their son … once a lad I looked up to when they visited us … has a son of his own. Though there's some bad blood between them when he married a woman not of the family they wished."

"How dreadful." She turned her head to Hannah and mouthed Fenella's name.

"I dare say, Mistress Eleanor," the captain tugged at his collar, "there is something most intriguing about your beauty today."

"Is it my hair?" She touched her head where Hannah had hastily clipped on the switches closest in color to her own hair.

"Perhaps. Your face is aglow though. Was your journey strenuous? How did you get here from the ship? Where did you stay last night?" His face wrinkled into a frown.

Hannah reached over and patted Eleanor's hand. "Captain Luxbury, it was not an ordeal. We were helped by two fine Scotsmen to whom we promised a reward. Should they return in a day or two or three, we should hope you'll allow us to present them with a healthy purse."

"Of course, of course." Luxbury acknowledged Hannah, but kept his eyes on Eleanor.

***

"I CANNAE STAY and wait for this redcoat to appear," Thomas complained. "Me farm needs me."

He was riding between Logan and Keir, walking their horses toward the nearest village and scouting the lanes for a carriage and an English soldier who'd be escorting the Hanover heir to the Beldorneys' estate. Hubert was trailing behind.

"I think we should all turn back," he shouted over his horse's head. "I'll come back in a few days wi' me son. 'Twon't be suspicious. I'll check on the lads, maybe meet the king's future wife." He chortled and his horse nickered as if the dumb animal was a part of the conversation.

Keir turned in his saddle and nodded. "If ye can stand us for a week or so, me brother can tend to yer chores and I'll help ye build that extra room ye'll be needin' by summer's end."

Hubert puffed his chest. "Fenella told ye, did she?"

"Aye, she did." Keir winked at Logan. "Should we tell wee Logan where bairns come from?"

The men all laughed and Thomas, now in the lead, began to change directions. Logan rode next to him, but Keir reined Copper back to ride alongside Hubert.

"She also told me yer sister is up the sprout ag'in." He waited until Hubert nodded. "And she'd like the cousins to ken one another."

"Aye, she's mentioned it. She doesna ken I've been sneakin' off wi' Huey so's he can meet his *Seanmhair*."

Keir looked away. "Aye, the lad only has one grandmother. He should feel that love."

"Aye, an' speakin' o' love ... were ye goin' ta tell me of yer up-comin' nuptials?"

Chapter 9

B Y THE FOURTH day Eleanor was confident in her manners, poise, and feminine disguise. Mrs. Beldorney, who insisted she be called Baroness as Eleanor could not rightly pronounce the Gaelic term *Banbharun*, showered her with kindness, taught her the most modern aristocratic manners that Lady Beth had failed to teach her, and pampered her with beauty treatments that neither Eleanor or Hannah had ever heard of.

"Your education is going rather well," the Baroness said, keeping her accent and syntax faultlessly British. "You were a lovely lass three days ago, but now ..." she lowered her voice "... your beauty could compete with Helen of Troy or Cleopatra or Queen Charlotte herself." She quickly put her fingers to her lips to stop herself. Then she continued in a conspiratorial tone, "I do not approve of the more gruesome parts of this plan. I have met Queen Charlotte, you know. She was barely seventeen when she married the King." She clucked her tongue. "She married George the same day they were introduced and has been churning out his issue like a barn cat ever since. It would not surprise me if she died in childbirth." She waved her fingers near her nose. "And that would relieve me of some guilt that I am a part of this." Her hand went to the piece of embroidery she'd been working on before Eleanor entered.

"Baroness ..."

"Yes, sweet Nora?"

The corners of Eleanor's mouth swept up at the nickname the Baroness had given her. "I was hoping that you'd allow my maid to accompany me on a ride. Bernard is leaving tomorrow to collect some soldiers and he offered to show me the rest of the grounds here."

"Oh, my, my, no. Bernard could not find his way from one pasture to the next. Why, when we visited his parents in England last, they were most concerned about his prospects, but someone handed him a commission and *voilà,* he seems in control of his future, however dangerous it may be."

"Baroness?" Eleanor lowered her chin exactly as the Baroness herself had instructed her to do when making a request. She looked out from under blinking lashes.

"Oh, listen to me, blathering on like an old lady. Well, I am an old lady, a grandmother now. I told you of my daughter's new babe, the one we were visiting when your arrival was delayed. But I have another. A grandson. Huey. Seven years old. I expect him to visit any day now. Perhaps today." She lifted her eyes from the stitches she'd begun. "Oh … your question about a tour of the grounds … I will allow it. But take the new carriage and have Briggs drive it. You won't need your maid for a chaperone then."

Eleanor nodded. She was anxious to get outside. The rooms were bright and spacious in this castle, but she needed sunshine and fresh air and some peaceful time in the stable. She'd tell Hannah to remake herself as Pascoe—they'd hidden those clothes under the bed—and be ready to follow the carriage. She suspected that one of the McKelvey men might make contact soon. Her heart fluttered at the thought that she might meet Keir again. She put a hand to her chest and absently touched the brooch she always wore now.

"Pardon me, ma'am," the butler stood at the doorway, "your son and grandson are here."

"Oh, Briggs, send them in immediately." The Baroness set her embroidery down and looked to Eleanor. "Remember this morning's lesson: a lady's tongue is the last member she moves." She rose and walked toward the door, but stopped suddenly as a streak of young flesh pitched into her. She swung her arms around the child and let loose a high note of joy. "Huey! Huey! My how you've grown this spring."

The child looked around his grandmother's skirts at Hannah and gave her a shy smile.

The Baroness kissed the top of the boy's head and looked up at her son.

"Mum."

"Hubert. How good to see you. You're an uncle again. Have you heard? Rhona has had a daughter." She leaned over Huey to receive a kiss on the cheek from her son.

Eleanor kept her hands in her lap and waited. Half of her wished Hubert would recognize her as the lad pretending to be a lass, but she was equally hopeful that there would be no spark of recognition with these finer clothes and hair style.

"Hubert," the Baroness said, putting her hands on her grandson's shoulders and stepping behind him so he could face Eleanor, "and Huey … let me introduce you to our houseguest. This is Nora, from England, another distant cousin of yours, Hubert. Bernard brought her. You remember Bernard Luxbury, don't you? The little lad that tagged after you when we stayed in London?"

Hubert nodded and crossed the room to stand two feet before Eleanor. "Miss Nora." He bowed deeply. "'Tis most pleasant ta meet ye." He lifted his head, stared intently at her, and extended a hand.

Eleanor watched for a glimmer of detection, but Hubert gave nothing away and certainly his son, who'd shared his loft with her so recently, acted as if she were a stranger. Of course, she thought, she did have her head piled high with a hairdo Carla had fixed this morn. A cockernonnie, she'd called it. And then this new dress was absolutely a distraction. She hadn't recognized herself in the mirror.

She accepted Hubert's hand, carefully nodded her head in greeting, and said, "Your mother has told me such nice things about you." She noted admiration in his gaze. Hannah had predicted she'd have men falling at her feet. She hadn't believed the mirror, but perhaps it was true: she was beautiful. And this man that she knew, did not know her.

"Then she's forgiven me." He straightened, turned, and lessened the distance between himself and his mother. He put an arm around her. "Have ye forgiven me yet? For if ye havnae given me pardon yet fer marryin' a McKelvey and not a McDonough, I have news that will hurry me exoneration … Fenella is wi' child."

The news was not expected. The Baroness slipped out of the English accent she'd been using and into her natural Scottish brogue. Eleanor barely understood another thing that was said between mother and son, but the tone and the excitement made her smile. She waited a bit and then made an excuse to leave the room. She needed to warn Hannah that Hubert was here and to send her out where he could find her on his way home.

She stopped a moment outside the door to listen.

"Is she really royalty, ma? Have ye gotten yerselves into mischief and intrigue? Or will ye break wi' the rebels and have a ball instead to marry her off?"

***

KEIR AND LOGAN were finishing the chores when Hubert and Huey returned home.

"I saw her," Hubert said as soon as Huey ran off to play. "I saw the royal heir."

Logan brushed the dirt from his hands and asked, "What name does she go by? I been meanin' to think up a name fer me horse."

"Nora."

"Och, a fine name fer me mare. Now if I'm the one to happen upon the princess she'll nay be leery of me when she hears me say 'Whoa there, Nora' or 'Easy, Nora.'"

Keir ignored his brother, leaned on his shovel, and said, "An' did ye meet the princess?"

"Aye, we did." He glanced at the house. "Ye ken I love Fenella, yer sister is a bonnie lass, but the princess's beauty is beyond compare. There be a glow upon her. An' a knowledge, as if she kent me from the heavens afore I was born."

Keir cocked his head, a smirk forming. "Beauty can betray a woman."

Logan frowned. "An' did ye see El or Pascoe?"

"Aye," Hubert gave the reins to Logan to hold and began to unsaddle his horse, "met Pascoe on the trail out the side. Dressed in the rags we first saw'em in. Musta wore'em under the dress so he could sneak out. Clever lad."

"Mm," Keir nodded, "and he told ye what?"

"He said El is one of the maids who attends the princess, stays by her side, fetches things fer her. I dinnae see her as the princess was alone wi' me mum. Pascoe mostly works in the kitchen, catchin' bits o' gossip whilst he's pretendin' to be a lass choppin' carrots and boilin' porridge." He gave a slight chuckle and pulled the saddle off. "But we have a problem. The redcoat. 'Tis Captain Bernard Luxbury. Ye'll nay guess it, but he be a faint relation of mine. Up me English line somewheres. I kent him when we was lads. I cannae have him killt. Ye'll have to call off Thomas."

Keir nodded again, but kept his words to himself.

Hubert glanced at the house. "When the princess left to go fer a carriage ride with Bernard, me mum told me there's to be a ball. She's agreed to invite me wife at last since I told her of the new bairn comin'." He walked to the small shed and heaved the saddle onto the railing there.

"An' I learnt she already sent an invitation to Castle Caladh. I think she means to subvert the plan in her own way."

"A ball?" Logan groaned. He led Hubert's horse to the corral, and called over his shoulder, "All six of the McKelvey lads and lassies in the same room? There's sure to be trouble."

Keir laughed and Hubert raised his brow. "I'm jist hopin' Fenella dinnae give her best gown away to the lads."

"There be plenty of gowns at Caladh. When is the ball?"

"A week Sunday."

"She needna fash aboot it. I'll ride back and send along a trunk of dresses. An' a sister or two."

***

"BRIGGS, YOU DROVE the horses too fast," Luxbury complained. "The lady and I will sit here and recover while you unhitch the horrid creatures."

He turned his head to Eleanor; they were seated close together and once again she could feel his breath on her face. She'd endured the carriage ride, bumpy and uneventful, and now had to endure a few more moments completely alone with Bernard.

"You're doing a lovely job, my dear," he crooned. "Already you have mastered the art of conversation with someone cultured, like me, but … I'm afraid you do not sound, shall we say, royal enough to fool the aristocracy."

Eleanor planted a contrite expression on her face. She was anxious to get back to her room and very much aware that Bernard was slithering closer as he spoke.

"Dear Bernard, you are so kind to be honest with me. Whatever shall I do? The Baroness has planned a ball in my honor, nine days hence."

"I shall pray that you succeed in rising to their standards. But should you not … I would be most honored to spirit you away. To the colonies. To America."

"Oh, Bernard. You would surrender your commission? For me?" She fought the urge to gag.

"Of course, my dear. I'm … I'm in love with you, you know."

Another inch closer. She squirmed. Thought fast. Let out a howl of a low-class laugh. "Oh, you amuse me so, Bernard. Thank you for the lovely tour of the estate. I almost wish I was a Beldorney." She moved to rise.

A voice outside caused them both to be more alert. "Eleanor?"

Bernard quickly exited and helped Eleanor down. He turned to Hannah and scowled. "There is dirt on your face, Mistress Hannah, or whatever they call you here. And you are to address the princess as Nora; it is what the Baroness has decided."

"Yes, sir," Hannah gave a slight head bow, "I will remember, sir. Mistress Nora, I am here to escort you inside." She smiled at Luxbury and moved so Eleanor could walk beside her.

Once inside, they wound their way through the halls and up the stairs to their suite of rooms. Neither spoke until the door was closed.

"Oh, that was dreadful. I wish the captain would go back to England. He's going to make it hard for me to escape."

"What? You've changed your mind again?"

"Yes, since I saw Fenella's husband today and he did not know me, I've been thinking."

"I saw him, too. I changed to the boy's clothes and met him on the trail like you told me to. I delivered the lies you suggested."

"Good. Also … I didn't tell you before … there's to be a ball. A ball, Hannah, with guests and musicians and dancing and feasting. I don't think I'll survive it."

"But we used to spy on the galas at Ingledew. You always dreamed of one day—"

"Yes, I know," she interrupted her, "but the McKelveys will be invited."

"That's wonderful," Hannah trilled. "I'll see Logan again. Oh, I hope I'll be allowed to attend." Doubt tainted her words. Her face suddenly fell.

"Well, of course you will. I'll insist. But … the captain wants to take me away to America if I fail at … this whole enterprise." Her face changed as she repeated what he said to her.

"Oh, El, so many choices. But you wouldn't consider marrying the captain, would you?"

"I don't know what the right choice is. Be a princess, marry a king, run away to America, stay in Scotland, search for my mother … my decision seems to change daily." She sighed. "I do want to see Keir McKelvey again. I wonder if his betrothed will attend the ball."

"I can check the guest list from Mrs. Perkins. Do you remember her name?"

"I do. It was Anabel MacLeod. Keir cut his brother off with an angry growl the moment he mentioned the name. Remember? It was when we got to the gate, riding sideways in our dresses."

"Ah, yes. Mostly I was enjoying the warmth of Logan's breath on my neck and not paying so much attention to their words."

"Hannah ... I've never been anybody. Now I'm ... important. I'll give myself till Sunday next to decide. What happens at the ball will help me make up my mind."

"I have to ask again. Is running off with the captain still a possibility?"

Hannah ran her finger down her neck and stopped at the brooch. "Maybe. But first I must meet this Anabel MacLeod."

Chapter 10

K EIR ENTERED CASTLE Caladh by himself, leaving Logan to help the stable boy unsaddle and groom their horses. His first thought was to find the maid he'd flustered the week before. He needed to apologize for throwing an assortment of flower vases across the stone foyer floor and leaving the mess for her to clean up.

He found her carrying an armful of dirty linens out of his sister Rory's room. He bowed deeply, and offered a dimpled smile along with a sweet apology.

"Elspeth? I must beg ye fer forgiveness." His smile faded and a look of true contrition fell over his countenance. "I let me temper get the best o' me. I hope ye dinnae have too much bother cleanin' up the pottery."

The maid's wide-set eyes went wider and a reddening blush crept up from her neck to her cheeks.

"'Twas no trouble, sir." She curtsied twice and clutched the linens tighter against her bosom. "Thank ye fer yer kind words." The blush deepened and she curtsied again. "I shall tell Cook ye're back and bring ye somethin' to yer room."

"Thank ye, Elspeth, but that won't be necessary. I can wait fer the mid-day meal."

Elspeth nodded, backed up a few steps, hesitated and then scurried off as if in a race. Keir watched her go, thinking how dissimilar she was to Anabel, and wondering if there was some way to put Elspeth's gentle spirit into haughty Anabel.

He passed Jack's empty room and Logan's, ignoring the stares of his ancestors from their portraits on the walls, before entering his own large suite. The fireplace was clean of ash and several dry logs were piled ready for his return. The room was chilly, but it didn't bother him; he'd light the fire later. He noticed the vases had been removed. He could imagine his father ordering Elspeth to collect them all. It made him chuckle.

But it also made him sad. His mother had been a relentless gardener and required the servants to keep most of the castle's thirty rooms filled with flowers as the seasons allowed. In her honor, his father continued the tradition. The momentary thought stabbed his heart with fresh grief. Apparently, after his temper tantrum, the Laird of Castle Caladh had ordered his room to be stripped of fragile urns.

Keir gathered some clean clothes and headed to the pond beyond the stables. The sun was out, but the pond, though shallow, had not heated up enough to lure his sister here. He had the cool water to himself and could bathe in relative seclusion if his brothers didn't join him. He swam about, noting the musky scent of wood anemones and the unpleasant smell of the celandine flowers. Perhaps he might send a bouquet of those to Anabel MacLeod. Would she get the intimation? He hated the thought of her, but now that he was home, he'd have to face his father as well as the consequences of the choice he needed to make. There were two disparate paths.

He paddled around slowly, thinking, and ignoring the growing iciness of the water. If he decided to marry the lass ... *och*, he could not envision the union, imagining such a future was too bitter. To be harnessed to a mule for the rest of his life seemed a hefty price to pay for peace with his father. And yet, if he didn't marry her, there'd be dishonor, humiliation, and, most likely, banishment. Could he leave Caladh forever?

America. The thought came to him along with the troublesome feeling he'd had when that word was spoken by the lad. He could see El clearly in his mind, standing in the wagon, holding a dress to his flat chest. He couldn't meet the boy's blue eyes. There was something about El ... *no*, he wouldn't dwell on that puzzling feeling now. The chill of the water as he floated around had worked its way nigh into his bones. He wished he'd lit that fire in his room; he was going to need it.

"Hello, don't mind me. Just picking flowers." It was his sister, Rory. Only ten months older, Rory held a special place in his heart. Whereas his oldest sisters, Fenella and Elsie, had mothered him as a child, Rory had been his playmate. The younger boys, Logan and Jack, were tag-alongs and nuisances.

"Join me. I don't mind." Keir stood up. The water came up to his waist, the cloudy silt he'd stirred up shielded the part that would have made any other lady of the realm swoon. Rory laughed.

"Ye're a fool, Keir McKelvey. I'll nay be yer plaything to dunk and splash."

"Fine, then, Rory. Turn yer heid. I best be wearin' a kilt when we have the talk I'm expectin' ye'll gi' me. I can see ye've got somethin' on yer mind."

"Aye, the *cèilidh*." She turned and sat square atop a mound of buttercups and started talking. "I'm sure they won't be servin' bannocks and brose puddin' at the Beldorneys' castle. 'Twill be a feast of finer things and we're to go a day early. Ye ken already, I suspect, that we've been invited to a spring *cèilidh*, along with the McDoons, the Campbells, the Stewarts, and … the MacLeods. Ye'll be dancin' all night with yer intended." She laughed, her back still turned to him.

"'Tis naught to laugh aboot. There's a McDoon lad I could bribe to run off with that arrogant Anabel. What think ye o' that?"

Rory rose and brushed off her skirt. "Dylan McDoon, I suppose ye mean? He's been moonin' over Anabel since summer last. But she's betrothed, dear brother, to the finest man in Scotland, who'll be gettin' a fine settlement as well. 'Tis a waste o' yer time to be dislikin' her. 'Tis almost as big a commitment as loving someone, and it carries none of the benefits."

"*Och.* The benefits. Ye mean Laird McKelvey will be receivin' a particular pasture from Clan MacLeod."

Rory tilted her head at Keir. "Aye, our father will benefit, fer sure, but as the oldest male, ye'll be Laird of the Castle upon his passin'."

Keir shook his head. "I've heard o' lands as green as our hills … across the sea." He saw the look she gave him. "Aw … dinnae fash. I'll nae leave ye." He finished dressing.

A smirk took over Rory's face. "Ye havnae heard, then? 'Tis I who'll be leavin' these hills and this castle. Our Elsie has convinced her husband's brother, Rennie Carlyle, to wed me … and quickly too."

Keir, who started to smile, instead puckered his face in anger. "Quickly?"

"Aye, and ye've no right to be angered. I've saved the last of the dowry our mum brought to Castle Caladh. She too was with child when she wed our father. 'Tis true love so ye'll nay be blamin' me … and I wish ye the same, should ye give Anabel a chance."

Keir clenched his teeth. If his three sisters got to choose their mates, why could not he?

***

CAPTAIN LUXBURY REMOVED his hat and bowed low enough to touch the rug with it. "M'lady, I've returned and the Baroness has informed me that you are in need of an experienced dance partner. I would be honored to teach you."

Eleanor would have heaved a sigh of disdain at the thought of having to dance with Bernard, but since Lady Beth had grossly undereducated her, she needed the lessons. She was excited to learn and it was that excitement that brought a smile to her face and reddened her cheeks. "Thank you, Bernard. I'll admit I am intrigued to try. As a child I used to love to watch the carriages full of women wearing glorious gowns come to Ingledew. And then we'd spy from under the tables set up behind the musicians. The swish of skirts and the clink of swords was fascinating. I never understood how so many people could float around the ballroom and not bump into each other." She set down the book she'd been reading and stood up. "Hannah, you must learn too."

Luxbury looked confused until he saw Hannah sitting at a desk on the other side of the study, a quill in her hand hovering over a paper full of the alphabet letters she'd been practicing.

He covered the snarl with a cough at seeing they weren't alone. "Oh, quite, yes of course. I'll teach you both the steps and tomorrow we shall do it to music. The Baroness has sent for one of the musicians to come by tomorrow afternoon." He smiled, closed-lipped, and set his hat on one of the chairs.

The afternoon was surprisingly pleasant and both girls laughed almost continuously. Luxbury divided his time unevenly between them, claiming that though Eleanor was a quick study, he'd be remiss in his duties if he didn't give the princess extra attention. Eleanor scolded him for calling her a princess, but Hannah reminded her that the Baroness was going to introduce her as such.

It was a while later when, half out of breath and giggling over how ungainly Hannah was, the three of them collapsed into chairs the very moment that the Baroness glided into the room.

"How are your students doing, Bernard?" The Baroness signaled for a servant to enter and set a tray of drinks on the side table.

The captain hopped back up onto his feet and bowed. "My lady, they are most fortunate to be swift of mind and fleet of foot. They will dance expertly at your ball with effortless coordination."

"Mm," she smiled, "I feel as though I've had a hand in that Frenchman's story, *Cendrillon*. Consider me your fairy godmother, Nora."

Eleanor frowned, then quietly thanked the servant who handed her a glass of fruited water.

"You don't know the story?"

Both girls shook their heads. The Baroness took a seat. "There was a poor unfortunate orphan, much like you—beautiful and kind—who, with help from fairies, went to a ball, met a prince, and fell in love."

"Oh, the French," Bernard hissed. "I've not heard this tale, but fairies … well, that sounds more Scottish than French."

The Baroness raised a brow, but went on. "Cendrillon, or Cinderella in English, left the ball without the prince knowing her name. She lost a slipper there, though, and the prince charged around the country looking for the girl whose foot would fit it. Oh, it's a lovely story. I used to read it to my daughter when she was little." She stared off at the shelves on the far wall where dozens of books were displayed.

Eleanor sat straight and wiggled her toes in her shoes. The story appealed to her and she realized she'd been picturing Keir as the prince, then suddenly her stomach soured as she caught Bernard eying her like a cat watches a mouse.

"Guests will be arriving this Saturday." The Baroness reached over and patted Eleanor's free hand. "There will be lads and lasses your age, Nora, but most will be older. If all goes well," she glanced at the captain, "we shall send word to our contacts in London."

There was nothing ominous in her voice, but Eleanor knew what sending word meant. There'd be poison for Queen Charlotte, a period of mourning, and then she, Princess Nora, would be introduced to the King. Her stomach did another flip flop.

***

HANNAH POKED HER head out of the room, expecting to see a horde of servants if not a herd of elephants, which was what she'd exclaimed to Eleanor must be tramping through the halls. Her cheeks were still high, having risen like bread dough with their laughter, when she caught sight of three handsome Highlanders following three footmen laden with baggage through the passageway. She recognized two of the men in kilts. Her cheeks lost their puffiness when her jaw dropped. Her mouth formed a silent O, but it was too late not to be noticed. Her sudden appearance drew their attention.

The tallest one, Keir, put a finger to his lips. Logan glanced at her and gave her an imperceptible nod, but the third man, obviously a Mc-

Kelvey brother in the same tartan colors, stopped following the footmen and stepped toward her.

"Greetings. May I have the pleasure of introducin' ourselves to ye? I'm the youngest of the McKelvey clan. Jack McKelvey at yer service." He laid a hand on his heart and bent at the waist.

Hannah, with one hand clutching the outer door latch and the other making shooing motions behind her back in the hopes that Eleanor would stay out of sight, gave the young Jack a lop-sided smile. He was obviously closer to her age and not as handsome as his brothers, but there was a mischievous look about him.

"And these be me wayward older brothers, Keir and Logan."

"Our pleasure," said Logan.

"Indeed," echoed Keir.

Hannah gave a hurried nod and hoped her body blocked the view into the room.

"This way, m'lords," one of the servants indicated the room across the hall and disappeared inside.

Keir and Logan stood, hands on hips, and waited for Jack.

"May I ask yer name?" Jack grinned.

"H-Hannah." She glanced from Jack to Logan in the hope that he would do something. He did.

Logan linked his arm in Jack's and said, "Excuse us, lass, me brother is a wee bit anxious as it's his first ball. There'll be proper introductions at dinner."

Hannah lowered her eyes as Logan pulled Jack away and into their room. She could hear Jack protesting under his breath that it wasn't his first ball. Keir stepped a few inches closer and whispered to Hannah, "Good job, lad. Ye look far and away more fetchin' than I'd have ever thought possible. Ye fooled me baby brother." Then his face fell into a more serious attitude. "Ye should be stayin' in the attic … so … is the special guest ye're tasked with watchin' … stayin' in there?" His eyes roamed up and over her head and he looked into the room.

Hannah pulled the latch and closed the door. "She is," she whispered back.

"And the other lad? El? Where might I find him?"

"I … I haven't seen him of late. Mrs. Perkins found him out. Took the dress. It was good he wore the breeches underneath." She gave a nervous laugh. "Perhaps he beds in the stable. It is only I who …" she bit her lip "who pretends to be a woman and tends the … the princess."

Keir's forehead filled with wrinkles. "Hubert said ye worked in the kitchen. Ye tend her? With her dressin'? That can't be proper. Did she not bring her own maid?"

84

Hannah realized her mistake and still whispering said, "Oh, yes, yes, m'lord. I meant I am employed as a companion ... when I'm not helping the cook." She thought of what she might do to remain in character and yet, since Keir thought she was a lad, to remind him of that. She pressed her thumb against the knuckles of the other hand and cracked them. No proper lady would indulge in that habit.

Keir's forehead smoothed out and he gave Hannah a light punch on the shoulder part of the puffed sleeve of her dress. "I'll talk wi' ye later, Pascoe. And tell El I'll find him later."

He turned and marched into the room across the hall as the three footmen came out. They gave her slight head bows as they passed her. She waited a moment then slipped back into the room, closing the door tightly.

"Eleanor, Eleanor, you'll never guess. The McKelvey brothers are across the hall."

Eleanor nodded. "I thought that might be why you waved me back. I couldn't hear what you said to them."

Hannah sat on the bed and recounted the brief conversation, but Eleanor, who was pacing, wanted to know more. "How did he look?"

"Handsome, more handsome since he was cleanly shaven."

"And he wants to see me?"

"Yes, in the stables. I told him you sleep there and that the housekeeper thinks you're a lad. You'll have to sneak out wearing the old shirt and breeches."

"Unless he recognizes me when we meet at dinner tonight." Eleanor thought a moment. "Oh, Hannah, why did you tell him that? What if he says something to the housekeeper? Mrs. Perkins knows we're girls. She's assisted in our baths."

Hannah shook her head. "I'm sorry. Keeping everything straight has gotten as confusing as the lacemaking Lady Beth was having us do."

"Deception," Eleanor sighed, "I fear we cannot perceive its consequences."

Hannah perked up at the sound of another carriage. She left the bed and went to the window. She watched for a moment then said, "I wonder if that's Keir McKelvey's future bride." She glanced back at Eleanor who was hastening toward the window.

"Oh," she said, pulling the drapery aside, "she's beautiful."

***

LUXBURY WAS WAITING at the top of the stairs to escort Eleanor, and by default Hannah, down the grand staircase. Thirty people were mingling in the Great Vestibule, waiting for the entrance of the Baron and Baroness's special guest. The gentlemen were nicely dressed, most in kilts, and the ladies were decked out in what were probably their second-best dresses, saving their fancier gowns for the next night when there'd be an orchestra for the ball and twice as many guests.

Hubert stood near his father with Fenella on his arm. Behind them the McDoons and the Stewarts speculated on the guest of honor's parentage. Throughout the festive greeting room other small conversation groups had formed. Lampstands flickered along the walls and the two large chandeliers that hung from the high ceiling had been set ablaze from the balconies. The scent of candle wax mixed with ladies' perfume.

Footmen were stationed at the doors and the hosts, the Baroness in a saffron yellow gown and her husband twitching and itching in an ancient wool kilt, laughed merrily with the Campbells before pulling their son and Fenella into the conversation.

The McKelveys stood as far from the MacLeods as possible, but Keir kept his eye on Anabel in case she started to move toward him. He had two escape routes planned, one back up to his room and the other out to where Copper was stabled. He wasn't sure if the news of his engagement had reached the Beldorneys, but he was hoping it hadn't. Voices echoed off the stone walls and reverberated throughout the spacious room and he thought he heard his name mentioned in the din. The volume suddenly diminished by half and heads turned. Keir followed the gaze of the woman nearest him.

He saw the Englishman first. His redcoat struck a nerve and not just with him. Most of the men made gruff sounds or spat out derogatory epithets. But their wives and daughters hushed them and soon all heads turned toward the staircase. Keir spotted Hannah on Luxbury's right arm, but the other woman, this mysterious heir unapparent, was on the captain's left and back a step.

Jack nudged Keir. "Look, brother. There's the lass I met this mornin'. Is she the secret princess?"

"Hush."

The Baron moved a couple steps up the staircase and turned to the crowd. "Ladies and gentlemen, may I introduce to you, on the arm of Captain Bernard Luxbury and attended by the lovely Anna," the Baroness signaled him, "er uh, Hannah … we have Princess Nora of … of Beldorney." He started the clapping and stepped down as Luxbury brought the ladies to the halfway point and stopped. There were oo's and ah's, comments on the sea-green gown, her hair, the natural beauty of the princess, and a few lingering disparaging words for the presence of the English captain. Keir noticed how nervous both women looked; if Pascoe, posing as Hannah, should look his way, he was ready to offer a sympathetic nod or an encouraging wink. He couldn't imagine being in the lad's position, impersonating a fine lady with such aplomb.

The Baroness smoothly pushed her husband to go up and escort the princess the rest of the way. Reluctantly he pounded up the steps, held an arm out to Eleanor, and preceded the captain and Hannah down. As if prearranged or instinctively known, the various heads of clans filed past, bowing and making introductions.

Keir held back and observed. The MacLeods practically elbowed their way to the front of the line. He watched the princess as Anabel curtsied, bowed, and otherwise bobbed her way through her introduction, swishing the skirt of her scarlet gown. He had to admit to himself that though the princess was certainly a fine-looking woman, her beauty could not compare to Anabel's. But this Nora was not proud or condescending in demeanor as he would expect and when Anabel walked on, Keir clearly saw Anabel's bearing devolve into her usual unpleasantness with a smirk and a swagger. Suddenly her beauty disappeared. And if he read her lips correctly, she whispered to her mother an insulting opinion of the princess.

His eyes flitted back to Nora. The woman looked toward Anabel with a most curious expression, something between pity and envy. Then she held a hand out to the next guest, smiled and spoke a few words. The smile changed her countenance entirely. Keir jumped as Jack poked him.

"Come on, brother. Logan's already walkin' up. We'll be the last to meet her. Look, the Baroness has ushered the captain and the lass I met in to the dining room. Perhaps one of us McKelveys can lend an arm to Princess Nora. I dinnae mean ye, o' course, as Anabel seems to be awaitin' fer ye, see?"

Keir grunted. "I'll nay be offerin' me arm to that *nicnevin*." He squinted his eyes at Anabel.

She raised a delicate brow at him and lifted her chin. Keir was obliged then to give Anabel a slight nod, but he did not smile at her.

He put his hand on Jack's back and pushed him toward the end of the greeting line, behind Logan. Watching and listening to his brothers as they met the princess gave him time to evaluate her. He deemed her pretty enough, but he wondered if she could bake bread, ride a horse, tend a bairn, sleep under the stars …

It was his turn. He bowed and then, caught in her gaze and her amazing smile, he stumbled through giving his name.

"K-Keir Douglas McKelvey, at yer service, m'lady, er, Yer Highness … Yer Royal—"

"Just Nora will be fine, if I may call you Keir?"

Her voice had all the familiarity of an angel, he thought. Hubert was right. It was as if they'd met in Heaven before they were bairns.

"I … I'm sure ye'll have hard enough time rememberin' all these names, Yer Ladyship … Princess, Princess Nora." He bowed again, felt the perspiration bead up on his skin. She was bonnier up close, but still was not the beauty he expected, and yet he'd rather stare at her soft features all night than contemplate the MacLeod lass for a lifetime.

"Are you not married, Keir?"

"Nay, but," he glanced toward the dining room and saw Logan and Jack escorting Anabel in between them. "Och, may I take yer arm, Princess, and find ye yer seat at the banquet?"

***

ELEANOR'S HEART HAD never pounded as fast nor as hard as it did when she walked down the staircase, her skirt spilling down the stairs behind her. She was ever so thankful for the captain's arm to steady her. Then the Baron, whom she'd barely had two words with since she arrived, escorted her the rest of the way. She'd had a chance to scan the unfamiliar faces and count the few she did recognize. Keir stood out, of course, and once she saw where he was, she didn't look that way again. She knew there was a third brother and her attention lingered on the young man. Hannah had commented that he seemed as if he could be a rambunctious cousin of the Chadderton boys, though better-looking.

As she stood for the main introduction, she spotted Hubert and Fenella with the Baroness. She gave them both a smile. Earlier, the Baroness had brought Fenella to her room as they were getting ready. She seemed stiff and formal and before she left, she heard her ask Hannah in a whisper where Eleanor was. Good, she had fooled the woman who hadn't been fooled when they posed as lads. That, at least, was a good dose of confidence-builder—something she needed for when she would come face to face with Keir.

Anabel MacLeod was another matter. No woman anywhere could be confident around such overwhelming beauty. The lass had perfect features, a grace about her poise, and manners and speech to better act as princess than Eleanor. Their introduction was short and all Eleanor could think was how lucky the girl was to be betrothed to Keir. As Anabel walked away, Eleanor's eyes lingered on her, and her heart fell to her toes. What she wouldn't give to trade places with her.

Stupid thought. She wasn't worthy. Had never been valuable. Would never be desirable. What a sham this all was. She'd never pull it off. Her lungs expanded; the room swelled around her.

It passed through her mind, though, that Anabel might be a clever ally in this dangerous plot in which she was the center figure—for both sides—and was hampered by, of all people, Keir.

And there he was in her peripheral vision. Her heart pumped harder. She swallowed, trying not to feel the tremor of anxiety working its way through her veins. She took her time with Jack's introduction and especially with Logan, who should have recognized her, but didn't.

When it was Keir's turn, she held back her smile while he stuttered through his name. Then she let the grin grow. He took her gloved hand and held it as he bowed. She glanced over his head to see Anabel scowling at her. She returned her attention to Keir and noticed his perspiration. He was nervous to meet her. Could it be because he thought he might have to kill her? She thought quickly for something to say. She meant to be clever, certain there were words in her head she could craft into a reasonable statement or perhaps a question, but they disbanded before she could marshal them into any kind of order. What was left was a burning question.

"Are you married, Keir?" She stiffened, hiding the way his serious gaze made her breath hitch.

"Nay, but," he glanced toward the dining room and she looked too. Logan and Jack were escorting Anabel into the dining room. Did that bother him? Perhaps not, because he looked at her then, a tiny dimple emerging, and asked, "Och, may I take yer arm, Princess, and find ye yer seat at the banquet?"

"Of course." What else could she say? She forced herself not to beam at him and took his arm. She pressed her other hand to her chest and gasped, forcing air into her lungs. She was short of breath and a flash of fever spread over her. Was everyone looking at her? Her cheek muscles twitched. Her face grew hot. They were not near enough to the candles to feel their heat. Was it the closeness of Keir? His touch? She might faint. She'd be exposed as the fragile English fraud who could not stand the pressure of this deception for a single evening.

"Are ye all right, Princess Nora?" Keir's voice cut through to her bones and curled warm around her whole body. She looked ahead at all the guests standing behind their chairs, waiting for her to be the first one seated. Their chattering and whispering tapered off. The silence that replaced it seemed ominous.

But she found Hannah's reassuring face, breathed easier, and answered Keir. "Yes, Keir, I'm fine." She dropped her hand from her bosom. "A little wine and I'll be fine." The candle closest to her let off a thin ribbon of sable smoke.

Keir held her chair, bent a bit closer, and whispered, "Whatever's meant to happen to ye, will happen to ye."

Eleanor thought her heart might have stopped with those words. She watched him find his seat, across from Anabel. He didn't look back at her. She, as she'd been instructed by the Baroness, picked up the wine glass and immediately a footman stepped up to fill it from a glistening bottle. Other servants, lined along the walls, also moved in to fill the goblets. Cheery voices rose in volume again, but sounded more and more muffled to Eleanor. The drubbing of her heart became one long hammering. She couldn't catch her breath.

Once all the wine was served the Baron rose to make a toast. Glasses clinked; the guests drank. Eleanor sipped and had a difficult time swallowing.

A moment later she leaned left toward the Baroness and whispered, "I think I'm going to be sick." She rose and rushed toward the door as the Baroness raised her voice to assure the guests that all was well and that Princess Nora had a delicate stomach like so many of the royal household.

Chapter 11

E LEANOR WAS DIZZY and seeing double by the time she raced up the stairs, found her room, and threw herself into the chair by the sputtering fire.

It was a threat. A palpable threat. Against her. Keir had threatened her life, hadn't he? *Whatever's meant to happen to ye, will happen to ye.*

She sprang back up. Poured herself a cup of water from the pitcher by the bed. Gulped it down.

She had to do something. What could she do?

She hurried to the wardrobe and looked at the clothes there. No, what she was looking for wasn't there. She stooped to look under the bed. Aha, that's where Hannah hid them last. She struggled to get out of the dress then knelt down at the night table and peered under the bed again, reached a hand out, and pulled forth the breeches and shirt they'd found on the ship, the things old Tavish made them put on.

She dressed at once then sat at the dressing table to put a wet cloth to her face and wash away the powder. She didn't have time to be careful about removing the hair switches and wefts.

She pulled and winced and succeeded in extricating every lock. She still looked like a girl. The small mirror said so.

She poured a little water into the washing bowl and dipped both hands in. Ran her wet fingers through her hair until it was flat against her head.

Nothing to tie it with, no ribbons anywhere. She tried out a curse she once heard Cook use. It didn't help. She'd have to find something in the barn where she could hide until morning. Perhaps she'd find a length of straw or a leather cord there. *Why am I preoccupied with my hair?*

The panic she felt would not subside. She had to run *now*. Hannah would understand. She glanced at the writing table. She could leave her a cryptic note and hope she could decipher it.

The brooch. She'd need the brooch and the money Lady Beth had sewn into the hem. Where was the bag they put it in? She hurried through the connecting door into Hannah's room and searched. Found it. Took half the coins out and put them under Hannah's pillow. Tied the sack to her waist.

She listened at the door. Opened it an inch. Peered out. Slipped through. Closed it quietly. Stared a moment at the McKelveys' room across the hall.

She couldn't stop herself. She scurried across the hallway and entered their room. Looked about among their things. Found a leather cord she could tie her hair with. Hoped she was stealing it from Logan or Jack and not from Keir. She looked for weapons. Found none.

She hurried back out and down the hall the other way, toward the servants' stairway. With all the servants busy with the dinner, she had no problem sneaking out the lower side door into the dark evening. The heady scent of honeysuckle filled the air but did nothing to calm her. But at least she was outside.

The brooch. She forgot the brooch. She turned to go back when the door opened again and a kitchen maid stepped out with a basket of carrot tops and turnip peelings.

"Oh, here boy, ye can save me a walk to the stable." She thrust the basket at Eleanor. "Bring the basket back when ye come fer breakfast."

Eleanor stumbled back with the basket as the maid slipped inside and pulled the heavy door closed.

Fine. Did she really need the brooch? Her breathing still came in huffs and puffs, but slower now. Calmer. She needed to think. The alarm she'd felt at Keir's words was fading. Perhaps he meant something completely different.

Perhaps, she thought, he did recognize her after all. He was a better actor than she was. Was that it?

She looked into the basket and picked out the single potato peel, something toxic to horses, turned toward the stable, and munched on the skin as she walked—long boyish strides—and thought.

The stable was dark. Not a candle or a lantern. No flowery scents either, but the horsey odors were comforting. Where were the livery men, the stable hands?

"Hello?" She called out a little louder and was answered by a few lonely horses nickering and snorting. She smiled and worked her way into the dark barn, her eyes adjusting.

"Here you go." She held out a handful of the treats and the first horse nibbled at the gift. She reached up and gave him a rub on his nose and moved on. Ah, this was where she belonged, not in a frilly gown at a banquet table.

There were several stalls in the Beldorney stable, each quite large, holding up to four horses. The guests that were staying the night had arrived by carriage or, in the case of the McKelveys, on horseback. She thought she might recognize Keir's horse if she could see better. Nevertheless, she walked along the stalls and offered the treats to whichever horses stuck their heads out.

She rubbed foreheads, patted necks, and cooed gentle words, keeping her voice low and husky. She remembered Keir's horse's name and called it out. She was rewarded with a neigh and a bobbing head out of the last stall. Of course, they were first to arrive and their horses would have been led to the back.

"Hello, boy, how are you doing?" She shared the last of the carrot tops with Copper and the two horses with him. She set the empty basket down and continued talking to the horse, asking the questions that were on the top of her mind: "Where should I go? What should I do? Huh? Any advice for me? I'm in a quandary and need to make a decision." She wiped a bit of horse slobber off her arm and inhaled the warm scent of stable air.

"A quandary, eh?"

The voice was all too familiar, sonorous and mellow. Eleanor froze.

Keir strode the length of the stable as if he could see like a cat in the dark. "I wondered when I'd see ye, El. Pascoe's doin' a nice job o' bein' a lady. At the dinner." He chuckled. "But I couldn't get close to her. And then she ran off durin' the second course. To check on the princess."

Eleanor stayed still. Any words she might have uttered plummeted to silence as if they'd stepped off a cliff and couldn't find the bottom.

Keir brushed against her at the stall, reached over the rail and patted Copper. "Ye've been givin' 'im treats, have ye?"

"The … the kitchen maid sent them." She stared his way, could barely make out the jut of his chin, the shape of his nose.

"So ye've been workin' in the stable and lettin' Pascoe do all the lady things? And now ye're thinkin' on where ye should go and what ye should do? Yer quandary?" His laugh made her insides flutter.

She tried not to sound as nervous as she felt. "Did you … did you meet Princess Nora? I don't think she's … I don't think she's as beautiful as … as one of the women I saw arrive this noon." She waited for his reaction.

He grunted. "I ken which one ye speak of. But the wee folk cursed that one with a streak o' meanness. Anabel MacLeod, me betrothed … Och, ye dinnae react to such news with the surprise I expected."

Eleanor dared to say, "Whatever's meant to happen to you, will happen to you." Her cheeks flexed but she couldn't manage a smile or a frown.

"Aye, lad, 'tis truth ye speak. I said the verra same to the princess. The Good Lord has a plan. I'll nae fash over me future."

His response lightened her fear. "And the princess? What did you think of her?"

Keir harrumphed. "The princess has her beauty on the inside … a lovely soul. I can feel it."

She felt better still, but had to be sure of one more thing. "But … but you're going to kill her." The clouds outside parted and a shaft of moonlight coming in the stall window put a spark in Keir's eye. Eleanor studied his face.

He sighed. "'Tis in God's hands, her life. I cannae take it."

"But you'll have Thomas do it."

"Nay. Thomas would kill the redcoat, but as fer sendin' a princess to Heaven … or a queen or a king … he's nay fer that. And I'm havin' second thoughts, too."

They stood side by side in silence. Keir rubbed Copper's face between the eyes. Eleanor sensed her heart rate returning to normal.

"El … can I tell ye somethin'? Man to man?"

Eleanor stopped breathing. Then sucked in a lungful of the pungent stable air. "I'm hardly a man. Barely eighteen years."

"Have ye ever had feelin's fer a woman?"

Something like a laugh escaped her mouth. "No. Never."

"Well, ye love yer mum, aye?"

"I don't remember her."

"So ye dinna understand the feelin' o' love? Or do ye?"

"I love horses. And …there is someone who has … stirred my soul." And with those words her heart picked up its pace again.

"Stirred yer soul? I havnae heard such an expression, but I like it."
He stopped rubbing Copper and turned toward the moonlight. "The
princess stirs me soul, El. Do ye understand? I cannae be a part of this
revolution ... this upheaval, anymore. 'Tis wrong."

"Because the princess stirs your soul?" Eleanor squeaked out the last
word, breathless.

"Aye. I've a mind to spirit her away."

***

IT WAS A crazy idea. Ridiculous. But Keir had spoken the thought
aloud. And to the lad, of all people. That strange feeling he'd had for El
before dissipated, replaced by a male camaraderie that emboldened him
to speak his changed mind to the lad, though he considered the youth
might not understand.

He rested his arms on the rail and tucked his forehead against his
elbow, closed his eyes, and groaned. "'Tis a betrayal of sorts. But also
a rescue."

He lifted his head at the sound of shouts.

"Somethin' is afoot." Keir looked toward the sounds. Two
stablehands bolted into the barn, one carrying a lantern. "Ho! Ye'll nay
be startlin' the horses, lads. Or startin' a fire."

"Sir," the boy huffed, catching his breath, "the liveryman from
Kilmahew Castle was teachin' us a new gamblin' game. In the attic.
When the alarm went up. The maids are asearchin'. We thought to look
here."

"Searching?" El's voice wobbled.

"Fer the English lady. The one they're makin' a fuss aboot. The
redcoat captain has sent fer his soldiers that be campin' near the river.
She's done and gone. Kidnapped, methinks."

"Or captured by fairies," the second boy claimed. The other one
raised the lantern high and peered into the first stall.

"She's nay here, lads." Keir stepped back from Copper's stall and
the lantern's light sent his shadow large and looming against the far
wall. The boys took one look, hurried out and left them in the dark again.

Inside the stable, with no lantern-fall, their ears detected a rustling
as if the lads left a draft to stir the straw-littered floor, yet the air
remained dead-still.

"The lass was ill, the Baroness said, but she seemed fine to me."
Keir cocked his head at El. "She'd need help to run away." He put a
large hand around El's upper arm and squeezed a bit. "And bein'
English yerselves, I ken the temptation ye might have to aid the lass."

He let go of his grip on her arm and neither said a word.

Time slowed as he breathed and thought and strained to determine El's expression. "When ye and Pascoe masquerade as lasses, do ye learn any of the Princess's secrets?"

"Secrets?" The lad's voice was as high as a girl's.

"We ken that her ancestors are Caroline and King George the Second and her father must be their third son. Deceased now, but the mother ..." He stared down at the lad who blinked repeatedly. "Do ye ken who she might be?"

***

IT WAS A decisive moment for Eleanor. She cleared her throat. "She, the princess, told Pascoe her mother's name. She has a brooch she claims belongs to her ... to Mary, uh, Mary Ainsworth Fletcher."

She could barely see his face, but she could tell he was mulling this new information over. She added, "And she told Pascoe she wants to find her mother ... before she'll consent to marrying a king."

She determined he was scowling.

"Perhaps this redcoat has agreed to help her find the woman." He shook his head. "But I can nay uncover a reason Princess Nora would leave Beldorney now. She must be in her room, or sulking in some quiet spot. The library or study."

"They won't find her. She's not in the castle."

He grabbed her arm again and she winced. "Have ye seen her then?"

"I'm sure ... if you would give your word to help her find her mother ... I'm sure I could get word to her ... Pascoe will know where to find her. They walk the grounds together. And then—"

Once again he let go, kicked at the bottom of the stable door, and said, "Aye, I'll make that promise. 'Tis a special thing to find yer mum. As ye must ken, El, not rememberin' yers." He kicked the door again. "I feel compelled to do all I can for the Princess." He cuffed Eleanor on the shoulder. "She stirs me soul, lad. Indeed, she does."

***

HANNAH HAD NOT meant to raise the alarm about Eleanor's disappearance. It was unfortunate that a servant had entered the room to tend the fire just when Hannah had removed the brooch from Eleanor's gown and stuffed it in her bosom.

The maid, a homely girl of twelve with spindly arms and a dirty face, dropped the logs in the scuttle and pointed at the gown. "Is the dress bewitched? I saw the princess run from the dining hall in it. Did she ... did she turn into a ... a fairy?"

"No, of course not." Hannah spread the dress neatly on the bed. She had been surprised to see Eleanor hightail it from the dining table, but her face was as red as the time they'd eaten all the strawberries in

96

Cook's pantry. Hannah assumed she perhaps had a reaction to the wine and therefore wasn't as concerned. But then the Baroness signaled her during the second course to go and check on Eleanor. And so she had, and found the rooms empty. "Princess Nora is just ... not here."

The maid used the end of a log to push the coals around and then set several logs on top, mumbling about fairies and gowns and missing persons.

Hannah waited until the girl left and then looked under the bed. "Oh, no," she whispered Eleanor's name, "you didn't." Eleanor's boy's clothes were gone, but the second set of male attire was still there. Hannah grunted. She wasn't going to put them on and go hunting for Eleanor. She knew exactly where her friend would be. Give her time, she'd come back. But now, Hannah's job was to go back to the dinner and reassure the hosts that the Princess was resting comfortably and would not be joining them tonight.

She took her time descending the stairs and returning to the dining hall, but upon reaching the doors several of the footmen burst through, one half dragging the fire-tender still muttering about fairies kidnapping the princess.

"Oh, Baroness, I'm sure she'll return to her room soon." Hannah didn't know what else to say. The dinner guests seemed stunned by the interruption. Hannah noticed all were still seated, but there was one other empty spot besides Eleanor's. The eldest McKelvey was gone.

***

"YOU WOULD HELP her?" Eleanor spoke slowly, knowing her mouth would betray her and spill out the wrong words, suggest the impossible, reveal the hidden truth.

"Aye, lad, if the princess were to stand before me this instant and beg fer me help, I'd be honor-bound to extricate her from this terrible plot."

Eleanor took a deep breath, pulled the leather cord from her hair and shook her hair out. "When you met the princess an hour ago, she asked you 'are you not married, Keir?' and you replied 'nay' and then you looked at Anabel ... and then back at the princess ... at me. You asked if you could take my arm and seat me at the banquet. Keir ... it's me. I'm Eleanor. I'm Princess Nora." She expelled the last of the air in her lungs.

She could tell he was squinting at her. She stepped to the side, crushed the basket with her foot as she angled herself under a beam of moonlight, and said again, "It's me."

Keir burst out laughing, his horse whinnied, and he clapped his hands a couple of times. "I cannae believe it." More laughter. Then he

97

got silent, quite serious, and cocked his head. "So ye impersonated the princess, did ye? And the English captain went along with it? Why, lad?"

Eleanor gulped back a sob. "You still don't understand. I'm not a lad. Your sister knows. Pascoe plays Hannah so well because she *is* Hannah. And I am the daughter of Mary Fletcher. You saw me as I really am, Keir. I *am* Eleanor ... or as the Baroness has named me: Nora."

Keir leaned toward her, not in a threatening way, but curious. "Now, lad, ye best be truthful. Old Sylvan hired ye to play a part, a lady in waiting, a spy, but ye're not to be confused by all the plottin' and mischief and call yerself a princess. Why yer no more a lass than Copper here is a goat. If I yank yer shirt over yer head—" He grabbed at the bottom of the shirt and did as he threatened. There was barely enough light to see, but see he did, and immediately he thrust the shirt back at her and twirled to give her his back. "Och, m'lady, a thousand pardons." He dipped his head and whispered, "I dinnae ken." Even the horses grew quiet.

Eleanor wiggled back into the shirt and started to cry. She sank down to the ground and completely crushed the basket, put her head in her hands, and blubbered out in short spasms what she could to tell him her tale. Her heritage. Her life at Ingledew. The journey with Luxbury. How they pretended to be the hired lads when Tavish found them on the ship. When she finished, she realized he'd lowered himself to the straw, too, and held his arm around, but not quite touching, her shoulders.

"I dinnae ken," he kept repeating.

"What shall we do? They're looking for me. And I don't want to be Princess Nora." Her face was mere inches from his. He lowered his arm the last inch to wrap her in his embrace.

"Ye shall come wi' me. 'Tis good fortune that yer room is across from mine. 'Twon't be a problem to sneak ye back into yer role."

"But ..."

"Dinnae fash, princess, I'll keep yer secret. But ye must resume the royal role until I work out the solution wi' me brothers and wi' Hubert. He kens Luxbury. We'll dispatch him back to England. Do ye ken if that's where yer mum might be?"

"No, no, she came to Scotland ... oh ... fifteen years ago. You'll help me? You'll help me find her?"

He put a finger under her chin as if to bring her lips to his, but he smiled instead. "Aye, *lass,* I'll help ye."

Chapter 12

ELEANOR BEGAN TO strip off the shirt and pull down the breeches as soon as Keir closed her door. She slipped on a nightdress and burrowed under the bed covers. Her heart hadn't slowed down. True to his word, he sneaked her from the stable to her room, told her to feign illness, and promised to have a solution by morning.

She shivered, more from excitement than cold. The temperature hadn't yet dropped outside and the fire in the fireplace looked to be recently tended. She pulled the quilt up to her nose anyway. A moment later she threw it off and leaped out of bed. The boys' clothes were where she left them, on the rug, near the door. It wouldn't do to have someone enter in search of her and find them. She balled them up and stuffed them under the bed.

She still trembled. She put one knee up on the mattress, then changed her mind. She scurried barefoot across the room to Hannah's door.

"Hannah?"

"Oh, thank goodness. I thought you ran away. I found the money you left me." Hannah embraced Eleanor and hugged her tightly. "Here," she said, letting her go, "I have your brooch, too." She went to her own bed, lifted the pillow, and brought back the coins and the jewelry.

"He's going to help me … us. He … Keir. He found me in the stable. I told him everything." The weight of her deceit lifted from her spirit.

Hannah's chocolate brown eyes went wide. "We don't have to pretend to be …? But …"

"I know. It's a miracle."

"He knows you really are the princess?"

"He knows." Eleanor shifted from one foot to the other and back again, rubbing her arms, and bobbing. "Hannah, he was so close to me. He touched my face. I thought … I thought he was going to … I mean … he confessed that … oh, I can barely say it, but he confessed that I stir his soul. He has feelings for me, Hannah."

"He told you that? To your face?"

"Well, he thought he was speaking man to man." She cut her laugh in half. "But he said the princess stirred his soul."

"He must have been struck dumb when you told him you are the princess."

"He laughed. He didn't believe it until … oh, Hannah … he looked beneath my shirt."

Hannah's hand flew to cover her mouth.

***

FENELLA SAT ON the edge of the bed and stroked Huey's leg as if he was a lamb sleeping through a storm. Because storm it was between Hubert and Keir. Words like quiet thunder.

"If ye cannae believe me, ye can ask yer wife. She kens the truth."

Hubert, pacing in front of the fireplace looked from Keir to Fenella.

"'Tis true, husband," she stopped petting her son, "they be lasses. English lasses. I dinna mean to keep a secret from ye, as I kent ye'd find out on yer own. But I dinna ken she was the verra center of the … the rebellion. She was simply a lost lass, lookin' fer her ma."

Hubert shook his head.

Keir patted him on the back. "I found her in the stable, no longer in that fancy gown. No wig. Disguised again as a common stable boy, feedin' the horses."

Fenella left the bed and joined the men at the fire. She poked a finger at her brother. "Tell me, Keir, are ye smitten with the lass? Will ye be helpin' her out o' love or duty?"

Keir snorted, picked up a smaller log from the scuttle and tossed it on the fire, though the room was warm enough. "Pity. 'Tis pity. And a bit of duty. I've changed me thinkin' on the nasty politics of it all. The woman should be free to find her mum."

Fenella crossed her arms and stared at her brother until he relented.

"Aye, ye see through me, don't ye? Always have. I'll nay call it love, but … the lass … she awakens somethin' in me." He plopped down onto one of the side chairs.

Hubert took another loop around the spacious room, came back to the fire, looked at them both and complained, "I cannae think a single word that will appease me mum or me father if we whirm her off and spoil the plan. 'Tis their hope to find a place at court." He took hold of Fenella's hand. "And they only this week allowed me bride to visit here."

Fenella tisked her tongue at him. "If ye were hopin' to one day be laird of this castle, I'll have ye know I'm happy on the farm and want fer nothin' more."

Hubert smiled at her. Keir stood back up. "We have to deal with the English captain."

"Luxbury? I can reason with him."

Fenella dropped her husband's hand and waved hers in his face. "Nay, ye cannae do that. He'll nay be swayed wi' words. Eleanor has captured his heart. I could see it in his face as he walked her down the stairs. I suppose ye two only had eyes for the vision she was, floatin' down the steps like a fairy, but I could see the captain's expression. And how he shrank with contempt to release her to the Baron."

"So I'll need more than purposeful words and a good argument." Hubert glanced at Keir.

Keir dug out his sporran and filled Hubert's hand with gold coins. "Will this do?"

***

"YOU DID WHAT?" Eleanor's jaw dropped.

"I didn't think we'd need those clothes again so I threw them in my fireplace." Hannah held her hands out in supplication. "They smelled bad anyway."

Eleanor glanced around the room. There was a tray of food on the writing desk, the draperies had been opened by the maid who'd brought the food, and a plain dress was lying over the back of one of the side chairs. Plain. Like the one Hannah was wearing. Then her eye caught a slight motion at the door. Something was slipping through the crack at the bottom.

A note.

Hannah saw it too and retrieved it, handed it to Eleanor, and sat on the bed with her.

The corners of Eleanor's lips curled up as she opened it. Who else but Keir would send her a note? There would be instructions … the solution he promised.

But no. "Oh, it's from Bernard. He says he'll be joining us in the Beldorneys' second carriage for the ride to the parish kirk." She set the note on her lap. "Do we have to go?"

"All the guests will be expecting to see you, rested and recovered. You'll have to play the part until—"

"I'm not playing a part anymore. I am who I am. I accept it now … because Keir McKelvey knows." She looked square at her friend. "I have some power now. I'm not a pawn in all this intrigue."

"You're not the queen either. At least not yet." Hannah picked up the note and ran her fingers over the ink. "Are you sure that's what this says? I can't make out all the letters."

Eleanor read it again. Word for word aloud.

"I guess I need to practice more." Hannah rose and got the tray of food, brought it back, and together they gorged themselves on the breakfast fare.

They chatted a bit about the previous night and Hannah raved about the two courses of food she'd enjoyed before she was sent to check on Eleanor.

"And there were plenty of desserts left. I went down to the kitchen after you went to bed. They treat me like another servant, which I rather like. There were cakes and sweets I'd never had before."

Eleanor smiled. "We won't be enjoying this rich life if Keir helps us find my mother. She must be poor or she'd have sent for me long ago."

"But Keir is rich. He'll be laird of Caladh one day."

"He's engaged to Anabel MacLeod. She's the one who will enjoy the riches." Eleanor sighed.

Hannah's face darkened. "But he's seen you, uh, he's seen your womanliness. He should have to marry you."

"He didn't touch me. He has nothing to repent of this morning. It was a simple mistake. He's betrothed … but … he doesn't love Anabel."

"He loves you."

"He didn't say that. Only that … oh, Hannah, why am I so flustered thinking about the man?"

Their laughter was not in the least full of humor, only confusion. They left the tray on the bed and Hannah helped Eleanor don the dress.

There came a knock at the door and as Eleanor called out permission to enter, a different maid appeared. "My ladies, I am here to tell you the carriage awaits." She eyed the girls and frowned. "Your hair, princess … shall I find you a bonnet?"

***

THE RIDE TO the kirk was bumpy and jarring. Eleanor kept her chin high and avoided Luxbury's eyes by looking out the carriage window to catch glimpses of the McKelveys at the turns.

The road smoothed somewhat as they came to a low row of bushes lining the last hundred yards to the stone chapel. The kirk was larger than Eleanor expected and, from the direction they came, was preceded by uneven rows of headstones.

"What a funny cemetery," Bernard said. He'd been commenting on various things along the way—a picturesque loch, a thatched-roof hut, a patch of new heather—trying to draw Eleanor into a conversation, but Hannah was the talkative one.

"It does look odd," Hannah nudged Eleanor, "not all the rows are straight like at Ingledew."

"Mm." Eleanor turned her head back to the other window and watched those on horseback trot by.

They had to wait as the Beldorneys' coach let out the Baron and Baroness along with Hubert, Fenella, and their son. Then their carriage moved closer to the door, the horses' hooves scraping on smooth stones, and stopped. Luxbury stepped out first and held a hand out for the ladies. Eleanor made her reluctance to have him touch her obvious as she kept both hands on her skirt to lift the hem. She stepped down unaided, much to Luxbury's embarrassment. There was a rather loud snort of amusement from a McKelvey. Eleanor was sure she knew which McKelvey it was.

She took Hannah's arm and rudely pushed passed Luxbury, whose red coat made him stand out even more against the backdrop of the grey stone church and a cloudy morning. The air hinted of impending rain.

At the doors Fenella took Eleanor's other arm and whispered as they entered. "Me brother asks that ye find him during prayers. He'll be waitin' behind yer carriage. I'll make an excuse to me mother-in-law … say yer delicate constitution be rearin' its ugly haid ag'in." She snickered softly, squeezed her arm, then turned to shush her son as he made loud exclamations over the stained-glass scenes.

Eleanor's temperature rose. *How could Keir expect to have a clandestine meeting here? And at their coach? Wouldn't the driver hear?*

She followed the Baroness into her pew and sat stiffly, waiting. There were already several parishioners in attendance and the Beldorneys' guests were still crowding in. Eleanor glanced back to see the men who'd ridden horses standing against the back wall along with the carriage drivers. *Oh, that's good. But how am I supposed to sneak past them during prayers?*

Perspiration began to bead up on her forehead. She loosened the bonnet's bow under her chin.

Fenella scooted closer as Hubert took the last spot in their pew. Now how would she get out? She was trapped amid the entire Beldorney family. A tiny groan escaped her lips just as an exceptionally old man in a long robe passed up the aisle.

The Baroness cocked her head toward Eleanor. "My dear," she whispered, "you don't look well." She clicked her fingers at her daughter-in-law. "Could you take her out for some air, Fenella?"

Fenella rose and put an arm around Eleanor to walk her out the side aisle. Eleanor kept her focus on the slate stones under her feet. The whispered suspicions of the guests reached her ears. One in particular made a rude comment about the princess's health. She raised her head enough to see the speaker was Anabel MacLeod, sitting in the last pew, directly in front of Keir. She could think of nothing to say or do in response, but Fenella, a hand on Eleanor's elbow, hissed at the beauty before directing Eleanor out a side door.

"That woman," Fenella growled, "I could spit. And to think our father has exchanged Keir's future for that lass and a chunk of land he coveted." She herded Eleanor toward the carriage. "Do ye ken?"

"That Keir is betrothed to Anabel? Yes, I know."

Fenella growled again. "Men! And ye, too, supposed to marry the king, and him an old senseless man, his wife not yet dead even."

"Do you know what Keir wants to talk to me about? He said he'd help me find my mother."

"Aye, I spoke to him aboot that brooch ye showed me and I told him of the lad I saw. I suspect he has a plan. Can ye ride a horse astride? In that dress?"

Eleanor tightened the strings of her bonnet, then touched the front of her dress; she'd fastened the brooch to the inner lining, out of sight. "I can ride any horse, but …"

"I best get back to Huey. Me husband is helpless at keepin' the lad quiet durin' the service. I'll tell them Keir escorted ye back, ridin' our brother's mare, to lie down before tonight's ball." She put both hands on Eleanor's shoulders. "Ye've decisions to make, lass. I'll ken what ye've decided by whether I see ye tonight … or not."

Eleanor pulled her shawl tighter across her shoulders once Fenella walked away. She could see Logan and Keir hold the door for her. Fenella slipped in and Keir eased himself out. He took long strides toward Eleanor, his hat in his hand. The closer he got, the more he scowled.

"Princess, ye look pale. Are ye ill indeed?"

104

"I … I may be. Nerves, perhaps. Should we be meeting like this?" She met his gaze, unflinching and waiting.

He put his hat on his head, then placed a hand on her back and directed her to the other side of the carriage, out of sight of the church doors.

They stood inches apart, Keir looking down at her, his compelling eyes searching hers, his hands roaming down her arms to her hands. He took each in his and held them up to his lips.

"I dinnae ken how to address ye anymore. I feel both awe and comfort in yer presence."

"Call me Eleanor. Or just El if you want."

"I promised to help ye. I have two plans and when I explain them to ye, ye'll either think me mad or genius." He looked up at the sky. "'Twill start to rain soon. We best head for the vicarage. We'll take cover there until the kirk empties out. Two hours at most."

Chapter 13

THE VICARAGE STOOD behind the kirk, a modest stone hut with a thatched roof and shuttered windows. Keir led his horse and his brother Logan's mare and tied them up under the back eves. The door was not locked and he opened it for Eleanor. There was a single chair at a small table nearest the fireplace, a longer table stood against the wall holding a few simple supplies, a cooking pot, a dish, a cup, a spoon, and nothing more. Two buckets sat under the table. Against the fourth wall a pallet bed lay upon the floor, neatly covered with a blanket. On the wall a cloak and a robe hung from hooks.

Keir set his hat on the table and held the chair out for Eleanor. "Please sit." He crouched before the fire and poked at the coals that still glowed orange. "Are you warm enough?"

She could tell that her plight, her prospects, scratched at him like a poorly sewn shirt seam.

"Yes." She kept her hands in her lap and her eyes averted from the bed. "What are we doing here?"

He cleared his throat, put a single stick on the coals, and stood up. "I rode out here early this morn. Copper kens the way now." His chuckle sounded strained. "I spoke to the vicar. He's agreed to it."

"It?" Eleanor pulled her shawl tighter.

"He'll help us … he'll marry us." He thrust his hands out in an imaginary stopping gesture. "Now, ye needna fash aboot it. 'Twill be a marriage in name only. 'Twill thwart the plan to have ye marry the King and …" his eyes flashed "'twill free me from me father's oath to the MacLeods. They'll nay be happy, but …" He gave a short grunt, his hands back at his sides. He looked over at the buckets, took one, flipped it and made it his seat. He sat with his knees almost as high as his chin. Eleanor thought he looked more like a child than a man who'd just proposed the most irrational thing she could think of.

"M-marry us?"

"I'll nay bind ye to the oath. We'll barely whisper the vows. I'm payin' the vicar fer the parchment. 'Tis all." He ground the last two words between his teeth, demolishing them before they exploded like pine tar in the charged air.

Eleanor took in a slow and long breath of air and let it out as slowly. Outside the rain began and though she heard no plinking sounds upon the roof, the stones outside started to echo the tiny splashes. A healing sound was how she'd always imagined the rain drops on Ingledew's stones. And this was a healing rainfall, undeniably. She gulped, thought of a dozen questions. Would they still go to the ball? Would they leave to search out her mother right away? Would he allow Hannah to come too? What would Bernard do? Would this news get back to Lady Beth? Would King George and Queen Charlotte be safe now? How much did Keir have to pay to bribe the vicar into performing a false marriage? Would Anabel be crushed by the news?

Oh, what did she care about Anabel?

Nothing. Nothing at all. Unless Anabel was one to plot revenge somehow. To hurt Keir. She'd die before she'd let that woman or anyone hurt this man. She clenched her lips to school the trembling that compromised them.

"Eleanor? Are ye thinkin' it over? I cannae read yer mind."

Her body answered before her mouth. Her head began to bob, a smile lifted her lips, and then at last she found her voice. "Yes, Keir. I'll marry you."

There was no lightning bolt for punctuation, no sign from God, no flash of flame as a victory of the devil's lies.

But his face … she could read it well enough. Keir was elated.

"'Twill be a good thing, El, ye'll see. We'll go to Castle Caladh first, get supplies, another horse. I ken ye're a good rider. I've planned it all out. Ye'll hafta dress in Jack's old things if we're to travel fast, but we'll have some lady things as well … fer when we find yer mum … and ye'll want to be presentable."

Their gaze held fast a moment.

"Och, ye're beamin'. The plan pleases ye, I see."

The blush mounting in her cheeks made it impossible to speak, so she gestured helplessly. He understood.

***

KEIR HAD NO hesitation that he was doing the right thing, but he'd been afraid he'd be unable to convince Eleanor. He almost fell off the bucket when she said yes. He sputtered through a list of what they'd do, trying to hold back the smile he felt throughout his body. *She said yes, she said yes.*

There was a brief moment when he thought he could see straight through to her soul. She was the one for him; he had no doubt. He told her she was beaming, told her he could see the plan pleased her. Now he waited for her response.

"Yes, you've thought of everything," she looked at her hands, "except for Hannah." She looked back up at him. "She's been with me since we were little. We've never been apart."

"'Twould be harder for the three of us to travel, but dinnae fash, I've talked it over wi' Logan. He and Jack will take her to Castle Caladh and there she'll be safe wi' me sister." He studied her, intent on every detail of her expression.

The subtle change in her countenance set his heart to thumping. He'd pleased her again and the little lines that formed around her mouth, the beginnings of another of her precious smiles, made him want to breach the two feet of space between them and kiss that mouth.

A flash of light startled them both, followed immediately by a crack of thunder.

Keir said, "Och, the priest must be preachin' a sermon on hellfire and brimstone. The Good Lord is addin' his tuppence worth."

Eleanor tilted her head slightly, the faint smile still there. "Or perhaps He's sending a sign of caution to us. Is marrying in vain like taking His name in vain?"

Keir gulped and reached for her hands. "I'll nay hurt ye, El, the Lord kens me heart." He didn't let go; she didn't pull back. He looked at their joined hands, hers soft and trembling, his rough and holding tight. And then a second flash came, but it took longer for the snap to follow. The heavens rumbled.

"There," Keir proclaimed, "ye hear Him? 'Tis settled." He gave her hands a final squeeze and let go, grabbed a stick to throw on the fire, and rose. "I mean to check on Copper and the mare. I'll only be leavin' ye a minute. Here, I'll light one of the vicar's candles." He did so, set it on the table and took his hat.

He was out a moment, but when he came back in his hat and shoulders were wet. This time he set the hat on the floor by the fire.

"Copper doesna mind the rain. And he's spun a *sian* on the mare."

"A *sian*?"

"A charm … a spell that's keepin' her calm in the storm."

He leaned against the wall and talked of horses. Eleanor had plenty to say and he enjoyed the fact that here was a woman who knew the withers from the muzzle, a mare from a gelding, a fetlock from a forelock. When she told him she'd helped a mare foal, he dropped himself onto the bucket seat and wrinkled his brow.

"How is it a princess spends so much time in a stable?"

She told him more of her history. The night before, when she'd cried in a heap at his feet in the stable, she'd only said she'd been raised at Ingledew. Now she told him how Lady Beth had kept her hidden. That she'd worked as a lad, dressed as a lad, played like a lad, endured beatings like a lad, and had only learned the feminine ways most recently.

"I was not raised as a princess. I don't think or act like one. I'd rather remain a secret princess."

Keir shook his head. "'Tis hard fer me to believe such a thing. Beatin's ye say? A salty oath comes to mind. I'd give a beatin' meself to the one who laid a hand on ye." He muttered under his breath. "And yet, ye tricked me over an' over with yer boyish looks and ways." He reached for the strings of her bonnet. "May I see yer real hair?"

Eleanor finished tugging on the strings, pulled the bonnet back, and let her hair come loose. It fell almost to her shoulders. Keir gently touched the ends then drew his hand back. "Aye, ye fooled me when ye slicked it back. Did ye wear it shorter still?"

Eleanor put her fingers to her ears to show him. They talked on about Ingledew, her life, and then about Castle Caladh and Keir grinned as he described his older sisters, his father, and lastly his mother.

"I miss her so," he said, turning toward the fire which had sparked to life. "If I can help ye find yers, it'll be a wee bit like honorin' me own."

The rain lessened and Keir got up to look out the door. As soon as he opened it, he could hear faint chanting from the kirk. "They'll be finished soon and the vicar will arrange for two witnesses. We'll go back when the Beldorney coaches leave." He closed the door.

Eleanor fixed her hair back under her cap and said, "What about Captain Luxbury? I'm sure he'll come looking for me."

"Nay. Fenella can be quite convincin'. She'll have everyone expectin' to see ye at the ball."

"But we'll be on our way to your castle?"

"Aye. The storm willna slow us down. We'll be suppin' at Caladh afore the ball begins." His brows knitted together. "Ye'll nay be sorry to miss it, will ye?"

Eleanor rose. "I'm relieved, actually. The thought of dancing … well, I've only just learned."

"The minuet?"

"Yes."

"I've heard there be a type of dance in far-off Austria where a man holds his partner in his arms." Keir took a long stride toward her. "Like this." He drew her close and looked deep into her eyes. There was no space between them. He shouldn't have been able to feel her heat, but her chest was heaving, and the wild beat of her heart matched his.

The door opened. They both stepped apart.

"The vicar says to come now." A young man, one of the acolytes, held the door and motioned for them to follow him.

Keir grabbed his hat and caught Eleanor frowning at the weather outside. The rain had stopped, but there was fog, and there were puddles. Her shoes were going to get ruined. He swept her up into his arms and ran ahead of the acolyte.

***

ELEANOR KEPT HER eyes tightly closed. She didn't know if she should enjoy it this much that Keir was carrying her in his arms. To the kirk. To get married. To ride off with her to a castle. A castle that would be hers should they stay married.

Ah, the feel of him. His strong arms holding her tightly but protectively. His ginger-stubbled face, so handsome and only an inch or so from hers. The warmth seeping off his skin, like summer sunshine, like Cook's best stew, like warm apple pie, like … ah, the bath.

Her eyes popped open. What was she thinking? How could she be so brazen in her thoughts? She'd laughed with the Chadderton boys when they talked boldly about things not said in polite company. She'd overheard the maids telling tales of midnight trysts and cuckolded husbands. This base perspective was rising from the suppression she'd exerted on it these last days spent learning the feminine arts.

But, he was so close. Holding her. Moving with the strength of a bull. Taking long strides with a purpose. Ah, she marveled in the moment. Ignored the damp chill in the air, the muddy scent, the latent drops of rain shaking off new leaves. There were better things to feel. His body. Her body.

And all too soon they were at the side door to the kirk. He set her down on the stone threshold.

"Can ye stand, El?"

"Yes. I'm fine," she answered in a whisper as a blush climbed her neck. But she was not fine. Trembling overtook each muscle. Had he not kept an arm around her waist she wouldn't have been steady enough to walk through the nave and up to the altar.

A second acolyte stood behind the old priest, a rolled piece of parchment under his arm and quill and ink in his hands. The priest eyed Keir from under hooded lids, but did not look at Eleanor. He coughed and beat his chest twice with a closed fist. "Best ye sign it now and pay yer due." He clicked his fingers at the acolyte who hurried to lay the items out on the altar.

Keir bent low to sign, handed the quill to Eleanor who, when she finished with her careful strokes, tendered the quill to the priest. He snatched it from her fingers, dipped it in the ink and made his marks, coughing again as he straightened. The acolyte picked the parchment up and, in the absence of blotting paper, he blew on the signatures.

Keir produced the money and Eleanor watched it disappear into the priest's robe.

"Now we will begin." The priest motioned for the other acolyte to come forward. "We have our witnesses—" A third coughing fit struck the old man. He clutched at the front of his robe and pounded harder on his chest. "I ... I ..." He stumbled backward against the boy with the parchment who dropped it as the priest clutched at him then fell.

Keir rushed forward and knelt by his side. The two acolytes stepped off to the edge.

"Is he all right?" Eleanor dared to move further into the space she was sure was consecrated and off limits to mere parishioners. The priest's face had gone as grey as the pewter candlesticks, but he'd stopped the racking cough. And gone still. She knelt across from Keir and pressed a shaking hand to the old man's neck.

Keir did the same. "I'm afraid he's passed from this land to the next. And right afore our eyes." He looked at the acolytes. "Shall I carry him back to his bed? Do ye ken what ye must do, lads?"

"Our father will come fer us. He'll ken what to do."

Keir nodded, glanced at Eleanor, and said to the closest lad, "The vicar has nay need of gold or silver now." He found the pocket and withdrew the money he'd paid. "Here, lads, ye'll have earned this if ye dinna tell a soul that this lass was here. Understand?"

He rose from his knees, dropped the coins in their palms, and helped Eleanor up.

"Come," he said.

"But ..."

"The vicar will be tended to. Dinna fash." He bent down to swipe the parchment, rolled it tightly and stuffed it in his shirt. "'Twill serve fer now."

Eleanor nodded, found her voice, and said, "I trust you, Keir."

***

DESPITE THE WEARINESS brought on by miles of travel and the shock of death and a plan gone awry, Eleanor kept her balance in the saddle. Her skirts were bunched and wet, her bonnet kept slipping back, her shawl was sodden, but her excitement still danced in circles in her stomach. When they could, they rode side by side and talked. First it was about the vicar's tragic death and the fright on the acolytes' faces, then, with the sky brightening, they found happier topics. He seemed as animated as she felt. She wondered if he was truly happy to be with her. Perhaps the burden of the plot against the king was lifted from his soul now that he'd committed to helping her instead.

She certainly was happy, and surprised that she didn't think more about Hannah being alone. She trusted Keir's brothers to come through with their promise to see to her welfare.

It was tempting to relax herself, but somehow conversation felt safer than the tense closeness of silence.

"The poor Baroness," Eleanor said when they came to a narrower path and she had to follow, "she's going to be embarrassed to be throwing a ball for a princess who has disappeared."

"Och, if I ken me sister, and I do, she'll endear herself to the Baroness by thinkin' up the right excuse."

"Or maybe Hannah can play my part. With the wig I wore last night and the best dress, perhaps no one will notice. I hardly spent a moment meeting each of yesterday's guests. And there will be new people tonight."

They guided their horses through the trees. Keir had insisted she take Copper as he wasn't as sure about the mare's disposition. The rain had finally stopped a while ago; there were still some clouds, but between them the sun burst through with warming rays.

"Aye," he chuckled, "she deceived me as easily as ye did. And when I first saw her in a dress … well, no wonder me brothers are besotted wi' the lass. I wouldna bet against one o' them takin' her fer a wife."

"But … she's not of their station. They would not marry Hannah Pascoe of Feock, Cornwall, a servant from Ingledew."

"Was she nay a ward of Lady Beth?"

"Yes." She reined in Copper when he started to trot.

"Me brothers, like me sisters, can marry who they choose. 'Twas only I, as oldest male heir, who seemed to be destined to accept a match of me father's choosin'."

"What will your father do when you tell him … whoa, Copper, slow down." Eleanor yanked on the reins.

"Copper kens the way now. We're but a few arrow lengths from home. Ye best hold tight and not give'im his heid or ye'll be racin' fer the barn." He urged the mare forward and took the lead. "I'll block yer way a bit, but when we crest yon hill, ye might hafta show me yer ridin' skills."

Eleanor smiled. She'd like nothing better than to gallop. Lose the bonnet, let the shawl fly away, feel the spring air on her face.

"I'm ready," she shouted at his back when they got to the top of the hill. But Keir stopped and so did she. The view took her breath away. She could see for miles. The seedtime sun seemed to bow and fill the valley, making the white flowers in the grass shimmer like stars. A pair of golden eagles soared over the loch. There were mountains in the distance, but what stood out was much closer: a castle, a pond, fields of heather, meadows of gold, flocks of sheep. There were small homes as well, with thatched roofs and small corrals, dotting the pastures wherever there was a tree to shade it.

"This is the most beautiful place I've ever seen, Keir.

"'Tis indeed. And when we get to the castle ye'll see … there'll be arbors an' benches an' birdbaths waitin' fer ye beside carefully laid stone paths. But I ken another spot, a secret place, I hope to show ye."

Chapter 14

SHE WAS SAFE, she was dry, she'd been given a hunk of bread and some ale, but she never expected to be put here … in a dungeon. She thought of the wet afternoons at Ingledew, the stink of the stables, the brisk rattle of Lady Beth's voice, Cook explaining the proper making of a savory pie. Little things that flitted through her mind, but they meant home. What had she gotten herself into?

It had all been so magical … seeing Castle Caladh for the first time, taking in the beauty of the land, the stateliness of the castle, the multi-green expanse of the Scottish Highlands … all with the magnificent Highlander at her side and indelicate thoughts in her head. And then the worst thing happened.

That blasted Captain Luxbury. He and six of his soldiers rode toward them from the north, suddenly surrounding them, weapons aimed, words shouted, horrible punishments threatened. They'd escorted them the rest of the way to the castle. Keir demanded that she be allowed to rest in what he called the wine cellar, led there by a servant named Elspeth, with a young English soldier to guard her.

Now she sat on a folded horse blanket on an ancient chair in a low-ceilinged room with a single small window, waiting, trying to ignore the red-coated guard at the door. She scratched her fingernails across the

114

table top and flicked away some crumbs, wondering if they were still having the ball right now at Beldorney Hall.

***

KEIR WAS FURIOUS. His father was giving fair attention to the spewing lies from the mouth of this wallydrag of an Englishman.

"Laird McKelvey, we have proof your son is an insurrectionist." Luxbury puffed his chest out. He held the parchment he'd taken from Keir as well as two letters he had, their seals broken, and waved them all in the Highland laird's face. "Coded letters from Horace Sylvan to Keir McKelvey and a copy of such to Hubert Beldorney, your son-in-law, I believe?"

Laird McKelvey nodded, grabbed the epistles from Luxbury's gloved hand and perused them. "Aye, I see, I see. And that parchment?"

"Treason!" He unrolled the document and pointed at the signatures. "Your son has spoiled the princess. Forced her into a marriage to thwart the future plans of English men far wiser than any Highland blunderbuss."

It was all Keir could do not to grab the nearest vase and shatter it in anger, but he knew he had to hold his temper in check if his father were to believe him.

"She wasna forced. Ye can ask her yerself. What makes ye think she be a princess? What royal name is Fletcher? See her scribble?" He snatched the parchment and pointed to her scrawl. "She signed it Eleanor Ainsworth Fletcher. Not Hanover or Stuart or Barclay or Bruce."

Laird McKelvey looked from his son to Luxbury, and glanced at the remaining men in uniform, then back to Luxbury. "We shall solve this like civilized Scots if ye'd be so kind as to accompany me and me son into the library? And leave yer men here."

***

THE DOOR OPENED, and a shaft of candlelight fell across the floor. Eleanor breathed easier when a lovely young woman, red-haired and freckled, spoke kindly to the guard, offered him a plate of bread and cheese, and then entered the dismal room and closed the door behind her.

"Hello. I'm Rory. Those are my skirts yer wearin'."

Eleanor hopped up. "I thank you. I'm Eleanor … Eleanor …" She burst out crying and blubbered that she didn't know her last name.

"Och," Rory said, sounding like her brother, "dinna fash." She gently pushed Eleanor back into her seat. "I've heard yon menfolk blatherin' on aboot ye. The lass who rides a gallopin' horse like a lad, with short hair to match." She scanned Eleanor's face. "Ye can call

115

yerself McKelvey now, since I ken ye married me brother, Keir …
though I'd sooner be expectin' such behavior from Jack or Logan,
impulsive little cubs. I cannae imagine Keir elopin'. Ye've captured his
heart, must be. I've nivver known him to change his obstinate mind …
except fer someone he loves." She seated herself on the second chair
and placed her hands on the table between them.

Eleanor clasped her hands in front of her to keep from fidgeting with
her borrowed skirt. She bit her lip and didn't respond to the lie of their
marriage. If Keir was somewhere in the castle making a case for a legal,
binding marriage, then she'd not say a word against it.

Rory cocked her head and smiled. "Ye're not as pretty as Anabel
MacLeod, but there's a gentle spirit aboot ye. A fairy glow … that I
sense … and I expect Keir feels it too. Can I ask ye why he married ye
so quickly?" Her plumpish face tilted in curiosity.

The sigh was heavy. "It seemed the right thing to do. Do you know
the particulars of … hmm … a princess coming to Scotland to learn to
be a queen?"

Rory's face gave her answer before her tongue. "'Tis aboot that
secret letter I helped him decode? He aimed to dissuade the princess and
…" Her hand went to her mouth. "Are ye the princess?"

She dropped her gaze. "I thought at first he meant to murder me, but
his heart is kind."

"Aye."

"And once he learned my story, he pledged himself to help me. To
help me find my mother." Eleanor sighed again. "But now I'm here,
imprisoned I suppose, in this dungeon."

A quick laugh from Rory echoed once against the stones. She glided
her fingers over the lace at her sleeves, the sound of her breathing giving
warm life to the chamber's seclusion. "Castle Caladh has no dungeon.
This was once a storage room, fer wine … with a secret passageway.
I'm sure Keir himself convinced those English jackanapes to put you
here, where they, too, would think ye'd be imprisoned and easily
guarded. Ah, but we could wrest ye back without their knowin'." She
leaned closer to Eleanor and whispered. "I'll be leavin' ye now, but ye'll
hear the clang of the hilltop irons soon, as I'll be callin' in the clansmen
that'll help us persuade the English to leave us."

***

LAIRD MCKELVEY SLAPPED his kilted thigh and squinted at
Luxbury. "Ye'll think me mad, captain, but I insist ye leave and take yer
soldiers with ye. Ye're in Scotland now, and this parchment stands." He
pressed a hand against the rolled document now lying crosswise on the
library desk. His back was to an impressive wall of shelves filled with

expensive leather-covered books. "I ken ye wish to take the lass to England, but she's bound to me son now and here she'll stay."

As if lending punctuation to his words there came the resonant sound of metals, a portentous clang from the hill behind the stable.

Luxbury put his hand on his sword handle and spoke slowly. "I dare say the princess would not have married a Scot on the very day she met him."

Keir interrupted. "I've kent Eleanor since the day she disembarked the ship ye brought her here on. I spoilt yer plan, aye, but she'd rather be wed to me than ... than the King of England." Keir took a step toward Luxbury.

"Step back, sir, or I'll be obliged to call in my soldiers." He turned his head toward the father. "Laird McKelvey, I swear the parchment must be a forgery. Let us speak to the maiden and set things right."

"Ye have me word, captain, that we'll speak to the lass, but first, if ye'll wait outside a moment, I'd like the favor of havin' a harsh word or two wi' me son here."

Luxbury tightened his grip on the sword. "I'll take back the traitorous letters." He held his left hand out to receive them.

The laird pressed them into his palm with a grunt. "They prove nothing."

"I'll not have you burning them." He turned on his heel and left the library, his boots barely making a sound on the red and gold rugs that covered the stones.

Laird McKelvey glared at Keir, his dark jade eyes going darker, and the lines on his forehead deepening. "Since yer mum died ye've been a changed man, Keir McKelvey. What were ye thinkin'? Ye've lost us the MacLeod lands. Ye've risked yer life fer some palace revolution and then ye turned yer back on the verra dissidents ye meant to work with ... and stolen this woman." He slammed his hands on the desk between them and growled. "Now ye've put me in an impossible position. We'll have the whole of Scotland and England ag'inst us." He lifted his hands, turned, and went to the window to look out. "Yer sister sounded the alarm. Did ye nay hear it? The hall will be filled with men willin' to fight fer us ... fer ..." He growled again. "Fer ye and fer yer sister's worthless farmer, too. Fenella could 'ave wed a McDoon or a —" He stopped speaking.

"Father," Keir moved to stand beside him at the window, "ye loved me mum, aye? And she loved ye back, I ken. There wouldna be a moment o' love between Anabel and me, but there's somethin' growin' between me and—"

"Yer princess? 'Twould be best if she'd deny the princess part."

"She may. She hasna seen her mum since she was a wee lass. I promised to help her find this Mary Fletcher. Her mum can name the father or deny him. Without a link to the royal lineage …"

"Aye, I see yer point. Perhaps we can make a deal with the captain … to search alongside ye. 'Twould be an appeasement o' sorts. And if ye could get the mum to say the father was a commoner …"

"Och." Keir looked to the hills and watched several men heading toward the castle. Directly below stood a soldier holding the Englishmen's horses. "He'll hafta send the troops back. I'll nay have Eleanor suffer the attentions of a dozen eyes upon her. 'Twill be nuisance enough to have Luxbury trail us."

The laird grunted and moved back to the desk. He unrolled the parchment again and studied the document. "She could barely write her name, if that's her real name. And this vicar who signed … the signature is faint, nearly illegible, and where are the witnesses' names?" He looked up at Keir who now stood next to him. "Son, yer face has paled."

"Father … the vicar died … before we said the vows."

***

BERNARD LUXBURY HAD left the father and son in the library, gathered the four soldiers that stood in the great hall of the castle and told one to alert the man holding the horses to be ready for a quick get-away. He told a second soldier to go down to the cellar where the servant had taken Princess Nora and bring her and the other guard up. To the two remaining soldiers, his most trusted men, he spoke quietly and told them to ready their arms. He reminded them they were here to rescue the princess and to expect some resistance as they carried out their orders.

He spoke roughly and with great authority to his men, keeping his hand on the hilt of his sword to evoke the urgency of his words.

Laird McKelvey strode out of the library, Keir at his heels. "Where be yer other men, captain?" His voice echoed in the great hall. His brows snapped together and his eyes burned with the question.

"Readying our horses, sir … and we shall collect Princess Nora and be off."

The laird stopped, folded his arms across his chest, and nodded at Keir. "Out wi'ye. See to … our new guests."

Luxbury frowned and whispered to the soldier on his right, "Follow him."

Alone with the laird and a single soldier, Luxbury smirked. "So … your son has confessed? The marriage is a sham, is it not?"

The laird narrowed his eyes further. "I'll let the lass tell ye." He looked beyond Luxbury where Eleanor was coming into the hall, flanked by two of his soldiers.

Luxbury turned his head enough to discover what held the laird's attention. He twisted all the way around. "My dear Eleanor!" This was not a woman for whom he should be feeling any sort of amorous inclinations, and yet he was. He bowed deeply, hand still on the sword. "I'm so sorry for the ..." He stopped speaking when he realized she was without bonnet, cap, or wig. "What have they done to you? Your hair ..." Suddenly he was repulsed by her appearance.

Eleanor glanced at the large entrance doors then at the Highlander who looked so much like Keir. She stopped, dropped her chin, and curtsied. "Lord McKelvey?"

The laird's face cracked into a grin as wide as Keir's and he strode quickly toward Eleanor. The soldiers on either side of her snapped into a defensive stance, but stepped aside as the older McKelvey embraced Eleanor.

"Daughter," he said, with false affection. He kept a hand on Eleanor's arm and said to Luxbury, "Ye may ask her yer question, captain, and if her answer is yea ye must leave her to her husband."

Luxbury stood shifting his weight from one boot to the other.

"Did you marry that Highlander of your own accord?"

Eleanor held his scrutiny, candle light from the wall sconces glinting in her eyes. "I did."

Luxbury huffed. His contemplation of the fact might have taken longer, but a roar of voices sounded outside and his eyes went wide. The great doors fell open and light and sound exploded in.

"'Tis a riot, aye." The laird spoke calmly. "Our neighboring clans dislike the Sassenachs. Perhaps we can achieve a compromise. Me son tells me his lady wishes to find her mum. 'Tis likely ye'll learn of the lass's true parentage if ye travel wi' them. She may be a princess," he nodded pleasantly at her, "or she may not. But either way, I claim her as a McKelvey now."

A crowd of men, led by Keir, pushed the soldiers inside. The soldiers' hands were tied behind their backs, their faces contrite.

Keir yelled across the great hall. "We'll nay hurt yer men, Luxbury. They'll be free to return to England and you and I can hunt for the truth together."

Luxbury dropped his hand from his sword and motioned to the soldiers with him. "Go. Get back to England ... and not a word of this to anyone."

***

ELEANOR FELT AS exposed as she would if she'd been found bathing in a lake. The laird's embrace, Bernard's capitulation, the clansmen's stares … it was all too much. Why hadn't Rory given her a bonnet? Or a shawl she could hide herself with?

And there was Keir across the hall, now marching toward her, getting closer, his face a mask of emotions she couldn't read. The yells and hoots from the Scotsmen at the doors met her ears in waves. She wished she'd hunted for that secret passageway. She could have escaped on her own, stolen a horse, ridden to …

To where?

Luxbury was saying something to her as Keir reached her side. What was it? Something about never letting her out of his sight? What was going on? The voices seemed to go mute, but mouths were still moving. The edges of her vision darkened. She couldn't catch her breath. She'd felt this panic before. But why now? Wasn't she safe? Keir was beside her, his arm around her waist.

Ugh, his grasp on her tightened as her knees bent, her head bobbed forward of its own accord. She couldn't get a frightened word out of her mouth. As she collapsed completely onto Keir, her head fell back, her eyes barely open, but she could see up. A balcony. A servant girl. Rory. Flowers—

Her body crumpled like the tip of a spent candle, her mind no longer registering the people around her.

…

She woke in a soft bed, Rory at her side.

"Och, ye're alive." Rory laughed. "'Twas the right thing to do, yer faintin' like a baby bird. The men go all a'muddle and forget they're a'fightin' each other."

Eleanor pushed up on her elbows. "I fainted? I never faint."

"Well, then, ye ken how to fall into a deep sleep and stay that way 'til things settle themselves." Rory rose from her chair and walked toward her wardrobe. "I've been gatherin' things and then sittin' a spell to watch ye. Here," she swung a hand toward a trunk, "are the clothes I think will fit ye best and travel well." She grinned at Eleanor. "And look," she held up a gorgeous gown, "'tis trimmed in green velvet with a matching bonnet. It should make a fine impression upon yer mum when ye meet her."

Eleanor swung her legs over the side of the bed and perused the room. It was as luxurious as Lady Beth's suite at Ingledew. There were two fireplaces, a writing table and a dressing table with tall-back chairs, an embroidered lounge settee, and a standing mirror with hardly any glass waves, trimmed in brass. The bed she now rose from was piled with quilts and pillows, the headboard intricately carved with a meadow scene of deer and trees and pond and ducks. This was the bedroom of a princess. She looked again at Rory and marveled at how different she was from Keir, his dark-haired brothers, and the laird himself.

"You must favor your mother. Keir told me a bit about her." Unconsciously she ran her palms along the soft fabric on the bed.

"Aye, all of us female McKelveys have the scarlet-hair blessing and the fiery temper curse. When ye birth Keir's bairns, ye'll see. The lads'll be dark as minks and the lasses will glow like foxes."

The heat that rose up her neck when Rory mentioned having Keir's offspring, cooled quickly when Rory lifted an improbable pair of trousers. "These troosers I keep hidden fer when I take it in me mind to ride one of me brothers' horses. I best get Keir's permission a'fore I lend them to ye."

A servant knocked on the door and Rory called her in.

"M'lady, dinner is served. Shall I bring a tray fer …" she sneaked a glance at Eleanor "yer guest?"

"Are the Englishmen still here?"

"Only the one … the captain. The village men saw to it that the others rode off." The girl kept her eyes on Rory.

"Good. No tray then, just make sure there's a place set for … my new sister. Elspeth, this is Keir's wife."

The girl's face showed her surprise, but she quickly suppressed it, curtsied, and backed out of the room.

Rory tilted her head at Eleanor. "Ye do feel up to it, aye? But we'll make them wait a bit, while I braid what I can of yer short locks. A few ribbons on the ends will make them seem longer." She pulled open a drawer at the dressing table. "Come sit here. May I call ye El? It seems to suit ye best."

The use of her shortened name brought a lump to Eleanor's throat. A pang of homesickness wrenched her. Hannah always called her El. She missed her so much, and yet, this sister of Keir's seemed a remarkably soothing replacement.

***

"THE GREAT HALL is used for clan meetin's, feasts, and large gatherin's," Rory told Eleanor as they came down the stairs. "We've a smaller dining room me mum liked to use when we used to have the eight of us here." She chattered on about how long her sisters Fenella and Elsie had been married, how often Keir was away, and how much she hated being the only female left in the castle. "Tonight 'twill be nice to have you with me. Last night I had to endure a lonely meal with me father. I'm so happy fer yer company."

"Thank you." Eleanor's comfort around Rory was undeniable, but the closer it came to the time to be with the McKelvey men, the more nervous she became. Her eyes darted around the castle when they reached the bottom step. "Perhaps we won't be away long."

"Oh, 'tis me hope. 'Twill be wonderful to have yer companionship … and advice … I'm to be married soon."

They entered the dining room which had a long table with seven armless chairs and one that resembled a throne, with a higher back and sturdy arms. Plates were set at both ends, but the other three place settings were grouped near the bigger chair.

Rory whispered in Eleanor's ear, "He's put the Sassenach away from us."

Eleanor smiled to herself to think how insignificant and small Bernard might feel sitting at the far end. She took a seat next to Rory and across from Keir which meant their eyes connected often throughout the meal. The conversation was stilted and strained as Captain Luxbury either fumed or pouted, then threatened or pleaded from the distant end. Rabbit stew, bread, and cheese completed the first course. Eleanor could not have described the food as bland or spicy, since her other senses were busy enjoying the sight and smell of the younger McKelvey. Right there, so close. His foot once touched hers and their gaze met between bites of food she wasn't hungry for. Yet this, she knew, would be a most memorable meal.

Elspeth brought a pie that steamed. She kept their wine glasses full, though she never poured more than an inch into the captain's.

At last the topic turned to the search for Eleanor's mother. A plan for travel was laid out, but the men could not agree on a direction to start.

Keir ignored every suggestion Luxbury made by taking a sip of his wine. When he finished the glass, he said to Eleanor, "Me sister Fenella spoke of a brooch ye had that may be a clue to find yer mum." He waved off Elspeth's offer of more wine.

Eleanor's eyes darted quickly left then right. Laird McKelvey and Bernard Luxbury were watching her intently. She had ignored the captain throughout the meal. Her hand went to her bosom to feel for the hard metal of the brooch pinned beneath the garment. "Yes, Lady Beth said my mother always wore the matching one, but Fenella told me she saw it on a lad … a long while ago … at a fair, I think." She tapped her fingers against her throat to obscure the fact she was confirming that the brooch was safely fastened underneath.

Keir nodded. "She gave me the particulars. Could ye draw us a picture of the brooch? So we'd know what to look for?"

Her mind flashed on the writing desk in Rory's room, then she thought of a similar desk in the room she'd had at Beldorney Hall and that made her think of Hannah. Her face drooped with sadness. She sighed. "Yes, I can draw its likeness."

"Make two drawings," Luxbury said. "I'll require one of my own." He swallowed violently, his Adam's apple seizing and jumping.

"Yes, Bernard, certainly." But the look on his face gave her a chill and she wished she was anywhere else but here. She did not want him to know she had the brooch and she did not want to draw him a picture. She lifted her glass and sipped the wine, thinking.

The laird, who suddenly seemed in a hurry to end the meal and the evening, said, "Rory, ye shall show the captain to Jack's room. Keir, ye may install yer wife in Fenella's old room. 'Tis closest to yers. But as long as the captain has a question about the authenticity of the parchment, 'twould be best to humor him, and leave yer nuptials till the facts are resolved." He gave a capitulating nod toward Luxbury.

Keir huffed. "There's a kirk not far. We could repeat our vows there." Before Luxbury could respond Keir added, "Captain, you could be our witness."

Chapter 15

THE HORSE SNORTED, and a pup raised its mangy body from the middle of the road and flattened its flea-bitten ears before slinking off. The three of them, Luxbury in the lead and Eleanor and Keir riding side by side, had traveled all morning. A fourth horse, laden with clothing and supplies, trailed on a long lead line attached to Keir's saddle. They were coming now to a small village, having missed the turn-off to the kirk Keir had mentioned. There would be no repeated vows yet; Eleanor was disappointed.

The night before, Eleanor had drawn a reasonable picture of a brooch she'd seen Lady Beth wear on occasion. This morning she handed it to Keir in front of Luxbury saying she only made the one drawing. Luxbury immediately snatched the paper and declared himself to be in charge of keeping an eye out for it. What he didn't know was that she'd shown Keir the actual brooch earlier. Keir had laughed at her duplicity, studied the brooch, and dropped it into her hand, lightly touching her fingers. He promised her he'd find a way to send the captain back to England. Without her.

"Ho!" Luxbury yelped. He reined in his horse.

Keir and Eleanor stopped too and Keir spoke with mock laughter in his voice, "What is it, captain? Is yer horse lame? Need ye a rest?"

Luxbury scowled at Keir, shook his head, and pointed. Up on the ridge stood three men with rifles pointed at them. The captain hissed at Keir, "They're aiming at us."

"Nay, they're aimin' at ye, captain. 'Tis yer red coat that riles'em." Keir raised his arm in a wide wave and yelled, "Guid mornin'. Keir McKelvey of Castle Caladh. May I have a word?"

Two of the men kept their sights on Luxbury, but the third lowered his weapon and started down the hill. Keir dismounted, told Eleanor to keep her seat, and motioned to Luxbury to get down. He handed his reins to Luxbury and started walking toward the other man.

Neither Eleanor nor the captain could hear the conversation when the men met halfway up the hill, but their body language put them at ease.

Luxbury put both sets of reins in one hand and moved as close as he could to Eleanor's side, using Copper as a shield. His face displayed disgust at the trousers Eleanor wore. He looked up at her. "I accept that you do not wish to be a princess or marry King George, but please know that you don't have to run away with that heathen. Eleanor," he boldly touched her knee "I'll wed you. I have money; we can sail to America. Lady Beth and Lord Edgeworth need not know." He glanced at the pack horse. "I suppose there are dresses in that sack?"

Eleanor bent her head down enough to appear as though she meant to whisper. Instead, she said in perfectly controlled modulation, "Bernard. How dare you ask a married woman to run off with you. I thank you for your help, but now perhaps it's best if you go back to England, too."

He stepped back as if slapped. His previous expression changed again. He narrowed his eyes at her and said, "I doubt your marriage has been consummated. And even if it was, I sneaked down at midnight and burned the parchment. You're no better than a whore now." He jerked Copper's reins in anger. "You, dear princess, shall marry the King and then, once he's been assassinated, you will do as we say or else," he cocked his head toward Keir who was finishing up with the man, "that man, your mother, your friend Hannah, and anyone else you hold dear, will die."

He snorted and moved the horses ahead of her.

Keir walked back to them, a quivering smile playing across his lips. "They'll let us pass. I explained our mission." He glanced at Eleanor, discerned her countenance, and looked quickly at Luxbury who turned to listen. Keir frowned then went on, "And I described the brooch. Asked if they'd seen a lad wearin' it pinned to his kilt." He stopped speaking and scanned the ridge and then the road before them. The men had resumed their position as lookouts.

Luxbury became impatient. "And? Have they seen him?" He jerked the reins as his hands expressed some exasperation. "Speak, man!"

***

KEIR SAW HOW stretching out his words could rile the captain. He looked up at Eleanor, sitting so straight on the back of his sister's favorite mare. He gave her a secret smile and she seemed to relax. Had she been afraid for the few minutes he was a short distance from her? He finally answered the captain, "Aye, they ken the lad. His mum lives beyond the valley, in a village called—he breathed in and out slowly—"in a village called … Auld Reekie."

He took a few steps toward his horses, slapped the pack animal's rump, and took Copper's reins from Luxbury. He mounted his horse and motioned for the captain to do the same. "Keep going straight up the road. It's quite a ways. We'll be a'followin' ye. Doan fash if the lady and the pack horse slow us down. We'll be along."

He allowed the captain's horse to get a good distance ahead before he spoke to Eleanor. "What happened, lass? Ye had the look me sister gets when me father loses his temper. Did ye fear fer me safety as I spoke to the sentry men?" He watched her face grow rosy.

"No, you didn't fear them and they laid their weapons down. It was Bernard who scared me. He wants to wed me and take me to America. He said he burned the parchment."

Keir nodded his head and pulled the reins back enough to slow Copper. The pack horse and Eleanor's mare slowed as well. "Aye, I figured he had the anger of a man spurned." He gave a gentle laugh. "Ye're nay thinkin' o' joinin' him and runnin' off, are ye?"

"Of course not. I may have changed my mind about this whole plan to dethrone the king, but I shan't change it again." She tightened her grip on the reins and stared at Keir. He liked what he saw in her deliberate expression.

"Ah, lass … El, will ye marry me … ag'in?"

***

FOR ONE WHOLE second Eleanor wondered if her heart could beat its way out of her chest. Was Keir serious? Should she scream *yes*? Perhaps he was joking and she should laugh. There was no decision to make because the next second her horse stumbled and she lost her balance and nearly fell off.

"Whoa." Keir stopped and reached over to halt Eleanor's mare. "Are ye weary, lass? Shall we rest a while? The horses can graze and ye can walk a bit." He straightened back up and eyed the clothing Rory had lent her. "I've seen ye walk aboot in men's breeches afore when I thought ye a lad. 'Twon't fret me none to see ye do it ag'in."

They dismounted in tandem and led the horses to a grassy spot.

Eleanor had her heart back under control, but her mind was another matter. She ached to know what was behind Keir's words. "Keir ... the parchment ... the marriage ... it was a way to travel together, to avoid having to go through with the plan for me to become queen, and, uh, to spoil your arranged marriage to ..."

"Ye're wonderin' if I meant it ... askin' ye to marry me."

"It was rash of us to go through with a secret marriage ... and since we never spoke the vows ... I wonder," her eyes scanned ahead to see the captain round a corner and disappear, "I wonder if you're asking now out of ... out of rivalry with Bernard."

Keir let go of Copper's reins and stepped closer to her. He said nothing, but the softening in his eyes told her what she wanted to know.

He drifted a hand across her cheek and into her hair. Every nerve in her body leaped.

He drew her nigh, lifted her off her feet, and found her mouth. The kiss was nothing like what she'd expected or dreamed of or ever thought possible. His lips traced hers, and she found the answer to her question in the supple corners of his mouth, replied in the broken breath of relief that escaped between her teeth.

Warm, wet ...

Thrilling ...

His lips on hers ... natural, perfect ...

Ah ... little noises escaped her throat ...

And he was humming too ...

Then a groan ... a desire ...

Her arms found their way around his broad shoulders, her bosom pressed against his chest ...

She felt his whole body as if they were entwined ...

Her heart danced past the beats ...

She trembled as he explored her lips and shuddered when his mouth slowly released hers.

She gasped for air, as did he. Then he whispered her name, "El ... Eleanor ... marry me." His dark eyes warmed to caramel brown in the light.

"Yes."

***

KEIR HAD WANTED to kiss her since he'd met her, and, he realized, the desire for her had been there even when he thought she was a young lad. Fenella once told him that when a lad met a lassie, their spirits

127

crossed on an invisible level. Now he believed it. He'd been in love with Eleanor from the beginning.

And now she'd agreed to marry him, not out of necessity this time, but out of this spiritual bond they had. Was it love? He'd do anything and everything to be with her. Yes, he loved her.

He let his breath out in one long sigh. Satisfied …

But Copper was straying farther away, trailed by the pack horse, of course, while the mare was nibbling grass right behind his beloved's feet. His beloved. So quickly his thoughts of her had bloomed. His lips curled into a contented smile.

Eleanor looked up the road, suddenly seeming shy. "I wonder how far Bernard is. Will he wait for us or go on to Auld Reekie."

Keir chuckled and touched her face again to direct her eyes back to his. "Auld Reekie … aye … he'll ask fer directions and be told the way to Edinburgh. I doan suppose ye English ken that Auld Reekie is the former name of Edinburgh."

"So that's not where we're going?"

He was still holding her in his arms … feeling her heart beat, noting the heat of her breath. It wasn't only his soul that she stirred. He forced his gaze from her lips as a breeze moved his hair off his forehead.

"Nay. He'll be searchin' out yer family usin' that picture ye made and lookin' in the wrong city." He tossed a look back down the road where they'd come from, released her, and stepped back. "The Scot I talked to … he directed me, but nay to Edinburgh. At the next village, Luxbury will nay doubt head east whilst we'll go west. There'll be a big surprise fer the Englishman the moment he gets to the city. If they dinnae jail him, they'll be sendin' him home, banged an' bruised. A red coat in Edinburgh willna be respected nor tolerated."

He turned his head toward Copper and whistled. The horse's head came up and he started walking toward his master. A startled pheasant flushed out of the grass and both Eleanor and Keir laughed at Copper's reaction. He used his muzzle to nudge six pheasant chicks out of his path, snatched some long grasses, and chewed noisily as he led the pack horse toward Keir.

***

CAPTAIN BERNARD LUXBURY was too proud to look back. The princess and McKelvey would follow. If that Highlander had plans to desert him, he was certain that Eleanor would put her precious foot down and ensure that they follow the captain. He meant what he said: he'd kill her cherished friend Hannah, the mother she hadn't yet met, and even the Highlander. He was confident she believed him.

He'd vacillated on his feelings for her. He'd been quite taken with her when he first met her at Ingledew. She was comely, innocent, and somewhat mysterious. She wasn't as beautiful as he'd hoped, but when he saw her again at Beldorney Hall, she had inexplicably changed. The only word he could think of for her transformation was blossoming. She had blossomed into an acceptably nice-looking woman. He wouldn't hesitate to bed her.

But now, deep into the Scottish countryside, he picked up on her distaste for him. Was it always there? She spoke to him with cold words, averted her gaze often, and when their eyes did meet, he sensed revulsion. Did she think him ugly? *Crivens!* He almost hoped she'd defy him. He'd like to see the look on her face when he thrust a sword through that McKelvey jolterhead.

Another hour's walk and he was bored. They hadn't caught up with him yet, but he wasn't worried. He could feel them back there. Sometimes he heard their voices, a man's deep tone and a woman's tinkling laugh. It rattled him, but he never looked back.

He'd gotten foul looks from the men he passed and a few hurled nasty insults about the crown at him. He wished he could stop and argue the point, let the stupid Scots know he was doing something about King George.

His stomach growled and he pulled a hunk of bread from his saddle bag. That timid little housemaid had handed it to him as they left. It didn't take him long to finish it and it seemed enough to stave off his hunger for a few more hours.

He urged his horse into an easy lope until he saw a peddler's wagon on the road headed his way. Surely this man wouldn't curse at him; he'd want to sell his wares. Money was money.

Bernard halted and angled his horse crosswise on the road, painted a faux smile on his face, and waited. The peddler pulled back on his pony's reins and stopped near enough. He was a smallish man, wizened and wrinkled, obviously no threat to a strong young man, but Bernard was wary just the same.

"Heyo, ye be in need o' me services, sir?" The peddler filled in the gap between his missing front teeth with a curious tongue for the moment it took the captain to nod. "They call me CheapJack an' I've an assortment o' necessaries ye'll nay find elsewhere in yer travels." He pulled back a tattered blanket that covered most of the things in his wagon. "Spoons, bowls, leather straps, nails, flint, knives … whiskey …" he raised his eyebrows "… medicine to make ye sleep, heal the warts on yer fanny flaps …" He went on naming various items he offered for sale as Bernard guided his horse closer and circled the wagon, peering at the tools and gadgets, house supplies, and diverse sundries. He hopped down from the saddle and stepped close to the back of the wagon.

"Are ye meanin' to buy or snatch and run? Ye ain't said nary a word, Sassenach."

Bernard glanced up at the peddler, startled to see a rifle pointing at his head. His own weapons were unreachable, except for his sword, which wouldn't win against a gun.

"Uh, uh, yes, yes, I've need of one thing you mentioned … but I don't see it in your wagon." He inched back.

"Name it."

Bernard focused on the old man's face, the toothless grin, the long nasal hairs, the loud wheezing breaths the peddler took. His own fingers twitched above the hilt of his sword, but the long barrel of the gun pointed at him sent shivers down his spine.

"I could use a flint." He gulped.

"'Tis a fine choice." The peddler kept the gun level, but reached with one hand for a flint, palmed it, and said, "Any t'ing else?"

"Information. I need to get to Auld Reekie. Which road do I take?"

The peddler gave a snort. "Ye'll pay me a tuppence fer the flint."

Bernard found his coin purse and started to set the payment on the wagon bed. CheapJack clucked his tongue. "Nay. Think me a fool? Toss it here." He did so and the peddler caught it, glanced briefly at the coin, and tossed back the flint. "Ye're on the right road, Sassenach. I bid ye guid day and guid luck in—" he laughed, "—Auld Reekie." He set the rifle down, re-covered his wares, slapped the pony's rump, and rattled on.

Bernard remounted, scowled at the cart, shook his head, and wondered why the old fool laughed. He stuffed the flint in his pocket, rubbed his horse's neck, and then kicked its sides to get it going faster.

The road eventually widened, was more well-traveled, and brought him to a sight he didn't expect. Auld Reekie was not a small village. He trotted down the streets of a rather bustling city comparable to his hometown of York. Then he learned its true name: Edinburgh.

Luxbury swore.

If he'd known Auld Reekie and Edinburgh were one and the same, he wouldn't have come. He'd heard the tales of what they did to Englishmen who came here. He'd have had a chance if he had his troops with him. But here he was, sticking out in his red wool like a cardinal in the snow.

He swore even more when a force of six uniformed policemen surrounded him, disarmed him, pulled him from the saddle, and took him to a magistrate.

"These charges are false and nonsense," he shouted. He argued his defense until he was as red in the face as the presiding judge, whose complexion came by its ruddy flare naturally. "You can't do this to me. I'm a soldier of the crown. And … and I'm here to help you."

Two men stripped him of his red coat and ripped off his shirt, leaving him to stand plainly shaking in his boots.

The judge joked, "A soldier of the crown, eh? Where's yer ruffled shirt, yer sword, yer fancy red coat?"

"I'm Captain Bernard Luxbury of the—"

"Och, we'll add impersonatin' an officer to the list. 'Tis not a capital offence, but carries a penalty of at least five years in prison." The judge caught the eye of each of the men who'd brought Luxbury in. "Shall I be lenient, me friends?"

There were nods all around and Luxbury let his breath out in a mangled sigh of anger and relief, but then the judge said, "The fine is ten English pounds. Have ye got it, *captain*?" He snickered.

Before he could answer, one man offered to pay half a pound for his horse and another a few farthings for the uniform.

Luxbury fumed. He had a few pounds in a money bag he'd attached to his saddle, but not enough to pay the exorbitant fine. *Ridiculous.* "I'll not pay a penny!"

Without warning someone's fist connected with his jaw and he fell to the floor. Another set of hands pushed on his shoulders and held him down.

"Are you Scots imbeciles or ratbags?" he snapped, wrenching free and shoving to his feet. Sweat shone on his brow, and his hands were trembling.

"Well," the judge smirked, "ye be lucky today, Mr. Luxbury. I'm feelin' kind. We Scots havnae felt kind toward an Englishman since the battles. Flodden. Culloden. Oh, and let us nay forget Bannockburn. Why, just namin' those tragedies is wearin' away at me kindness." He looked from Luxbury to two of the men who'd brought him in. "Is the frigate Penelope yet in port?"

One spoke up in the affirmative.

"Take him there, men. I dare say the skipper will pay his fine to have such a strong young Englishman to swab the decks and man the sails, eh?"

"Right away, sir," the mouthy one said. "The Penelope sails tomorrow bound for the West Indies."

Wide-eyed and panting, Luxbury collapsed before another Scotsman could touch him. There was laughter all around, but he didn't hear it. They kicked at his ribs a few times, but he didn't feel it. Yet.

Chapter 16

ELEANOR WRINKLED HER brow in thought, rolling the word through her mind. She'd heard Keir call her his *hen* as he spoke to a farmer they'd come upon. The term melted on his lips, easing off his tongue as if they were a long-married couple.

Now Keir motioned to her, wanting the brooch itself to show the farmer. She handed it down, noticed how the farmer eyed her breeches, then the bonnet she'd hastily retied when they'd trotted up the lane and seen the old man in the field.

"Aye," the farmer's gravelly voice carried on the wind that had come up, "this belongs to the widow's son. Yonder." He swung an arm north. "Nay doubt they'll be happy to have ye return it. 'Tis a prized possession, worth more to the lad and his mum than all the world, so says me woman." He chuckled. "But I pay dearly fer listenin' to her. She can talk the legs off a donkey, ye ken." He handed the brooch back and scratched his beard. "I'm to wonderin' what's holdin' the lad's kilt closed wi'out that pin."

Keir talked a little longer with the farmer, gathering the proper directions in fits and bits as the man, hungry to speak to someone, took his time telling him how to find the widow and lad. Eleanor noticed Keir covertly retrieving a coin from his sporran as he listened to the farmer.

He let it drop by his boots, then nodded gratefully for the information, doffed his hat, and came back to the horses.

Keir remounted, gave the farmer a friendly wave, and clicked his tongue to get Copper moving.

"Keir," Eleanor said once they were a good distance away, "I saw what you did … leaving him a coin to find in his field."

"Och, 'twas but a wee bit o' charity. He's late in his plantin' and dinnae have 'nough seeds."

She smiled to herself. Thought about that kiss. They trotted a little further before she asked, "Why did you let him believe my brooch was the lad's?"

His shoulders moved in a quick shrug. "We're beyond the reach of Castle Caladh and now on the lands under protection of Castle Kilmahew." He glanced at Eleanor. "Ye may have met the Laird and Lady Kilmahew at the greetin' time the Beldorneys had fer ye. Ye remember the lads that were lookin' fer ye in the stable? They said they'd been learnin' a gamblin' game from the Kilmahew liveryman."

She nodded and he went on. "Gamblin' and gamin' are makin' poor folks poorer here."

He sniffed at the air. "Smell that? Smoke from a cookin' fire." He slowed Copper.

Eleanor reined her mare in and stopped. "Which way?" To her right a scraggly vineyard crossed the landscape, the vines twisted along the heather-stem cords strung to support them.

Keir pointed, a dimple playing on his cheek. "The farmer said to take the narrower, left-hand path at the grapes. We'll walk the horses in. A lone widow may be scairt to see three horses come a'trottin' up the way."

Suddenly Eleanor's heart jumped. Was this it? Was this the moment she'd meet her mother? Could this widow be the woman she was searching for? Her mind brought forth the portrait of Mary Ainsworth Fletcher that hung on her bedroom wall, that she'd stared at many times and especially the last night she spent at Ingledew. She drew in a sharp breath, pricked by the memory. Would she recognize her mother? Would her hair still be autumn brown or turned to winter grey? Would her face now be lined with wrinkles?

And then she thought: widow! Her mother must have married again, had a son, forgotten all about her. And of course, Mary Ainsworth Fletcher would not recognize a grown up Eleanor.

"El," Keir's voice cut through her thoughts, "are ye gonnae whitey?"

She didn't understand.

"Ye look sick, lass. Are ye gonnae spew yer guts?"

134

She dropped the reins, slid off the saddle, and did exactly what Keir had predicted.

Keir jumped down and raced to the other side of the mare, knelt by Eleanor, and put an arm around her shaking shoulders. "I'm so sorry, lass. I made it worse. I dinnae think. O' course ye'd be nervous to make such a momentous arrival." He gave her a squeeze. "Can ye stand?" She nodded and he helped her up. "I'll get ye some bread Elspeth sent wi' me and some wine to swish about yer mouth."

He left her for but a moment as he retrieved the items. The horses weren't fazed by the flurried and flustered riders and bent their noses to the fresh sprouts beside the lane.

"I should change into skirts," Eleanor whispered. She mumbled more advice to herself, trying to calm down. "I wish Hannah were here."

***

KEIR TURNED HIS back and kept watch on the road as Eleanor changed into something more appropriate. They would have to walk the horses in; he hoped it wasn't too far down the lane, but he thought not, since the smell of the smoke was strong. The widow's home—hovel, he suspected—should be close. The thought of El meeting her mother stirred feelings in him of his own mother, her hands on his face, the discipline she'd dealt him with nothing more than a harsh look, the pride she'd displayed at his every accomplishment. He missed her mightily.

"Ready?" he prompted Eleanor after a few minutes. When she didn't answer, he turned to see that she was changed and already several yards down the path, well out of earshot. He gathered the horses' reins and followed after her, not rushing to catch up, letting her be first to arrive.

When she rounded a turn where chimney smoke was thickest above the trees, he quickly tied the horses to the nearest branch, and sprinted after her, slowing when she was in his sights again.

"Hello!" he heard her cry out toward the wood and stone cabin—larger than he expected—that appeared at the end of the narrow lane. He watched her stand firmly, clutching the brooch, peering all around. Seconds ticked by.

Finally, barely disturbing the anxious quiet of the two of them, came the unmistakable sound of a latch being drawn. Keir's eyes darted from Eleanor to the door.

"Who are you?" came the answering call from the two inches of space the door had opened.

"I'm Eleanor … Eleanor … your daughter."

Keir's throat tightened at the catch he detected in Eleanor's voice. He stayed perfectly still, out of the line of sight of whoever was at the door. It opened wider. A shabbily dressed person stepped out, barefoot, wearing breeches and a loose shirt, hair pulled back at the nape of the neck.

To say this person was the spitting image of Eleanor would be to deny the gap of twenty or so years between them. And to further confuse things, Keir was not sure if this was a woman or a man. She—or he—strode forward, stopped abruptly and stared. Now Keir could make more comparisons. Same height. Same build as Eleanor.

Was this the lad Fenella had met, now grown? A half-brother to Eleanor? Or was this her mother, disguised to appear mannish when alone in the dangerous Kilmahew territory?

"Eleanor?" The voice broke. This was a woman, after all. No man would shed so many tears, so quickly, or drop to knees and then to all fours to keen such sorrowing cries. Then spill more tears, tears of joy.

***

ELEANOR RUSHED FORWARD, fell on her mother's sobbing body, and embraced her. As she repeated the one word she thought she'd never say, "Mother, Mother," the woman uttered "Ellie, oh Ellie," with such passion that Eleanor thought her heart might burst.

The first few moments were spent on their knees, then Eleanor lifted her mother up and they stood, still embracing. They swayed back and forth, hugging each other more and more tightly.

"Oh, Eleanor, Eleanor, I'm so, so sorry." At last the woman loosened her grip and leaned back enough to get a better look at her daughter. "However did you find me?" She brought her fingers to Eleanor's bonnet and loosened the ties, pushed the bonnet back, and studied her daughter's face. She ran her fingers over Eleanor's ears, and traced the line of her jaw.

Eleanor tipped her head at the touch, looked downward, and whispered, "Lady Beth told me you went to Scotland … she gave me this … said you had the matching one." Her mother's eyes went to Eleanor's chest and the brooch pinned there.

"Aye," she moaned, sounding a bit more Scottish than English in that word. "A gift from your father." She said no more, but caught sight of movement up the lane. "There's a man!"

"It's all right. That's Keir McKelvey. He helped me find you. His sister saw a lad wearing this … at a fair?"

Eleanor watched her mother's face relax, the edges of her lips trembled with a smile, and her whole demeanor changed to one of embarrassment. "Oh, Eleanor, I'm so sorry you found me dressed like this."

"I don't mind, Mother. I spent a dozen years dressed as a stable boy myself." She gulped back a laugh. "I only changed into this dress a few minutes ago." She ran a hand across the green velvet trim, then waved at Keir to come closer.

When he got six feet away, Keir stopped and bowed deeply, "'Tis a pleasure to meet ye, Mary Ainsworth Fletcher."

The woman's hand flew to her mouth. "Oh, shh … shh … ye mustn't give me away. I am Mary Rose Macfarlane, widow of Ross Macfarlane. Please dinnae gi' me away tuh nary a soul." She stressed the accent developed in the years here then whispered in perfect English, "Come inside, both of you. We have much to tell each other."

***

ELEANOR WASN'T SURE why her mother was shushing them not to speak her real name when they were off the main road, down a lane, and so close to the woman's home. Who would hear? They entered the cabin and she knew who immediately.

In a thick Scottish brogue, her mother spoke to the lad lying on a pallet by the fireplace, "Rise ye lazy dog. Up wi' ye, Colin. 'Tis past noon." She squatted next to him and slapped his rump. In a lower voice she hissed, "We've company, lad. I need ye tuh fetch us some water from the creek. Ye hear me?"

The boy rolled over and grunted, opened his eyes, and saw Keir first. He jerked the rest of the way awake and sprang to his feet, almost knocking his mother over. He clutched possessively at the pin on his kilt.

"'Tis a'right," she soothed him, rubbing his arm, "they be friendly. Jist get some water. Fer tea. Take two buckets."

The lad's eyes never left Keir's face until he reached the door, then a quick glance at Eleanor seemed to stun him even more. He visibly gulped and slipped out the door.

Mary motioned for Keir and Eleanor to sit on the bench. Eleanor took a moment to survey the room. Its size and general rustic nature reminded her of Thomas's cabin, where she first met Keir, but here there were beautiful embroidered cushions on the wooden chairs and the bench. The table was covered with squares of fabrics and a bowl filled with needles and threads. There were drapes hung at the windows, something Thomas's cabin did not have, and decorations on the walls to beautify the home.

"Did you do that painting, Mother?" Eleanor stared at the unframed picture of the hills of Ingledew. There were two figures in the forefront. She thought she might know who they were meant to be, one a man, one a small child.

"Aye … yes," she chuckled, "you'll have to excuse me … my … tongue. I've hidden my English vowels for so long that I believe myself to actually be Mary Macfarlane, widow."

"You're not a widow?" Eleanor was thankful for the silent warmth of Keir sitting next to her.

Mary turned a chair toward them and sat down. "Well, yes, of course. But Ross Macfarlane is a made-up name. I'll tell ye … you … the short of it, but as soon as the lad returns, so does my Scottish way of speakin'." She folded her hands upon the lap of her breeches and crossed her bare feet at the ankles. "The longer story is a sad one, starting with the day I had to leave you, Eleanor. I never meant to be gone for more than a week. I was coming back to take you to America. I was married to your father, but the palace claimed it was not a legal marriage. When he died … he left me some money and I had enough to arrange passage to America. I came to Scotland … I was robbed … beaten."

Eleanor leaned a bit into Keir's shoulder. "How awful. Could you not send word to Lady Beth? Surely she would have helped you."

Mary hung her head. "Lady Beth … yes, Elizabeth, my half-sister. I did write, but the return letter was from Clive … Lord Edgeworth. He threatened to … well, never mind. He let Beth raise you, but refused to send me support." She peered at Eleanor. "But you look to be well turned out. Accomplished, no doubt."

Eleanor huffed. "Barely. She kept me hidden. I wasn't telling tales when I said I dressed as a stable boy for most of my life." She pulled off her bonnet and shook out her hair. "It's only begun to grow out this last year." Keir took hold of her hand and she looked in his eyes for a moment, enough time to see his complete acceptance of her.

"But …" Eleanor looked back at her mother, "you must have married again."

Slowly, Mary shook her head from side to side. "The lad doesn't know, was too young to remember, but his real parents died of the pox ten years ago. I took him in. Raised him as my own." She lapsed back into her adopted speech, "'Twould kill'im tuh ken the truth. Proud he is. I gave him the brooch to close his kilt, told him 'twas a gift of his long-dead pa. The stories I tell'im of his father are true stories, but they're of yer father, Eleanor." She began to weep and Eleanor left the bench to pull a second chair next to her. She sat close and tried to comfort her mother.

Keir rose. "I'll see if I can help the lad with those buckets." He closed the door quietly behind himself.

Mary sniffled, wiped her face with her blousy sleeve. "Seems a proper high-born Scot that's brought ye here."

It was Eleanor's turn to explain a few things. But first she re-pinned her brooch to the inside of her bodice, out of sight for when the lad returned.

***

KEIR WENT TO untie the horses and took them down the path he found behind the cabin. It led to a fast-running brook. The buckets were full and sitting on a flat rock, but the lad was ankle-deep in the water, bent over with fingers splayed under the surface. Keir made himself known with a preamble of coughs and grunts; Copper added a snuffled snort. He held the horses' reins as they drank their fill, then tied them up again before addressing the lad.

"I believe yer mum wished the water fer tea. Shall I carry them back fer ye?"

The boy looked up, shook the water from his hands, and said, "Ye're nay from here aboot, are ye? Yer tartan, I cannae say I've seen that plaid 'afore. Are ye a MacDougal or a Duncan?"

"Nay, I'm Keir McKelvey of Castle Caladh." He gave the boy a simple bow, his dark hair falling forward, his big hands brushing it back. "Eldest son of Laird Finley McKelvey."

Colin cocked his head, squinted, and returned to what he was doing in the shallows. "Ha! Got one." A quick flick out of the water and into the air sent a silvery minnow to the shore. "Bait."

"Aye. Ye're a fisherman, are ye?" Keir removed his boots and joined Colin in the frigid water.

"I'm the man o' the house since me pa died. Pox, it was, me mum says. She was a fine lady once, but we've come upon hard times. She sews and I fish when I can. Mostly I work in the cotton mill. 'Tis a long walk and mum only lets me go three days a week, when she's willin' tuh work there, too."

Keir nodded. "'Tis hard labor, indeed."

The boy tossed two more minnows to shore as he agreed. "'Tis. But we work through the night and earn enough to buy bannocks and thread. She pretends to be me older brother."

"Ah," Keir scooped a handful of tiny fish and helped them fly to shore, "and so ye sleep on the floor and miss the daylight."

"Sometimes." Colin eyed Keir again. "Where is Castle Caladh?"

Keir pointed past the horses. "A day's ride south. Well past the lands of Kilmahew."

Colin scowled at the name. "I hate them." He splashed his way out of the shallows and stepped up onto the rocks at the shore without an explanation for his comment.

Keir thought it best not to pry, but perhaps an innocent question would calm the lad. "How old are ye?"

"Mum says I'm a man though I won't be thirteen till winter next."

Keir stepped out of the water. "We have a dozen for bait here. Where are yer hooks?"

Colin reached up into the crook of an old tree. He showed Keir his hooks and the woven threads his mother had braided into strong twine. Then he revealed his favorite spot to stand to throw the hooks out into the deepest water. He handed two lines to Keir. They fished in silence.

***

ELEANOR FINISHED TELLING her mother of her sudden change of circumstance, of finally being allowed to dress as a girl, only to be escorted to Scotland by Luxbury to learn the courtly manners. Mary tisked her tongue as her daughter summarized the plot to kill the queen, make her marry the king, and then have him dethroned. Mary let her breath out and smiled when Eleanor assured her she would never follow through on such a radical scheme. Next, she recounted her successive adventures, from being attacked by highwaymen to being kidnapped by a phony ship inspector to meeting Keir and then his sister, Fenella. Her mother sat in rapt attention, holding both of Eleanor's hands.

"'Twas God's will this Fenella told you of Colin's brooch. 'Tis the most precious thing we own and he kens it … he knows it. Must have shown it off at the fair. So proud, he was."

Eleanor continued her tale, describing the Beldorney estate, and often referring to her dear friend, Hannah. She skimmed over the part about the kirk and the priest and the tragedy there, but described how she and Keir were captured by Luxbury and his soldiers. Mary was intrigued and mentioned God's providence again that the soldiers would end up taking them to Keir's own home, Castle Caladh. Eleanor nodded, considered the coincidence a moment then spoke of the comfort she got from another of Keir's sisters, Rory.

"And this McKelvey, ye say ye married him, but there's no proof now?" She glanced toward the fireplace mantel. "Do ye love him?"

Eleanor nodded. "We never said the vows, the priest died suddenly. We had a parchment, but Bernard burned it."

Mary's blue eyes sharpened. "But ye will find another kirk, won't ye? Ye cannae … you cannot roam the highlands with such a man without the benefit of a clergyman blessing yer union."

"It was more important to me that I find you … and now that I have—"

Mary abruptly rose and went to the mantel. She opened a long box and retrieved a parchment, rolled tight and tied with thread.

"Can ye read? Did Lady Beth teach ye?"

"Yes." Eleanor watched her mother's fingers untie the thread.

"Me boy cannae … cannot … read. He thinks this bears the signature of his own pa, but o' course it does not. Here's yer proof that ye're a princess, truly." She spread out the parchment as well as a smaller document rolled inside the larger one. "Our marriage document, mine and my precious love's, your father. And here's yer baptism certificate."

Eleanor stared at the unexpected document. The ink was smeared in spots, but someone had carefully written her name in a flowing script she could decipher. It was the first time she saw her complete name. She put a hand to her chest and squeezed the brooch beneath the fabric of her dress. Her eyes lingered over the looping lines.

Eleanor.

Eleanor Mary Fletcher Hanover.

It thrilled her and just as deeply frightened her. Lady Beth had warned her of documents she must destroy. She knew in her heart that she must do a most terrible thing. And the sooner the better. Her eyes strayed to the fireplace.

The door opened and Colin burst in with a smile and a bucket of fish. Keir followed carrying the other bucket, sloshing the water. Eleanor threw him a look that made him set the bucket down immediately and stride to her side. She lifted the parchments and drew his attention to the signatures.

Mary alternated between praising Colin for the hearty catch of fish and scolding him for bringing them inside. She shooed him and the fish out the door, but before he left, he saw what held Keir's interest.

"Why are ye showin' 'em me papers, mum?" He whipped his head around, neck craning.

Mary's tone and cadence changed. "Out wi' ye, lad. 'Tis nay concern o' yers. Clean the nasty wee beasties and I'll make a fish stew fer our guests."

Colin grumbled and slammed the door on his way out. Eleanor immediately took the baptismal certificate and threw it on the fire. It crackled and burned. The edges curled. The smoke danced and the sparks shot upward.

"Heavens!" Mary gasped. "'Twas all I had left o' me daugh— … of you, Eleanor."

"You have me now, Mother, but I shan't be coerced into being a princess, not if there's no proof of my parentage. Lady Beth warned me to destroy it."

Keir put his arm around Eleanor, alarmed by the crimson surging into her face, and aimed a sympathetic frown at Mary. "Ma'am, ye should destroy yer marriage parchment as well."

Mary looked from Keir to Eleanor to the fire and then to the parchment. She picked it up and stared at it, as if memorizing a face, then crumpled it and threw it into the flames. To Eleanor she said, "You are a princess no more. Stay with me or ... or go with him and live a happy life, my sweet little Eleanor." Tears formed on her lashes. She dabbed at them, schooling her breath. She was not the only one to choke up.

Chapter 17

L UXBURY ROWED THE jolly boat to shore, unloaded the cargo, and rowed back and forth six more times, always under the watchful eye of the ship's chief officer. The righteous anger hadn't left him. At first, he was furious with the men who'd relieved him of his horse and uniform, then at the judge who sentenced him to an indeterminate length of time aboard a ship headed for the West Indies. But after the brutal treatment he received from his new shipmates and the realization that his life may never again contain a single pleasurable moment, he redirected his anger into planning his escape. And, in the back of his mind, he ultimately blamed that wretched Highlander and Eleanor herself for his present predicament. They had never planned to follow him to Auld Reekie and were undoubtedly somewhere west or southwest of here.

The ship had barely sailed an hour before landing at another Scottish port. Now he was on his last cargo run, watching for his chance to drop under the dock, or hide under a tarp, or run off toward the town.

He carried the final crate slowly down the dock, scanning right and left for a suitable opportunity. He set the crate down on top of another, wiped the sweat from his brow, and turned to walk back. The chief officer, arms folded, was staring straight at him, fifty feet up the dock. Luxbury hoped for a distraction, like a woman screaming, but there were none at this wharf. Or a horse rearing and upsetting a cart, but the nags he saw all looked ready to drop over dead, heads hanging low. Or … and then it happened: an unsteady and exceedingly hefty sailor, struggling with a trunk on his back, stumbled toward the edge and slipped. The trunk spilled into the water and the man nearly went with it. He clung, kicking and yelling, to the edge of the dock as another sailor and the chief officer himself rushed to pull him up.

Luxbury ran. He wasn't above stealing clothes, money, a horse. He'd do whatever he had to do to get away from these blasted Scots and out of this country.

***

ELEANOR TRIED TO protest when Keir used the saddle blankets and a straight branch he broke from a tree to make a temporary lean-to. The rough structure would shelter him and Colin for the night while she slept inside with Mary.

"But you could stay inside. It won't be improper to sleep on the floor. Who would know?" Eleanor frowned at Keir, a sliver of that recurring thrill beginning to creep its way through her. The sky was darkening and she stood in the same spot where, several hours before, she had clutched her mother in their first embrace.

"Yer mum kens we're nay properly wed. Best we honor her house."

Honor and manners and proper behavior were not on Eleanor's mind. This day was the best day of her life. Was she not a complete woman now that she'd met the one person she owed her life to? And was she not in these high spirits due to the magnificent Highlander an arm's reach away? She owed much to him as well. The only thing missing was her loyal friend, Hannah. She wanted to tell her how her heart could never be fuller than it was now. Her mother hadn't abandoned her after all. She'd struggled to survive, unable to save anything to pay for passage back to Ingledew, and afraid if she did return that Lord Edgeworth would make good on his threat to have her killed.

"Keir," Eleanor's voice softened, "where can I go? I cannot return to Ingledew or Beldorney Hall or Castle Caladh. I can't disguise myself forever. Should I … stay here?"

Keir closed the distance between them in one stride. He took her hands and lifted them to his mouth, covered them with kisses, and said, "El … I'll nay leave ye fer a day or e'en fer an hour. 'Twill be hard enough sleeping out here." He kept their clasped hands at heart level and gave a little grunt as Colin came up the path, interrupting them.

"Sister … I've pulled yer things from the pack horse," he jostled the sack of her clothes he carried, "and ye can settle into me spot by the hearth." He took the things into the house.

"Aw," Keir smiled at the door, "he's a wee brammer, so he is."

Eleanor gave him a questioning look.

"He's fallen fer yer charms, m'lady." He took her hands again. "As have I." He gazed at her and she let the feelings wash over her. "'Tis but a moment we have. He'll be out in two shakes of a lamb's tail." He bent, brushed his lips across hers, and whispered a promise. "We'll be wed at Castle Caladh. That's where we'll go. Tomorrow. I promise, ye'll be safe there."

The dulcet call of a night bird punctuated his pledge.

"El … ye're shiverin'. Ye needs get inside."

She wasn't cold, but his hands upon her arms, the way he cradled her shoulders to lead her to the door, made her shiver all the more. Tonight she'd have time to savor the anticipation of a real wedding. She'd barely understood the plan he'd spoken of at the kirk, had waited in the vicarage not completely absorbing the immensity of the sudden matrimonial scheme. But now … now it wasn't a scheme or an escape or a temporary arrangement to avoid some vile consequence. He wanted to marry her. And she wanted to be his bride.

They stopped at the threshold, the sounds of mother and son moving something inside muffled by the door. Keir placed a hand on the latch, insuring it would stay closed as he kissed her lightly on the forehead.

"But what about Luxbury?" The question escaped quicker than a mouse fleeing a broom. "And your brothers and Hubert? What about Lord Edgeworth? I'm certain my patron was to gain something from my royal lineage."

"Do ye ken Luxbury well? Will he hunt ye down, ye think?"

"I don't know."

"Ye've burned yer papers. Only yer mum kens yer lineage. Ye're naught but me own secret princess, El." He lifted her chin with his right hand, pressed a better kiss onto her lips, lingered there a moment. "Ye'd best go inside." He paused, then took her hand and placed it over the one he held on the latch. "I love ye, El. Ye are me special person and I am yers. I want ye to ken that, for the rest of our lives, whatever door we come to, we will open it together."

With that he, and she, pushed opened the door and Eleanor stepped in.

Two heads turned.

"Ahh," Mary said, "the boy's ready. He'll bring some coals to start a fire. There be the last bits of split wood beside the house."

Eleanor turned and gave Keir a modest smile, her heart still trying to settle down from this new excitement that seemed to flip her insides and twist her gut. Colin shuffled out the door behind Keir and she sighed as it closed.

Mary stood grinning at her. Eleanor noticed the straw mattress from the bed had been dragged to the floor.

"Yes," Mary said, "ye'll be sharin' the mattress with me, close to the fire. I can't have a princess sleepin' on Colin's dirty pallet." The smaller, thinner mat had been pushed to a corner.

Eleanor scoffed. "No longer a princess." She waved a hand to dismiss the subject. "Colin called me 'sister.' Are you going to tell him the truth?"

"Never. There's no point. I love him as me own and he loves me. It would hurt him to know the whole truth. But I told him a version of it, that I was widowed before I met his pa. That's true enough. And that you were born of that union and left behind with me sister. Truth again. He'll have more questions and I think I can satisfy his curiosity without too much lyin'. But I'll never tell him he came from another woman's womb." She shrugged her shoulders and began to undress. She pulled on a plain shift and laid her day clothes on a chair.

Eleanor enjoyed the instant intimacy. She felt as comfortable with Mary as she did with Hannah. She removed the dress she'd worn. To her mother she said, "This isn't mine. Keir's sister, Rory, lent it to me. All my things I had to leave behind at Beldorney Hall. I can only hope my friend Hannah has taken charge of the trunks and I'll be able to return this to Rory." She laid the dress across a chair and shook the dust off the bottom hem.

"Tell me more about this Hannah. I'm glad you have someone you can trust." Mary threw a log on the fire and straightened the blankets on the mattress. "My own sister … half-sister … is, I'm afraid, more loyal to her husband's ambitions than to me. But when you marry …" her voice trailed off in forgiveness. She knelt down on the mattress and patted the space next to her, a clear indication for Eleanor to join her.

"When you marry?" Eleanor repeated the question, prompting her.

"Mm-hm. You'll see. When you love a man … well, you never lose by loving him, unless you hold back." She reached over and pushed a strand of Eleanor's hair behind her ear. "And I see that you and Keir have something … something that you will always treasure. I'm sure he loves you passionately and will protect you fiercely. That's all you need."

Eleanor stared into the flames and contemplated her mother's words.

***

KEIR SAT IN the night shade alert to the sleeping lad's steady breathing, taking in the fragrance of honeysuckle, and ignoring the tree frogs and crickets calling to one another. His stomach was churning, not from the rather thin fish soup they'd eaten, but from the thoughts of the immediate future. He wanted to spend the rest of his life with Eleanor, no question, and he wanted that life to start as soon as possible. As husband and wife.

A Bible passage from the Song of Solomon his mother used to quote echoed in his mind: *I have found the one whom my soul loves.*

Eleanor was his heart, his life, his first thought. He loved her with all his soul.

But Eleanor's questions hovered around that first thought and were upsetting him. What about Luxbury? And how could he make her leave her mother so soon after she finally found her? And then there was the MacLeod clan to deal with when they returned to Castle Caladh. Blasted Anabel. Perhaps he shouldn't take Eleanor there yet. There'd be repercussions from the MacLeods.

No sense stewing about it, his practical side scolded him. Then the right answer came to him. There was plenty of room at the castle. Rory had said she was to marry soon; she would welcome the extra help from Eleanor and Mary. The castle would be bustling with wedding preparations — a happy time. His father, even if he objected, wouldn't do anything to spoil his youngest daughter's wedding season. Why couldn't he bring Mary and Colin back with them? Who could object to that? His father was old, but not so old he wouldn't find Mary attractive. Some new clothes, a long bath, a little help from the maids in making her look like the mother of a princess — which she was, though they'd have to suppress that fact — ah, he thought as he closed his eyes, a good plan. All will work out.

***

LUXBURY RODE ALL night long on his stolen gelding. He was tired and hungry, but still angry. He was smart enough to hide his English accent, dropping his g's and using ye instead of you when he encountered anyone on his journey. When he came upon a lone rider, a drunken horseman, he relieved the poor bloat of his coat, hat, pistol and a small coin purse. He took the horse too, but what did he need with two? After a mile he dropped the reins and left the animal to forage at will.

By dawn he'd reached a familiar stretch of road. He was careful not to take the fork to Edinburgh—Auld Reekie be damned—and to go more slowly, determined to deduce the Highlander's route.

***

KEIR SPENT MUCH of the night lying awake staring at the stars, imagining Eleanor so close, sleeping in the house. Well after dawn he

147

was startled out of a doze by the rustle of leaves under the feet of a young lad wielding Keir's own *claidheamh mòr*.

"Colin!" he shouted, his voice reminding him of his own father's quick temper. He took a breath and rose, assessing the boy's strength and form. "Och, ye've a natural talent." He chuckled at the memory of his nephew Huey barely able to hold the heavy sword above his head.

Colin resumed slicing the air and grimacing at imaginary foes.

"A wider stance, lad, and put yer shoulder into it. Aye, that's it." He'd teach him later about not touching another man's sword.

He gave him a few more instructions before walking toward the creek to check on the horses, relieve himself, and splash some cold water on his face. When he stepped back from the creek, he found a clump of wintergreen and pulled off a few leaves, chewed the flavor out and spit them onto the ground. He turned to find Eleanor coming toward him with a bucket. She was wearing breeches again and her hair was swinging freely to her shoulders. He didn't think he'd find her any more beautiful if her hair was longer; most women wore it braided and wound against their heads anyway. He rather liked this unconventional style.

"Ah," he smiled, glad he'd freshened his breath, "'tis me bonnie bride-to-be." He took the bucket from her and filled it. He put his other arm around her shoulder and said, "Did ye sleep well, me princess?"

"I tossed and turned a bit. I'm afraid I kept my mother up half the night." She smiled up at him and they started up the path together. "I call her Mother. It thrills me almost as much as …" she paused, averting her eyes "well, we talked and talked and … and I'll be so sad to leave her …" She peered up at him again and this time her facial expression reminded him of his sisters and how they'd grieved at their mother's passing.

"Och, ye'll nay be fashin' over a sad departure. I, too, was up half the night, a'thinkin'. If it pleases her and the lad, I'm offerin' a home fer'em … at Castle Caladh. The lad told me they have no ties here."

Eleanor stopped him in his tracks and hugged him tightly.

***

LUXBURY GROWLED TO himself when he saw three horses coming his way. One was heavily laden with packs and the others bore two riders each, a large man in front wearing a kilt of a familiar green pattern. Luxbury crouched over his horse's neck, pulled the purloined hat further down his forehead, and turned off onto a side path. He went a couple hundred feet before looking back.

Yes, he was right to suspect the Highlander was McKelvey. He scowled over his shoulder, glad to give the man nothing to see but his backside. When McKelvey raised an arm in friendly greeting, Luxbury returned the gesture, certain he wasn't recognized in these rags, slouched as he was, his face mostly hidden.

He lowered his arm and kept staring back. Ah, there was Eleanor. His heart thumped an extra beat at the sight of her, then his skin prickled to see how brazen she was to ride astride. And so close up against McKelvey. Waves of heat ran over him. He tore his eyes away from her and studied the other two people. He could well guess who they were.

He nudged the horse to keep moving. The Scotsman and his new family continued on and Luxbury circled back, intent on following at a distance. No doubt they were headed to Castle Caladh. Sooner or later, they'd have to stop and he'd make his move, shoot the Highlander, steal away Eleanor, and figure out their future once he got her over the border to England.

Chapter 18

KEIR FELT ELEANOR'S forehead against his back. Her arms were wrapped around him and her chest was tight against him. He cocked his head toward his left shoulder, whispering the words, "I swear I couldn't love you more than I do right now, and yet I know I will tomorrow." Copper stopped trotting and there was no longer the bouncing-rubbing friction between the riders.

Keir waited for her response, afraid maybe he'd said too much. They were a good thirty feet ahead of Mary and Colin and the pack horse was between them on the narrow lane they'd turned down. The spring sunshine cast faultless light on their faces on this clear, unblemished afternoon. *Had she heard him?* The seconds seemed like molasses, sticky and slow-moving.

Her voice was soft, tentative. "I've made few choices in my life. This feeling I have for you … came upon me when I first saw you. I didn't choose to … to love you … but I do … and now I'd choose you over … anything."

He pressed one hand over the two of hers that were clasped at his waist. Her words were like lyrics. He couldn't stop smiling, staring straight ahead at Copper's ears. He appreciated the effort she was making to tell him this. It couldn't have been easy, and perhaps impossible if they'd been face to face.

150

She chose him. It was utterly remarkable. He could imagine that Anabel, or any lass in Scotland for that matter, would not choose him over the chance to be a princess. But Eleanor did.

Behind them Colin's voice rang out. "Me mum is feelin' peely wally. Can we stop and rest a bit?"

Keir pulled on Copper's reins. "Aye, we can." A hint of laughter in his voice. "'Tis a spot good enough if we tie the horses over there." The smile was still planted on his lips. He was glad for the opportunity to get down. As nice as it was having Eleanor pressed so close to him, he looked forward to a chance to kiss her again, perhaps with Copper shielding them from Colin and Mary's eyes.

Mary croaked, "I'm sorry. I nivver rode much a'fore."

"Och," Keir groaned, his face falling as he glanced back. "Yer mum is gonnae whitey."

Colin slipped off the horse's rump and held his spindly arms up to help his mother. She landed on the ground, put her hands on her knees, and lowered her head. Colin took the horse and led it toward Keir and Eleanor.

"Let me help her." Eleanor withdrew her arms, but Keir caught her left one and held on as she mimicked Colin's dismount. With Keir's help she landed steady next to his leg. She ran to her mother.

***

ELEANOR'S STOMACH WAS as upset as her mother's, but for a different reason. She'd been straddling the horse, holding close to Keir, and thinking about a real marriage. And more specifically, about the marriage bed. She'd answered Keir truthfully; she did love him and she knew she would always love him, choice or not. She couldn't stop this emotion if she tried. She was rather proud of herself for voicing her feelings.

She reached her mother and put a hand on her back.

"I'll be a'right," Mary said. "I dinnae want tuh lose me mornin's porridge." She dropped most of the learned accent and whispered, "I hope we're not making a mistake. I feel we can trust this McKelvey heir."

"Heir? I've met his father. It'll be a long while till Keir inherits anything. Laird McKelvey is not as old-looking as Lord Edgeworth."

Her mother spat on the ground and straightened up. "Clive Edgeworth. That monster." Her tongue tangled, and she went back to her old language quirks, smacking the air with an unlikely English oath. "He stole away me older sister, paid me widowed mum off, then turned his back on her and me." They walked together toward a clump of bushes and rounded to the other side to put a screen of green between them and the men.

Mary went on with her rant. "And he demanded money of yer father when we came to hide our marriage from—" Mary gave a startled squeak and jumped. "Snakes."

At first Eleanor thought it was a commentary on the royal family, then she saw two serpents slithering beneath the greenery. She broke off a brittle branch and stabbed one, then the other.

"Well," Mary proclaimed, "'twas an action Colin woulda done fer me." She looked with greater care at Eleanor, put a hand to Eleanor's hair and patted her. "Daughter, ye be a stranger to me, but I'm verra glad to … to finally know you."

Eleanor shrugged her shoulders. The warmth from the sun seemed to dissipate and she heard a sound she didn't expect. Faint hoof beats. She looked over the bushes and saw their horses tied a good hundred feet from where she stood. Keir and Colin were out of sight. They must have walked a little farther to do their business. But she still heard the thumps. She turned. Someone was trotting up the path.

"Stay down, mum." She crouched with Mary and put a foot on the snake to hold its lifeless body against the dirt as she pulled the stake out. A sharp stick was the only weapon she had if she was to defend herself and her mother against a lone rider. She hoped there wasn't more than one.

***

CAPTAIN BERNARD LUXBURY, devoid of the proper uniform and personal weapons, decided to rely on his own cunning and the training he had in England, as well as the filthy and oily pistol he took from the drunken Scot. He spied his chance and took it. The women were separated from the boy and the Highlander. He planned to swoop in, snatch Eleanor, and gallop away. He might even shoot at the horses, marksman that he was, and if he didn't kill them, they would certainly scatter.

He came off the trail, hid his horse, and crept up close. Now he needed to creep back, mount, and charge. He reached the nag and was about to put foot in stirrup when a disturbing sound reached his ears. Loud as a mail coach on a bumpy road, came a carriage preceded by a horse and rider. The rider passed him without a nod from his dark-haired noggin, and headed straight for where he was sure to cross paths with Eleanor if not the Highlander. The coach came next; the driver nodded, cocked his head at Luxbury and slowed his horses. As well as he could tell, only two women sat inside the coach.

Luxbury gasped. He recognized one of them and quickly pulled his hat down. Then a head popped up from the back of the coach and hollered to the carriage driver. "Take care between the trees. The lane'll open in a wee bit. We're almost there."

Bernard switched his attention to this last Scotsman and swore beneath his breath. He figured it out. He knew exactly who these five were, and their connection to Eleanor and to that blasted Highlander who thought he'd married a princess. Ha! They'd all be bound for Castle Caladh, but he still had a chance to capture Eleanor.

He mounted up and wove his way through the brush and trees, trotting where he could, and smacking branches out of his way, sniffing the air like a hound tracking a wounded fox.

***

ELEANOR DROPPED THE stick when she realized it was Jack who was trotting up the lane, looking so much like Keir.

She touched her mother's arm. "It's Keir's youngest brother." She looked behind him and added, "And that's Hubert driving the carriage. Oh, Fenella must be inside. And there's his other brother, Logan, hanging off the back."

Mother and daughter stood watching, unaware of a different sound coming up behind them until a horse whinnied, Mary was knocked down, and a strong arm reached for Eleanor, grabbed her around her waist, and hefted her up and across the saddle. The breath was pushed from her lungs before she could cry out.

She bounced along, feeling the pressure of someone's chest against her back and the stiff leather of a saddle under her stomach, her lungs still empty. One of her arms was trapped under her torso, but the other one that the kidnapper had wrenched, hung limply, bobbing next to his leg. That's what she saw, what she registered: a leg in dirty breeches, a rather expensive boot, the ground passing beneath her in jarring spasms, and her useless arm.

At last, her lungs filled. She cried out, lifted her head in time to see the stopped carriage, now far away, and several wide eyes staring her way. Hannah! Hannah was in the carriage. And then she saw nothing.

***

KEIR JUMPED LOGS and twisted his way around trees to run to where the shouting was. He caught his foot on a root but managed to stay on his feet, dodged a tree and leaped over a mossy stone. He saw his brothers and Hubert first, then Hannah and his sister Fenella stepped out of the carriage that he recognized as one of the Beldorney coaches. Colin raced past him, shouting something to his mother. He followed the boy's trajectory and saw Mary on the ground beyond the carriage. *Where was*

El? Something caught his eye and he looked toward the horizon. A horse and rider were galloping off, the rider bent low over some kind of cargo—or dead body?—that flopped behind the horse's neck.

Everyone shouted at once.

"He took her!"

"Keir! Go after them!"

"Who's the woman? Where'd that lad come from?"

"Keir, what's going on?"

He scanned for Eleanor, didn't see her, and understood the crazy pieces of nonsense the shouted words meant.

"Luxbury!" he snarled. He whistled for Copper. The horse jolted hard enough to pull the reins from around the branch he'd been tied to.

***

ELEANOR WOKE SORE and aching. She could move both arms, but one sharply pained her. She lifted her head and might have screamed if she was anyone but who she was.

This was a startlingly obvious graveyard. The sun had set and shadows cast about her in eerie shapes. She'd played among the headstones behind the church Lady Beth and Lord Edgeworth attended when it suited them. She and Hannah used to trace the letters with their fingers before she learned to decipher the names and dates. This place wouldn't frighten her, *but where ...?*

She sat up and remembered. Hannah. She'd seen her in the carriage. Then ... *what happened?*

She rubbed the back of her head. There was something wet. *Blood?* She looked down where her head had been. A stone marker. *M c C a ...*

"Ah, you're awake. I thought I might have dropped you to your death at first." The chuckle was humorless. The voice not one she expected to hear. If there were ghosts in this kirkyard, the one approaching her seemed vaguely familiar as well as talkative.

"Bernard?" She smelled the inescapable scent of spilled ale on his clothes as he reached her. "Where am I? What happened?"

"You don't remember?"

She squinted at him and slowly moved her head side to side. He sat down on the ground next to her and took her hand. "My dear, you were kidnapped. It was most fortunate that I came along when I did."

"What?"

She tried to listen as he explained. It didn't make much sense to her.

"I was with my mother, her son, and Keir McKelvey. How was I kidnapped?" Now her head began to throb and she started shivering.

"Come," Luxbury got to his feet and coaxed her up, "I found the door to the kirk unlocked. We can rest inside."

154

Unsteadily, she allowed him to lead her toward the small building, past a snorting horse tied to an iron hitching post. The church reminded her of the kirk in which she'd almost married Keir, only this one was somehow much less pleasant. Two candles up on the altar gave a minimum of light to the small space.

They sat together on a pew and Bernard put a smelly horse blanket over her shoulders. Eleanor continued to frown.

"Where's Keir?"

"I suppose he's hunting for you, my dear. I can't imagine what happened. Highwaymen, perhaps? It's not the first time you or I have been attacked."

Eleanor held her hand out and concentrated on the smear of blood across her palm "I think … I think I'm hurt. My head …"

"I can go look for the vicar, if you'd like, or a neighbor. Perhaps there's communion wine …" He got up and scavenged through two low cupboards at the side of the church.

Eleanor peered at him in the dim light. "Where's your uniform?"

"You're not the only one to be abducted, my princess. I made it to Auld Reekie and was arrested, stripped of my uniform, and sentenced to serve a term on a ship bound for the West Indies, but I emancipated myself. Unfortunately, I had to dress as a tatterdemalion to avoid recapture." He came back to her with a goblet and a bottle. He poured a few inches and held it out to her. She took a couple sips and handed it back. There was something about his tone; the man was lying.

The urge to vomit suddenly overcame her. She leaned forward and splattered the wine on his boots.

She recognized the boots.

***

KEIR HOLLERED FOR Logan to grab the other horse and follow him. He expected that Fenella, Jack, and Hubert, along with Colin and Pascoe, or rather Hannah, would tend to Mary and take her to Castle Caladh. He didn't need any other help besides Logan to track down the miscreant who'd made off with Eleanor.

But as the sun set and the trails grew darker between the forests and the hills, he worried that they'd taken a wrong turn.

Logan had ridden in silence, well aware of his brother's feelings. This was a crisis. He did his best to watch for signs of hoof prints or obscure trails. When they neared a village, Logan spoke. "The clan MacLeod lives near aboot. Could ye see yerself askin' fer their help?"

Chapter 19

K EIR PACED FROM his horse, tied to the MacLeods' gate, to the iron door that was locked for the night.

"They should be here by now," Logan insisted. "Our carriage left when theirs did. Anabel was makin' 'em wait, beratin' the Beldorney maid assigned to help her. We could all hear her caterwaulin' after she learnt ye were missin' along with—"

"Aye. I can jist imagine her whinin'." Keir kicked at a clump of dirt.

"Ye dinnae ken the commotion yer runnin' away wi' the princess stirred. They went ahead wi' the ball, tellin' folks Hannah, er Pascoe, was the princess." Logan cleared his throat. "I danced the whole night with the imposter. 'Twas most disconcertin' ... given that I ken she's a he."

Keir looked at his brother. "She coulda been the princess as easily as Eleanor."

"Aye. She was. Er, he was." He made a gravelly sound in his throat. "Fenella arranged to bring her—him—to Castle Caladh. I guess she assured Pascoe ... uh ... we'd find Eleanor there."

"I almost married Eleanor, Logan. But the priest died before the vows were said. 'Twas the apoplexy what took him." He quickly explained how he took Eleanor away, how Luxbury and his men intercepted them, and burned the parchment Keir planned to use to

156

protect Eleanor. "But our clansmen sent those English buggers packin'. All except Luxbury. Father agreed to have him go with us to search for Eleanor's mother." He snickered. "We got separated. The poor Sassenach is, per chance, in an Edinburgh jailhouse now."

Logan nodded. "And was that Eleanor's mum back in the woods?"

"Aye. And her mother's son. Did ye see who took Eleanor?"

Logan shook his head. "It happened too fast. 'Twas some low country scoundrel."

Keir huffed and strode back to Copper and remounted. Copper gave a whinny and there was a distant answering call.

"Horses," Logan perked up. "Could be the MacLeods' carriage, now arrivin'." He gave his mare a long stroke on her neck.

A few minutes ticked by and they were rewarded with the sight of two lanterns dangling on either side of a large post-chaise driven by two men and followed by two more on horseback.

Keir called out his own name and his brother's, identifying themselves as friendly, and backing their horses away from the gate.

The carriage stopped and its fusty male occupant burst out of the door. Bram MacLeod.

"Ye've more nerve than an unbroke stallion showin' yer face here, McKelvey." MacLeod held the door and growled over his shoulder at the ladies inside, "Ye keep yer seat, Anabel. Callie, keep yer daughter still. I forbid her to speak." He slammed the door shut and faced the McKelveys. "What's yer business here in the dead of night, man?"

Keir lifted his hat and held it against his chest, his other hand on Copper's reins. The horse nickered quietly as if warning his master to stay calm. "Sire ... the princess ... she's been abducted—"

MacLeod let loose a string of oaths before saying, "O' course we ken she's been stolen. And by me daughter's own betrothed, though that weddin' will nivver take place as long as I live. Keir McKelvey, ye've disgraced yer family name," he raised a fist, "and ye shan't find any favors among the MacLeod clan. Have ye come to find lodgin' with yer princess hoor?" He snorted in anger.

Keir's tongue stuck tight as Copper pawed dirt with a front hoof. The foul label MacLeod had used infuriated Keir. He opened his mouth to protest, but Logan held up a shushing hand and twitched his gaze toward the coach. Keir could see Anabel's surly face catching lantern light as she poked it out the window.

Logan spoke for Keir. "Me brother was protectin' her, MacLeod. They—the English insurrectionists—meant to ... to use her. Kill the queen and send Eleanor to the King's bed."

MacLeod's brow furrowed more and he lowered his fist a few inches. The darkness remained predominant under the vault of night yet they could each clearly see the other's eyes.

Logan went on. "Keir took her to her family ... her mum ... and then he was bringin' 'em to Caladh when a highwayman nabbed her. I saw it wi' me own eyes. We chased after 'em and lost the trail. Can ye spare us yer men to help us search?"

MacLeod glanced at the driver and his mate and then at the two horsemen behind the carriage, his personal guards. He answered addressing Logan and ignoring Keir, "Aye, ye can take young Will and Alpin, but give 'em time to saddle fresh mounts and raid the larder for a bite. We've been travelin' hard this day."

The driver's mate jumped down and opened the gate.

MacLeod looked to his wife and daughter whose faces were still visible, though they'd finally sat back from the window. His wife smirked at him, her teeth flint grey in the dark. He gave her a warning, "Now Callie, doan be a thinkin' 'tis all patched up ... her troubles ... but these lads can have a bite alongside Will and Alpin. If the cook's asleep, have Anabel help ye." To Logan and Keir he said more severely, "Tie yer mounts at the trough and go inside, eat, and then go on yer trek. Take the lanterns." He cleared his throat, somewhat appeased. "Guid luck."

***

HANNAH AND FENELLA fussed over Mary who was obviously hurt and confused. They insisted that she and Colin sit inside the coach with them. Little Huey, who'd been soundly sleeping before, now sat wiggling on Colin's lap, asking question after question and ignoring Fenella's shushing.

Hubert drove the carriage, snapping the reins on the backs of the horses as Jack trotted alongside. They talked slightly louder than the sounds of the wheels and the clip-clopping.

"I'm ashamed of me father," Hubert said. "I kent he was a big part of the plan, offering to train up a Hanover offspring." He repressed a laugh. "Though I think Eleanor dinnae need much learnin'. She has a spark about her."

Jack agreed. "And Hannah too. Logan thinks he can woo her, but I danced with her as much as he did."

Hubert shook his head, a sly smirk on his face. "We'll nay talk of yer mischief wi' the ... uh, the ladies. I saw ye dance once with Anabel, too ... a *real* bonnie lass."

Jack's face reddened and he pressed his knees tighter against his horse. "Are ye plannin' to leave yer family at Caladh and go after Keir?

158

Or jist leave it to Logan? He shadows Keir whenever he can." He smirked. "I'll get a fairer chance with Hannah while he's away."

"Perhaps." Hubert groaned, "Och, 'tis gettin' darker and I dinnae have a way to light the lanterns."

Jack clucked at his horse and trotted out in front of the team. "I'll lead ye. Me horse kens the way by day or by night."

Inside the carriage, Huey finally settled down to play with a pair of round stones Colin produced from his pocket. Mary answered Fenella's last repeated question, "Aye, I havnae seen me dear little Eleanor since she was three." She glanced at Colin and measured her words. "'Twas a long time ago, fer sure. Do ye ken me daughter?"

"I met her a couple weeks past. She was dressed as a lad at first, but I saw through the ruse." Fenella smiled at Mary. "She's a bonnie lass. I like her."

The carriage hit a particularly deep hole and they all bounced uncomfortably.

"Oh," Mary said, "I may be sick again." Her brows narrowed and she looked from Fenella to Hannah to Colin and then to little Huey. "But where's me daughter?"

Fenella exchanged a look with Hannah. "Ye'll see her soon. Ye were knocked unconscious by a lone horse and rider. We best tend to yer injury quickly. We're close to the McKelvey castle."

"Castle?"

"Aye. Castle Caladh. Me sister Rory and me father, the Laird himself, will welcome ye and the lad." She patted Huey's arm. "And he'll be verra happy to see his grandson, Huey."

Mary put both hands to her temples. "But Eleanor? Is she with Keir?"

"I'm sure she is." Fenella changed the subject, looking at Mary's son, and addressing him. "Nice of ye to let wee Huey play with yer river stones." She stuck her head closer to the window and yelled, "Hubert! Slow down, I almost skelped me heid off the carriage top."

***

ELEANOR CURLED HERSELF into a ball on the pew and complained to Bernard that she might be sick again.

"I could go and look for help … wake the vicar … but I do not think it prudent to leave you alone here." His frown managed to scold and pity her simultaneously. "Just rest a bit. I … I need to tend to the horse." He strode out of the church as if he were wearing a stiff uniform and not dressed in peasant rags.

Eleanor lifted her head and studied the room. Two brass candlesticks were the only things she determined could be used as weapons. Bernard had her worried. She put her head down again and tried to come up with a plan, but her thoughts were foggy. When she heard him return, she closed her eyes and feigned sleep. He spoke to her anyway.

"The horse needs water. I could lead him. Do you think you could ride?"

Eleanor stirred, pulled the blanket tighter, and groaned. "You said before … about looking for a neighbor or the vicar … couldn't you … couldn't you go get help?"

Bernard shook his head. "I shan't leave you, Eleanor." He knelt beside her and ran a hand along her face. "My dear …"

"My head hurts, Bernard, and my stomach is unwell and my shoulder feels like it was twisted off. I don't think I can ride; I'd fall off. There must be a vicar or someone nearby. How else did the candles get lit?"

Bernard drew his hand back and rose. Even in the low light Eleanor could see his jaw clench. "Yes, my princess, you are correct, but I pounded on the vicarage door and there was no answer. Perhaps he is off serving at a deathbed or … drunk asleep." He moved to sit on the same pew beside her feet. "It must be past midnight. We shall both rest awhile and then we'll be off."

Eleanor drew her feet up away from him and sighed.

***

ANABEL KEPT HER nose in the air as she sliced a loaf of bread into four parts, shoving three of the pieces across the cook's work table at Will, Alpin, and Logan, and dropping the fourth at Keir's feet.

"Oh, how clumsy of me," she said, her voice shrill. "I am not used to doing servant's work. Ye must excuse me." She watched Keir retrieve it, brush it off, tear off a bit and chew. She turned toward the larder, stepped in, and stabbed a hunk of cheese with the knife she still held. She came back out and pointed it first at Keir. "Master McKelvey. Ye can crumble off a piece, if ye will." As soon as his fingers touched the corner of the wedge, she let go of the knife. It clattered to the stone floor, taking most of the cheese still attached. "Oh, I beg fer yer pardon." She had removed her bonnet before and now she swung her loosened locks across her shoulders, doing her best to look innocent of any wrongdoing. "I am meant to be served … like a princess …" she caught Keir's eye "… though I would never run off in such scandalous, outrageous, and shameful a manner as Princess Nora." Her posture was unnaturally stiff, her jaw tight. "Such a disgrace." Her face paled and looked as if it had been stretched by cruel hands into a sharp chin point.

***

THERE WAS NO way Eleanor could relax enough to fall asleep. Her head throbbed, her belly ached, and her arm twitched with shooting pain. She lay with her eyes closed for as long as she could stand it, knowing quite well that Bernard was staring at her, his fingers playing with the edge of the horse blanket at her feet. She suddenly threw the blanket off, gasping in pain from the movement, but quickly getting the words out of her mouth. "All right. We can go. Perhaps I can walk beside the horse until we find a creek or a well." She flung a hand to her head, dizzy.

"Come then." Bernard helped her up, squeezing an arm around her a bit too possessively.

***

KEIR COAXED COPPER on, but the horse was leery of the lantern Keir held. He handed it off to Logan and let him lead the way. Alpin held the other lantern and Will trailed after.

"Here's where we last saw tracks." Logan nodded at Keir, holding the lantern down by his boot and well out of his horse's field of vision. "Ah, there. We missed that they veered off." He raised the lantern and pointed.

From behind, Alpin said, "Aye, 'tis the trail to the kirk, if ye be walkin' and not ridin' in a carriage, but a horse can make it through well enough."

***

LUXBURY SET THE saddle back on the horse without the blanket and cinched it lightly. Eleanor wrapped the blanket around her head and shoulders for warmth. She walked alongside the horse and held onto the left stirrup to make Bernard think she was unsteady and needed the help. He walked in front, leading the horse and holding a brass candlestick and candle he'd taken from the kirk. The tiny flame lasted long enough for him to find the path past the graveyard, then a snort from the horse blew it out. He swore and tossed the useless item to the ground.

The smell of wax brushed under Eleanor's nose; the trees spiked the night sky above.

Eleanor heard the candle land, saw a moment's worth of red glow from the wick before it too disappeared, and quickly retrieved the possible weapon without Bernard knowing. She tucked it into the fold of blanket at her chest and argued with herself about whether to hit him on the head now or wait until they came upon a village or at least had some daylight.

Once their eyes adjusted it wasn't hopeless, blind wandering. She thought she saw bobbing light through the trees.

Closer.

A lantern.

Two lanterns.

A low hum of voices speaking in harmonic Scottish sounds with rolled r's and an inflection at odds with the King's English.

Bernard stopped the horse and Eleanor stumbled into him. He grabbed her roughly, silencing her by putting a firm hand over her mouth. But there was no way to silence his weary horse. Its high-pitched neigh was an apparent greeting to the approaching horses.

"You will say nothing," Bernard hissed in Eleanor's ear. He lifted his hand from her mouth and took out his stolen pistol. He pushed her in front of him and pressed the weapon to the middle of her back. Peering over her head, he watched the lights come closer.

The front rider's face was revealed.

Luxbury recognized Logan and assumed the big shadow behind him was that blasted Highlander. And there were two more riders. Luxbury pulled his hat lower to hide his own features. He swore in Eleanor's ear then whispered, "Bow your head, keep it covered, do not look up."

***

ELEANOR FELT THE pistol's pressure on her back waver. She'd seen what Bernard had seen and her breath caught. The lantern light revealed the thickness of the woodland they were in; there was little room to allow the approaching midnight riders to pass. Logan's voice called out.

"Hullo there. Have ye seen a … whoa, what have ye there, man? Is that a woman with ye?"

"Jist be on yer way, friends. Here, we'll let ye pass." Bernard flung her stumbling to the side and pulled the nag with them. They took several steps into the woods.

A jolt of panic electrified Eleanor's nerves. She stopped clutching the blanket and let it slip. Bernard swore loudly, now sounding exactly like the English foreigner he was.

"'Tis them!" Keir shouted. He leaped from his horse.

"Stay back or I'll shoot her."

Eleanor let out a short squeal and collapsed as if fainting, but in that sudden move she also twisted and brought the candlestick up hard between his legs in such a way as to instantly incapacitate him.

Bernard crowed in pain and pulled the trigger, directly aiming at Keir. But the pistol failed and he curled to the ground.

Eleanor raised the candlestick to do more damage, this time to her tormentor's head, but stronger hands reached for her, pulled her away and up into sheltering arms. There was commotion all around as three other men surrounded Luxbury, shouting and swearing, kicking and

162

hitting, their lanterns left on the forest floor to send flickering shadows on horses' hooves and on one Englishman's humiliation.

Chapter 20

MORNING SUN POURED through her window, spangling the floor with golden light and purple shadows. Eleanor sat up with a start and called for Hannah.

"I'm here," Hannah called back, rushing in from the adjoining room.

Upon their arrival Fenella and her family had taken rooms on the third floor and insisted that Eleanor and Hannah use Fenella's former rooms. Eleanor already knew how close she'd be to Keir, his rooms were next door. Colin was installed in the former nursery and Mary stayed in the eldest sister, Elsie's, long-vacant bedroom.

"Oh, Hannah." She held her arms out and Hannah jumped into the bed and squeezed her friend with all the strength she had.

"I was afraid I'd never see you again. It gave me such a scare when you left before the ball." Hannah sat back on her heels. "But Fenella assured me you'd be safe with Keir. Then that awful Captain Luxbury took off in search of you."

"And he found us, but Laird McKelvey sent his troops back to England and the captain came with Keir and me to look for my mother." Eleanor, breathless, went on to tell bits and pieces of the trip: separating from Luxbury, finding her mother, traveling back to Castle Caladh and being abducted by Bernard on the way. She described her rescue, but told Hannah none of the precious moments she'd spent in Keir's arms, or the kisses they shared, or how they almost married, but she did have one revelation to tell. "Oh, Hannah, I know my real name. I saw it on my baptismal paper. My mother had it safely stored all these years."

Hannah blinked repeatedly and focused on Eleanor's face. "And? Your name is ..."

"Eleanor Mary Fletcher Hanover."

Hannah's lips formed an O. "So it's true. You're a Hanover. You're royalty."

"There's no proof anymore." Eleanor shook her head. "I threw it in the fire and destroyed it."

Hannah's face fell. "But why?"

"Because Lady Beth warned me to. Without proof that I have royal blood, the insurrectionists cannot use me in their plan. I'm free, Hannah." Her smile was lop-sided.

Hannah bit her lip and frowned. "You don't seem happy about it."

"Well," there was a light knock at the door and then Elspeth, the maid, asked if she could enter, "yes, come in." Eleanor continued, "I would have liked to keep the baptismal certificate, but ..." she caught a glimpse of someone else at the door, a flash of tartan colors, before the door completely closed.

Elspeth curtsied, tray in hand, and announced, "I've brought ye our cook's special welcoming breakfast."

Both girls slid off the bed and settled themselves at the table before the fireplace. Elspeth arranged the food on the table then tended the fire.

"Mm, bacon." Hannah picked up a piece and sniffed it before taking a bite.

"Be there anythin' else ye need?" she asked as she straightened the bed covers.

"No, thank you, but was that Keir in the hall?" Eleanor asked.

"Yes, ma'am, yer husband ate in his room and said he'll be expectin' ye in the library this mornin'." She curtsied again and started for the door.

Once she was gone Hannah, whose fingers had dropped the bacon at the word husband, asked, "What did she mean? Are you married to that McKelvey? How could that possibly be?"

"Remember how I left the kirk ... kind of sickly? I went to meet Keir. Then we waited in the vicarage until your service ended and all of you, the Beldorney guests, left. We went back to the kirk. It was Keir's plan to marry me so I couldn't be forced to marry the King."

"Oh, I understand. Clever." She lowered her voice to a hush. "So ... are you truly a married woman, El?"

Eleanor sighed. "Not yet. The vicar died before we could pledge our troth." She bowed her head. "And now with proof of my lineage gone, he doesn't need to marry me, but ..." she looked up, a tiny hint of a smile coming to the corners of her mouth, "he still wants to."

***

"KEIR, TELL ME what happened!" Rory grabbed him at the bottom of the stairs and, arm in arm, walked with him toward the main doors. "Logan and Jack had conflictin' stories, and neither could tell me aboot the woman and son stayin' with us."

Keir told her the short version as they went outside and started walking toward the stables. "We lost track o' that scoundrel captain before we came upon Eleanor's mother. A fine woman is she and sorely glad to see her daughter again." He looked over his shoulder and added, "The lad's not hers, but we're to say he is. She took him in as a bairn when his parents died o' the pox. He's a meek one, but he gets along wi' me nephew, Huey."

"But Logan says the captain stole Eleanor away from ye and then ye stole her back." Her freckled face bore a confused frown.

"Aye," Keir explained to Rory, "we sent him to the MacLeods to be dealt wi' there. Alpin and Will tied him to the nag he rode and promised to trot the whole way. Lent us a lantern to find our way here, though Copper woulda done it on his own. 'Twas a frightful night." He opened the stable door. "Ho, Copper, I've brought ye a treat." He pulled out a carrot and headed for the stall.

Rory stayed back and waved the flies away from her head. "A last question, brother." She paused until he looked her way. "Ye dinnae take yer bride to bed last night. Was she ... hurt ... by the captain?"

Keir rubbed along Copper's neck and chuckled. "Nay, but I dare say the captain was woefully abused by me princess. She struck him a good one in the baws. And Alpin and Will bruised the rest of him."

Rory nodded. "Fer sure I like that lass e'en more. But ... me question, Keir ... are ye nay sleepin' together?"

"I confess to ye, Rory, that the priest meant to wed us, but gave up the ghost before we said the vows."

Rory gasped. "And ye went off with her? Alone? Unchaperoned?"

"Well, we had the captain fer most of the way, and then her mother. No better chaperone than a lass's mother, aye? We'll have a proper weddin', we will. Soon, if she'll have me." He gave Copper a final pat then caught the look on his sister's face. "Rory, ye're goin' all peely wally. I swear I dinnae wrong the lass."

"I was thinkin' on me own weddin', now jist three weeks off."

166

Keir tried not to glance at her middle, but he'd not forgotten her words from the other day and that she was to wed quickly. She hadn't definitively confirmed her situation and he did not want to assume anything. He closed the stable door, put an arm around her, and said, "Can we share the blessed day with ye? Two weddin's will save our father one feast and glad he'll be o' that."

***

FENELLA ASKED COLIN to come with her and Huey to the pond. The lad was happy to be choreless and rather delighted to play with another boy even if there was an age difference.

Rory brought Mary to Eleanor's room to offer her some of her older sister's discarded clothing, rather nice things that were still in the wardrobe. Since Hannah had brought her and Eleanor's trunk of clothes to Caladh they had plenty of items to choose from. Mary was overwhelmed with the selection and hesitant to borrow a dress, but the four of them had fun deciding what would fit, what needed mending, and what they could wear today.

Eleanor ignored the fact that her arm burned and her ribs throbbed in such a way she had to bite back a cry when Hannah helped her into a day dress.

"Shall we go down now?" Rory seemed anxious. "Me father is waitin' to meet ye, Mary. Doan let 'im rile ye. He's a bossy man, hard on the outside, but soft as fresh churned butter on the inside."

Mary looked toward the dresser mirror propped on its short side. They'd been admiring themselves once they'd changed clothes and now Mary checked her face with a bit more serious inspection.

"I've had a bit of experience wi' widowed men ... but not wi' the laird of a castle." She shook her head and amended her statement. "Well, I'll nay blether on aboot it, but there was once a McHenry what had an eye on me."

"Me father's a good man and will treat ye as a guest." Rory smiled and stared openly at Mary. "Can I ask ye a question?" When Mary nodded she said, "Ye speak like a Scot, but ye're English, aye?"

Eleanor spoke before her mother could. "Folks here aren't always friendly or forgiving of the English ... of us Sassenachs. Some folks, I mean. Your family has been most welcoming."

Rory brushed a strand of red hair behind one ear. "Aye, ye're one of us ... or ye will be soon. Now, shall we go down?"

They descended the steps in a chattering, laughing knot, then all four quieted as they entered the spacious room next to the library. Rory called it "mum's gallery." There were two divans and several carved walnut chairs, a low bench, and massive portraits set against dark paneled walls.

Velvet drapes framed two tall windows and the McKelvey crest hung between them.

"This was me mother's favorite room. When I was a wee lass, I'd stare at the coat of arms and me mother, nursin' Jack in that chair, would tell me and me brothers an' sisters all the meanin's of the symbols and colors."

"It's beautiful." Mary walked closer and stared at the tapestry. "I can guess the lion symbolizes courage."

"Aye," Rory sounded proud, "as well as strength and valor. Me brothers hold those traits, though we should add a monkey for Jack." She laughed and straightened a throw rug on the wicker seat of an arm chair. "The colors are important, too. The gold color is for generosity—makes me think of Keir—the blue is a sign of loyalty and black signifies grief."

"What does the red hand mean?" Eleanor sat on one of the divans and motioned for her mother to sit next to her. Hannah took another chair.

Rory held her own hand up. "Well, red represents warriors, but the hand is an emblem of faith. I didn't understand why they would go together until I was grown up. And the helmet denotes wisdom, protection …" Her voice trailed off and she looked at Eleanor. "I hope ye ken that Keir—" she stopped mid-sentence as her father strode into the room. All stood up to greet him.

"Guid mornin' to ye, lassies." He gave a somber nod to Eleanor and raised his eyebrows at Hannah and Mary. Rory made introductions. "Verra pleased to meet ye. Ye have a fine daughter, Widow Macfarlane."

"Just Mary, 'tis all I've ever been called."

"Mary, then. Will ye allow me to escort ye aboot the grounds? I saw Fenella take the boys out. I'll show ye a bit of the nature they'll be enjoyin'."

Mary hesitated and Laird McKelvey tipped his head toward Hannah and Eleanor. "And ye lassies must come, too, o' course."

Rory kissed her father on the cheek and said, "I'll show Hannah the castle while Eleanor meets with me favorite brother. I'm sure he wonders why I havnae brought her to him yet." She gave him an affectionate touch on his arm. "Be nice to Mary, father. Doan show her the McKelvey temper if the neighbor's sheep are grazin' on our hills."

"Och," he said in the same tone as his son, "ye may be thinkin' o' yerself. When have ye ever heard me raise me voice?" He laughed loudly over Rory's response and held his arm out to Mary. "M'lady, shall we?"

***

ELEANOR'S HEART SKIPPED a beat to see her newly found loved one set off with a man who looked so very much like her own Highland beau.

"Well, that went as planned." Rory chuckled. "I kent me father would take to yer mum, Eleanor. He always comes in here this time of day and stares at this portrait." She walked to the right side and lifted off a silk covering that hid a painting of her mother. The artist had blended three shades of red to capture the woman's hair, an exact match to Rory and Fenella's tresses. But her skin, creamy white, was a tinge lighter than Rory's.

Eleanor and Hannah made solemn comments, reverently admiring the Laird's deceased wife. Rory quietly recovered the portrait and said, "Off wi' ye, Eleanor. The library is on the other side of this wall. I've agreed to somethin' special wi' me brother. I hope ye'll like it."

***

KEIR PACED AROUND the library. He couldn't hear the words spoken in the next room, but he could hear the voices, especially his father's. When it got quiet, he knew Rory would come … with Eleanor.

Would she be amenable to the new plan? A ceremony set on the hill behind the castle? And in three weeks' time? Eleanor had agreed rather hesitantly to their first wedding plan at the kirk. He stopped pacing to remember. They'd met outside the kirk, the rain about to fall. He'd led her to the vicarage before the clouds opened up. She'd listened to him explain about entering into a false marriage to thwart the political plot he and she could no longer follow through on. She agreed then, but the priest died and the parchment was destroyed. Later, on the road to finding her mother, he'd asked her, in all seriousness, to marry him. She'd doubted his motive at first, but then accepted. Nevertheless, how would she feel now?

The large library door creaked open and his sister ushered Eleanor in.

"Here she stands, brother. I havnae told her our sly scheme yet. I'll leave ye to it." She gave Eleanor a hug and closed the door behind herself.

Eleanor looked at him. "Scheme?" She put a hand to her heart, thumb and two fingers caressing the brooch there. She wore a simple dress, light blue that favored her eyes. She stood slightly bent like a bean sprout.

He dissolved the space between them with a few quick strides.

"Are ye all right? Did ye sleep?" He put a hand gently on her hurt shoulder. "Are ye healin'?"

She opened her mouth to answer, but he pressed her close and they spoke in kisses instead.

"'Tis nae scheme in a bad sense," he finally said, his mouth but an inch from hers. "Will ye marry me, El, here at Castle Caladh on the verra day me sister and her beau will wed? 'Twill be a grand day. Twenty days hence."

A long two seconds ticked by, but seemed like hours to Keir. Then she spoke.

"I said I would marry you, Keir. And so I will. Here. Twenty days hence."

He let his breath out and smothered her again in kisses. "Ah, there's me bonnie lass. I love ye, El, I love ye more than words can express."

She started to speak, but voiced a squeal of pain instead.

"Have I hurt ye, lass?" He dropped his hands and stepped back a foot. "I'll nay touch ye again."

"I'll be fine, Keir. Nothing's broken. Just bruised and sore."

"Ye'll heal up strong and ready in twenty days' time. 'Tis hard to keep me hands from ye, but I shan't add to yer pain as I plan to be gone fer a spell. Two weeks at most."

"Gone?" Her face fell.

"Aye. There's a bit o' patter I must needs to have with Horace Sylvan. Ye may remember the name. I'll be away to England to mend that fence and pass on a few unkind words about Luxbury, too. He'll lose his commission and nivver return to harm ye. I'll see to it." He reached to stroke her good arm. "Ye look a might peely-wally, El. I'll carry ye back to yer room."

***

ELEANOR SNUGGLED AGAINST Keir's hard chest and ignored the throbbing in her injured arm as he carried her up the stone steps to her room. She memorized the feel of him, his scent, the cut of his jaw, the firmness of his gentle grip on her, and the strength he showed as he took the hard steps two at a time. She'd never been happier and yet there was that thread of sadness that he'd be gone for two weeks. She wondered if he was doing so now to allow her time with her mother.

"Keir," she said as he lowered her onto the bed, "can you not wait a bit to make your journey? I could go with you to England once we're married."

"'Tis a lovely thought and we shall make that journey and many more once we're wed." He sat on the edge of the bed beside her hip and stroked a hand down her cheek. "Ah, Eleanor, remember when I thought ye was a lad and I bared me feelings fer the princess—for ye, that is—that ye stirred me soul?"

"I remember." A blush crept up her neck. She moved herself a hair's breadth closer to encourage him to say more.

He leaned down and rested his cheek on hers, lightly, softly, and then he lifted his head again. "Ye stir me whole bein' and I dare give ye only one kiss more or else I'll nivver leave this room."

The attraction was always there, but now she enjoyed the anticipation, short as it was. There was no hesitation, rather a promise of things to come … weeks away perhaps, but that knowledge did not hurry this goodbye kiss. His lips on hers, their breaths in unity. Silence. Her ears refused to hear a thing. The castle fell silent, the birds outside were mute. This was a moment to remember.

Another longer kiss with her arms wrapped around him, no pain felt. Hungry mouths. Wet and hot and searching. Something new: a tongue.

Soft skin and hard muscles, two bodies tentative, but with growing insistence. His hand trailed down her side to hip and thigh, caressing her. His weight pressed upon her for a brief instant and then he broke away; she let go as he sat up. Her mind was stunned, blank with dizzy longing.

The bed creaked and he was up, standing before her looking down.

"I will be back. I promise. And I aim to bring ye the perfect weddin' gift."

Eleanor rose up on her good elbow as he left. She couldn't have stood up if she wanted to, she knew her legs would not hold her, but she needed to watch him leave. The broad shoulders, the sway of his kilt, that final backward glance. Again he said, "I promise," and she wondered what gift he could possibly bring her. She only wanted him to return to her. Safe and sound.

Chapter 21

TWO WEEKS PASSED slowly. Eleanor felt like her old self by the third day and joined in all the activities at the castle that Rory required for their joint celebrations. Fenella stayed on with Huey, but Hubert returned to their farm. Keir's oldest sister, Elsie, arrived to help.

They sewed dresses, weeded the May gardens, practiced weaving flowers into each other's hair, and consulted daily with the cook on what scrumptious dishes might be served for the wedding feast. Logan and Jack found ways to corner Hannah. Eleanor teased her friend that perhaps there might be a third couple standing before guests to unite in holy matrimony. Hannah always blushed and swore she'd rather run off with the stable boy than be bound to a lad as mischievous as either young McKelvey.

By the end of the second week Eleanor climbed to the castle's southern turret with Fenella, Rory, and Elsie. The sisters had stories about the tower—how their mother brought them up here to watch for their father's return, how they played with rag dolls while their little brothers tossed rocks from the windows, aiming at imaginary attackers.

"Remember how Keir threw a stone—he always had his pockets full of them—at a pair of ravens?" Elsie rested her arms on the opening facing due south.

Fenella nodded and Rory said, "I don't remember that."

"Ye don't? He hit one of the birds and knocked it out of the sky. It plummeted to the ground and landed next to the rock that killed it. Ye both started crying and mother let Keir race down the steps to see to it."

Fenella smiled at Eleanor. "He was always very caring. Ye're marryin' a man with a good heart, Eleanor. I nivver saw him throw a stone at a livin' creature again." She laughed. "But Logan and Jack sure did. They wanted to be like Keir." She turned to gaze out the northern window. "I think Logan and Jack are competin' fer yer friend, especially now that I told Logan the truth aboot Pascoe. Hannah will have her hands full whichever one she chooses."

Eleanor was speechless. She'd given little thought to Hannah's future, assuming she'd stay on at Castle Caladh, not as a servant, but as a dear friend. Perhaps her remark about the stable boy was to hide her feelings for one, or maybe both, of the younger McKelvey men.

Fenella broke through her thoughts with another startling observation. "Have ye noticed the other lovers in the castle?" She wiggled her brows at Eleanor and then at her sisters. Rory and Elsie seemed to know what she meant and looked meaningfully at Eleanor.

Eleanor frowned and waited.

"Our father," she paused, "is acourtin' yer mother. I've seen 'em in the garden and by the pond and out walkin' in the heathers. Have ye nay noticed their smiles at dinner?"

Rory put an arm around Eleanor's shoulders. "Ye may be lady of the castle someday, but yer mother shall rule here before the summer ends. 'Tis me prediction."

"Aye," Fenella and Elsie both agreed.

This new idea fell on Eleanor's heart with joyful satisfaction. Would there be no end to this happiness? And when Keir returned … oh, how she looked forward to that bliss.

"Ha!" Fenella's shout made all heads turn. Rory dropped her arm from Eleanor then crowded close next to Fenella. "There's a rider. See?" She stuck a pointing finger out the southern opening aimed at the farthest, highest hill. "'Tis but a speck o' green on a larger speck o' brown, but Keir promised me he'd come this day, this hour, and to have ye here in the tower awaitin'." She moved to the side to let her older sister see.

"I believe ye're right, Fenella." Elsie sighed. "Just like when we were kids. Fenella always spotted father first."

"Is it really Keir?" Eleanor pressed against the stones to lean out.

"If it is," Fenella laughed, "Copper should start to gallop of his own accord. Aye, look again. They're movin' faster. Go down now, Eleanor. Ye can meet him there, see? At the wild cherry tree."

Eleanor glanced at the three expectant faces, freckled and blushing and bright. The sisters began to shoo her toward the steps. What was she waiting for? She had missed Keir terribly. That face, those kisses, his arms, his words of love …

She took the steps as fast as she dared, clutching her skirts up out of the way, watching out for the pebbly debris that might trip her up.

At last she reached the bottom, out of breath, but steady. She lifted her head and tried to settle her breathing in order to walk as calmly as she could toward the cherry tree. Halfway there she could see for herself that the horse cantering across the field was indeed the copper-colored gelding she'd ridden on with Keir. She craned her neck to look up and behind her at the top of the turret. Three red-haired womenfolk stared and waved, then moved out of sight. She imagined them coming down the steps slowly to give her a bit of privacy to greet their brother. She realized then how they'd accepted her. At last she had a family. A complete family.

The horse and rider were closer yet. She reached the cherry tree and leaned her back against it, her eyes not wavering from the rider. Copper jumped a border hedge and Keir's dark hair fluttered back from his forehead, his kilt flapped up and down on the horse's rump.

Eleanor put a hand to the brooch on her dress and pressed it protectively against her madly beating heart. She pressed her lids closed for a mere second, but when she opened them, Keir was somehow much closer. He slowed the horse, stared at her with a smile that must have lifted her off the ground. She no longer felt the earth beneath her feet.

Copper neighed as Keir jumped down. He dropped the reins and let the horse continue its way toward the stable. He strode quickly toward Eleanor and she melted into his embrace. There was no one else in the world.

***

KEIR MCKELVEY, FUTURE Laird of Castle Caladh, had dropped the reins and marched himself to the side of the woman he loved. How he'd missed her. She'd been his every thought morning till night for the fourteen days he'd been away. But he'd accomplished all he set out to do.

He pulled her to him, not at all worried that he might hurt her. He knew she was healed, trusted that his sister had watched for him, and assumed that she'd just managed to tread the seventy-five steps up and then down the turret. If she was strong enough for that she could bear how tightly he meant to enfold her in his arms.

"Eleanor … my love," he barely breathed out the words before their lips touched.

Her bonnet slipped back and he ran his fingers up into her silky hair and let them get tangled there. He heard her purring moans, felt her soft hands along his new beard and the skin of his neck. The sweet taste of her mouth was all he thought of as he multiplied the kisses.

His sixth sense told him someone was approaching. He didn't want to stop kissing Eleanor, but the sound of a male clearing his throat finally broke through to his consciousness.

"Son," Laird McKelvey began, "if ye'll allow me a moment of yer time. I have somethin' of an important nature to discuss with ye."

Keir released a rather red-faced Eleanor, kept one arm around her, and faced his father. "Aye, father. Ye can say whatsoever ye please wi' me intended at me side." He smiled broadly and put his other hand on his hip near his sword handle, but resting on his sporran.

Laird McKelvey grumbled in his throat again and nodded at Eleanor, his own cheeks darkening and his hands nervously moving in a way Keir had never seen before.

"'Tis a conundrum, ye see." His eyes sparkled and he focused more on Eleanor. "I love yer mother, lass, and we intend to marry." He switched his gaze quickly to Keir's face and hurried on with voice and hands. "We'll nay intrude upon yer blessed day. 'Tis enough fer two couples to wed Sunday next. But we wish to claim some happiness fer ourselves and so we will. At summer's end, when the crops'll be aburstin' for pickin' and we host the Highland games …" his face nearly split with a smile "ye git what I'm suggestin', aye? We'll be needin' yer presence at the castle … and so …?"

Keir's face knotted into disbelief and then acceptance. He glanced at Eleanor who was clutching at her brooch and grinning ear to ear, her cheeks still pinkish. He looked back at his father's keenly animated face, now aflame with emotion.

"Aye, father, I ken yer meanin'. Me wife and I will be yer witnesses, by me oath." He released his hold on Eleanor and lunged for his father, grasping him in a bear hug like he used to do as a young lad.

***

THE BUZZ AND bustle among the servants at Castle Caladh was matched by the flurry of activities and excitement by the McKelvey clan in the final week before the double weddings of Rory and Keir. Each had a pair of sisters or brothers to help or hinder the preparations. Fenella and Elsie were great helps, hovering over Rory and also Eleanor, whose mother was less occupied with Eleanor's feverish plans than preoccupied with her own new love interest: the Laird himself. Hannah was strangely absent for hours at a time, concurrent with either Logan's or Jack's absences. Eleanor was too busy to question Hannah, assuming she was looking after Huey or watching Colin, and never suspecting that Hannah was enjoying not one, but two fledgling romances. It was enough for her comfort to know Hannah was somewhere in the castle. She meant to discuss Hannah's future with Keir, but so many other subjects took precedence—her future role, his plans for the lands, the clan's obligations—that she assumed the topic would resolve itself at some point after they were married.

Eleanor spent most of Keir's first day back wandering the gardens with him, then it was back to sewing and myriad other preparatory obligations. The following days they had only the hour before and after dinner to be alone.

Rory's young man, Rennie Carlyle, showed up with great regularity. Eleanor learned he lived with Elsie and her husband, Charles. He was Charles's hard-working and amiable brother, and had quickly and not-so-innocently wooed Rory during her many visits with Elsie. Charles and Rennie came the day before the wedding, as did several friends and relatives who'd traveled great distances. The castle was filling up and by mid-afternoon Keir had grown weary of it all. He searched out Eleanor.

"Come with me." He held out a hand and she rose from the divan where she'd been working on something. "Och, I'll lend ye some boots. It's a ways we'll be walkin' and the grasses are wet from last night's shower."

She followed him out of the room. He helped her into a pair of tackety boots, then, to her surprise, led her down what she thought of as the dungeon stairs, directly to the room she'd been held in by Luxbury's men several weeks before.

"Why are we in the wine cellar?" she asked, noting the table and chairs weren't where they'd been before. On the table sat a bulging sack.

"Ah, ye ken its original use, do ye?"

"Rory told me."

"I suppose she bent yer ear as well about the ghosts and secrets."

Eleanor touched the back of the chair she'd once sat in. "Nothing about ghosts." She looked around at the walls. "But she did say there was a secret. A secret tunnel for escaping. I thought I might have to use it."

Keir frowned. "Ye were always safe, El. I would have slain Luxbury and all his men if I'd had to." He moved toward one wall. "Here." He pressed his foot against a stone, then pushed his hands against the wall as if he could move it.

And he did. He turned to give Eleanor a satisfied look. "Are ye scairt o' the dark, me darlin'?"

"Not if I'm with you." She blushed.

"I'd light a torch, but the tunnel snuffs the flames and 'tis more frightnin' to go from God's light to the devil's dark heart than to start our journey blind." He walked to her, picked up the sack, and took Eleanor's hand. "Come along. I've a weddin' present fer ye. I'm hopin' it'll be the perfect gift."

Eleanor frowned, but trusted Keir, and followed along. For the first twenty feet of the tunnel, she could see her feet and Keir beside her, then they turned a corner, and the darkness enveloped her. He tightened his grip on her hand and told her to keep her other hand out to feel for the rough stone walls.

The ground was even and felt more like the carpeted library than the well-packed dirt it undoubtedly was.

"Is it far?" she asked.

"Do ye remember how the hill rises behind the castle and that there's a hedge that curves to the south?"

"I do."

"We're walkin' underneath the hill now, headin' fer the cliff. We'll come out among the boulders, walk along the other side of the brae, and then take a path to … well, ye'll see soon enough."

Before long Eleanor's eyes adjusted to the dark, then suddenly she could determine shadowy shapes ahead. Keir's grip loosened.

"Almost there." Twenty feet more and two turns and Keir warned her to duck down. They walked into sunlight as if out of a low cave opening, one that, upon looking back at it, she never would have discovered.

"'Twas an escape route planned by me great-great-great grandfather. Me brothers and me sisters learnt of it by accident and used to hide in this end, nivver suspectin' it led all the way home." His laugh was pure delight to Eleanor's ears. "Now, on to another of me favorite spots. 'Tis one me siblin's havnae found." He switched the sack to his other hand and put his arm around her.

They walked along a muddy gully and Eleanor was glad for the borrowed boots. "How much farther?" she asked after fifteen minutes of walking.

"Into these woods here," Keir assured her, "and then we'll come upon a hidden hollow. I've nivver shown another human this spot. Not even Copper kens the way here."

He let go of her to wave a hand toward a conical marker of stones. "I set the stones as a lad to mark the entrance. Ye'll have to duck beneath the evergreens." He reached for the lowest branch and lifted it. Eleanor bent low and stooped to go under his arm and the branch.

"It's like a green, living cave," Eleanor breathed out the words in awe. Once inside she could stand with enough room for Keir beside her. He set the sack against the trunk. It was gloomy within the tree's skirts, but not dismal. The dusky interior let several shafts of golden light through, enough to see each other's face and the expectant emotions there.

"Ye're shakin', Eleanor." Keir bowed his head closer. "Are ye afraid I'll take ye here, upon the pine needles?" He put his arms around her and pulled her to him. She rested her head on his chest and he put his cheek against her hair. "Ah, Eleanor, me secret princess. I brought ye here fer one thing only." He kissed the top of her head and put his hands on her shoulders. Pushing her just far enough back to look her in the eyes, he said, "I love ye, lass. I mean only to show ye how great me love is. I told ye I'd see that Luxbury nivver pursued ye again. The man doesnae walk the earth on this side of the ocean. Ye nivver have to fear him again." He blinked a few times. "And I learnt from Hannah of yer beatin's by the lord of Ingledew. That man is payin' fer those crimes under the authority of Judge Horace Sylvan, me friend."

"But ..." Eleanor screwed her brows together in a question, "but wasn't Sylvan the one who paid for two men to kill me?"

"Aye, that was the first plan. But all is straightened out now." He bent to retrieve the sack. "I spent five of the days I was gone from ye to search out the church ye were baptized in. I only saw yer parchment but a moment before ye threw it in the fire. I dinnae remember it all and so I went from parish to parish until—" He drew out a rolled scroll. "I found the original. Did ye ken they made one fer yer mother and another to hold in the church's register? I paid a bribe to the clergyman's maid, and a fair price to a scribe to make a copy." He unrolled the paper. "Here's yer certificate again, Eleanor. All the names are as they were."

Heads together, they read the artful inscriptions, the names, the date, the clergyman's signature. Eleanor touched her father's name and a beam of light sneaking through the branches lit it up. She looked up at Keir.

The first thank you was more breath than word. "Thank you. Oh, Keir, thank you. I can think of no better gift. How did you know I'd want this?"

"I saw yer face. I felt yer sorrow. Yer mother's too. She was wounded to her soul to lose both yer birth paper and her marriage parchment." He pulled out another scroll. "I found hers as well. Once I straightened things with Sylvan there was no need to hide your identity and so ..."

"Another copy? Oh, Keir, that's ... that's ... I cannot express it."

"Eleanor ... I must confess ... the church has the copies. 'Tis a stolen original ye have in yer hand. I've already asked forgiveness. The Lord is a forgiving God."

She flung her arms around him.

***

ELEANOR HUGGED RORY tightly, so grateful to be sharing this day with her. They, along with the sisters, and Hannah and Mary, were gathered in Rory's bedroom finishing their dressing rituals. From Rory's window they'd been looking down every few minutes to see how the crowd of guests was growing, but now the noise from below diminished and the sounds of a hired piper replaced them. The sisters sang the Gaelic words to the tune while the three English-born women listened and smiled, everyone still doing last minute details—tying shoes, tucking petals in their hair, or lacing tight-fitting bodices.

Mary nudged Eleanor and whispered, "I wish it was yer father who could walk ye through the guests or better yet, down the aisle of a church."

"I never thought much about it," Eleanor whispered back, "so I won't be missing it. It seems fitting that Laird McKelvey will walk Rory down and then come back for me."

The singing stopped and the piper's tune was a bit more solemn, though the high notes of the flute seemed happy.

"It makes me think of fairies," Hannah said.

"Oh," Elsie clapped her hands, "'tis the stone-passin' tune."

"Stone passing?" Hannah looked up from fussing with the wreath-like crown of purple heather on Eleanor's head.

Rory turned, careful not to disturb her own laurel of rare white heather. "'Tis an auld custom. The folks below are givin' their good wishes and blessin's onto the stones. We'll place our hands on them when we say our vows."

Hannah declared Eleanor ready and stepped back to admire her work.

"You are both beautiful brides," Mary beamed at them.

"We should go down now," Fenella said. "I hear the first drones of the bag-pipes warming up."

***

KEIR SCOLDED JACK and Logan when he saw the look in their eyes. "Och, ye'll nay be thinkin' of yer tricks."

179

Jack's face scrunched up. "But we kept the McDoons from comin' and doin' the blackenin' on ye. Ye must let us do the shootin'."

"Ye'll nay do it durin' the vows. Ye'll give me bride a fright. The English ways are different. Eleanor dinnae ken aboot the feet washin' or the blackenin of the bride and groom. Though she'll see it when comes yer turn."

"The piper stopped." Logan gave his brother a rather hard cuff on the arm. "The evil spirits are chased away. Ye'll have guid luck now, brother."

Keir huffed. "'Tis luck, to be sure, to find a woman like El, to love her and have her love ye back. Ye two should be so lucky."

A strange, vaguely hostile look passed between Logan and Jack.

Keir nodded to the other group of men. Rennie, his brother and another friend, nodded back. Rennie stepped forward, his groomsmen on either side of him, and started walking behind the first bag-piper up through the guests. The McKelveys watched.

Also watching from the side was Laird McKelvey. He strode over to his sons and embraced Keir, patted him heartily on the back without a word, then went into the castle. He reemerged a moment later with his daughters. The married girls went first and Rory clung to her father's arm, but kept her eyes fixed on Rennie, now standing under a floral canopy.

Once the first wedding party was settled in their places, Keir said, "'Tis our turn, lads." He took a deep breath and touched the plaid draped over his left shoulder, pinned in place with Eleanor's wedding gift to him: her brooch. Logan and Jack fell in behind a second bag-piper and Keir followed.

***

ELEANOR PRESSED HER hands to her ears. "Why are they so loud?"

Her mother laughed. "Ye get used to it. Are bagpipes still banned in England?"

Eleanor and Hannah nodded together. The castle door opened and the skirl of the pipes was louder yet. Laird McKelvey slipped in, his expression a confusing mix of pride, love, and sorrow.

"Are ye ready, lass? Me sons are under the arch."

"She's ready," Mary said. She handed Eleanor a bouquet and took Hannah's arm. They went out and Eleanor put her arm in the Laird's. He patted it, looked down at his kilt then at her dress, and complimented her. "Ye're a bonnie lass, Eleanor, and ye wear the McKelvey colors well. 'Twill be an honor to call ye daughter."

Eleanor's tongue cleaved to the roof of her mouth. She swallowed hard. "Thank you." Her lashes fluttered and she teared up. Blinking fast, she walked out with him and immediately saw a mass of unfamiliar faces staring at her. But up front stood the most important people in her life.

They began to walk over a trail of crushed petals. She heard her name in hushed whispers despite the overwhelming and distinctive sounds of the bagpipes. She recognized Colin's voice and little Huey and then there was one voice she had to force her eyes off Keir to look for. She gasped and smiled. Another gift from Keir, she thought, as she saw the round, plump face of Cook from Ingledew smiling back at her.

Halfway down the aisle time seemed to slow. The bagpipes faded and all she heard was her own heartbeat. All she saw was Keir's face.

***

KEIR NEARLY DROPPED the blessing stone the last guest passed to him. It was one from the cairn he'd made at his mother's grave, where he'd gone early this morning. He thought reciting their promises holding this particular rock would firmly set their vows in stone and not just metaphorically.

There she was. The woman he loved. He knew she was coming forward on his father's arm, but he only saw her.

Looking more beautiful than ever.

Wearing McKelvey tartan colors. The most Scottish dress he'd ever seen on a woman.

Her hair like a flower garden.

Her cheeks aglow.

Her eyes sparkling.

His own eyes went blurry. He blinked hard, felt the warm tears trail down his face.

"Eleanor," he whispered. He took her hand from his father's arm, barely acknowledging the Laird's presence. The bagpipes finished with a diminishing hum, leaving the silence broken only by the sound of Keir whispering, "I love you."

They stood facing one another under the arch of flowers as Rennie and Rory swore their oaths. When it was Keir and Eleanor's turn, he held the stone out in one hand and she placed both of hers on it. He covered them with his right hand and they made their pledges.

The ceremony was blessed by the religious officiate and deemed completed.

***

ELEANOR KNEW HER mother had helped make a *bridescake* and she knew its significance and to expect someone to break it over her head. It would mean a fruitful marriage if it broke into small pieces. What she didn't expect was the roar of the crowd upon the ending of the ceremony or the blasts of gunfire from several pistols.

She saw Elsie appear at Rory's side and in the same instant Fenella came to Eleanor. Both sisters had shortbread cakes in their hands and broke them in unison over the brides' heads. Crumbs caught in her hair and flowers, fell to her shoulders, and scattered to the ground in a hundred tiny pieces. She looked down and laughed. Keir also laughed, caught her in his arms, and kissed her with abandon. The guests cheered. Several rushed forward to elbow each other for a lucky crumb.

"They'll nay miss us at the feast," Keir said in her ear, "and I intend to indulge in some houghmagandie with me new wife." He scooped her into his arms, carried her through the shouting crowd and into the castle.

He took the stone steps two at a time, passed her room, and carried her into his. The suite was filled with vases of flowers, trays of food, and enough water and wine to last the wedding week. He set her gently on the bed then barred the door.

THE END

Up next: book 2 in the Loved by a Highlander series, THE HIGHLANDER'S ENGLISH MAIDEN. Hannah's story is next and starts a while back, at the kirk where Eleanor disappears. Both younger McKelvey brothers are drawn to Hannah; Logan still thinks she's a lad pretending to be a lady, while Jack thinks she's a lady pretending to be a princess to cover for Eleanor's absence. Hannah's heart beats wildly around both of them, but she knows she's too far beneath their status to hope for anything more than a dalliance. When she at last acknowledges which brother owns her heart, she's ready to risk banishment for a chance with him. Then rival Dylan McDoon comes into the picture to put everyone's future in jeopardy.

Order your copy on Amazon.

And if you haven't already, please leave a review for this book on Amazon.

MORE BOOKS by this author writing under the pen names of Debra Chapoton, Boone Patchard, and Marlisa Kriscott:

Young adult to Adult:

THE HIGHLANDER'S SECRET PRINCESS
THE HIGHLANDER'S ENGLISH MAIDEN
THE HIGHLANDER'S HIDDEN CASTLE
THE HIGHLANDER'S HEART OF STONE
THE HIGHLANDER'S FORBIDDEN LOVE

Unbridled Hearts – Sweet Cowboy Romance
TANGLED IN FATE'S REINS
RODEO ROMANCE
A COWBOY'S PROMISE
HEARTSTRINGS AND HORSESHOES
KISSES AT SUNDOWN
MONTANA HEAVEN
MONTANA MOMENTS
TAMED HEART
WRANGLER'S EMBRACE
MOONLIGHT AND SPURS
WHISPERS ON THE RANGE

Second Chance Teacher Romance – Christian romance series written under the pen name Marlisa Kriscott:
AARON AFTER SCHOOL
SONIA'S SECRET SOMEONE
MELANIE'S MATCH
SCHOOL'S OUT
SUMMER SCHOOL
THE SPANISH TUTOR
A NOVEL THING

EDGE OF ESCAPE Psychological Thriller - Innocent adoration escalates to stalking and abduction in this psychological thriller. SOMMERFALLE is the German version of EDGE OF ESCAPE

THE GUARDIAN'S DIARY Young Adult Coming of Age - Jedidiah, a 17-year-old champion skateboarder with a defect he's been hiding all of his life, must risk exposure to rescue a girl that's gone missing.

SHELTERED Young Adult Paranormal - Ben, a high school junior, has found a unique way to help homeless teens, but he must first bring the group together to fight against supernatural forces.

A SOUL'S KISS Young Adult Paranormal - When a tragic accident leaves Jessica comatose, her spirit escapes her body. Navigating a supernatural realm is tough, but being half dead has its advantages. Like getting into people's thoughts. Like taking over someone's body. Like experiencing romance on a whole new plane - literally.

EXODIA Dystopian Biblical Retelling - By 2093 American life is a strange mix of failing technologies, psychic predictions, and radiation induced abilities. Tattoos are mandatory to differentiate two classes, privileged and slave. Dalton Battista fears that his fading tattoo is a deadly omen. He's either the heir of the brutal tyrant of the new capital city, Exodia or he's its prophesied redeemer.

OUT OF EXODIA In this sequel to EXODIA, Dalton Battista takes on his prophesied identity as Bram O'Shea. When this psychic teen leads a city of 21st century American survivalists out from under an oppressive regime, he puts the escape plan at risk by trusting the mysterious god-like David Ronel.

THE GIRL IN THE TIME MACHINE Young Adult Time Travel - A desperate teen with a faulty time machine. What could go wrong? 17-year-old Laken is torn between revenge and righting a wrong. Sci-Fi suspense.

THE TIME BENDER Young Adult Alien Sci-Fi - A stolen kiss could put the universe at risk. Selina doesn't think Marcum's spaceship is anything more than one heck of a science project … until he takes her to the moon and back.

THE TIME PACER Young Adult Alien Sci-Fi - Alex discovered he was half-alien right after he learned how to manipulate time. Now he has to fight the star cannibals, fly a space ship, work on his relationship with Selina, and stay clear of Coreg, full-blooded alien rival and possible galactic traitor. Once they reach their ancestral planet all three are plunged into a society where schooling is more than indoctrination

THE TIME STOPPER Young Adult Alien Sci-Fi - Young recruit Marcum learns battle-craft, infiltration and multiple languages at the Interstellar Combat Academy. He and his arch rival Coreg jeopardize their futures by exceeding the space travel limits and flying to Earth in search of a time-bender. They find Selina whose ability to slow the passage of time will be invaluable in fighting other aliens. But Marcum loses his heart to her and when Coreg takes her twenty light years away he remains on Earth in order to develop a far greater talent than time-bending. Now he's ready to return home and get the girl.

THE TIME ENDER Young Adult Alien Sci-Fi - Selina Langston is confused about recurring feelings for the wrong guy/alien. She's pretty sure Alex is her soulmate and Coreg should not be trusted at all. But Marcum … well, when he returns to Klaqin and rescues her she begins to see him in a different light.

TO DIE UPON A KISS Gender-swapped Retelling of *Othello* - Several teenagers' lives intertwine during one eventful week full of love, betrayal and murder in this futuristic, gender-swapped retelling of Shakespeare's Othello.

HERE WITHOUT A TRACE Young Adult Parallel World - Hailey and Logan enter a parallel world through hypnosis in order to rescue a girl gone missing.

LOVE CONTAINED Christian Suspense - Trapped in a shipping container, sinking to the depths of the ocean … but this isn't the worst thing that's happened to Henry … or Max.

SPELL OF THE SHADOW DRAGON Epic Sci-Fi Fantasy - Four hundred years after colonizing a planet ruled by dragons, the future of the human race hangs in the balance once again.

CURSE OF THE WINTER DRAGON – Epic Sci-Fi Fantasy – Sequel to SPELL OF THE SHADOW DRAGON

A FAULT OF GRAVES – young adult thriller - A disastrous fall into the depths of our planet turns into a desperate fight for survival.

Non-fiction:
35 LESSONS IN THE PSALMS Ready to use Sunday School lessons and/or personal Bible Study Workbook

PRAYER JOURNAL AND BIBLE STUDY FOR MEN

PRAYER JOURNAL AND BIBLE STUDY (for women)

PRAYER JOURNAL AND BIBLE STUDY IN THE GOSPELS

GUIDED PRAYER JOURNAL FOR WOMEN

HOW TO BLEND FAMILIES This guide gives step by step advice from experienced educators and also provides several fill-in worksheets to help you resolve family relationships, deal with discipline, navigate the financials, and create a balanced family with happy people.

BUILDING BIG PINE LODGE A journal of our experiences building a full log home

CROSSING THE SCRIPTURES A Bible Study supplement for studying each of the 66 books of the Old and New Testaments.

300 PLUS TEACHER HACKS and TIPS A guide for teachers at all levels of experience with hacks, tricks, and tips to help you get and give the most out of teaching.

HOW TO HELP YOUR CHILD SUCCEED IN SCHOOL A guide for parents to motivate, encourage and propel their kids to the head of the class. Includes proven strategies and tips from teachers.

HOW TO TEACH A FOREIGN LANGUAGE Tips, advice, and resources for foreign language teachers and student teachers.

200 CREATIVE WRITING PROMPTS WORKBOOK
400 CREATIVE WRITING PROMPTS WORKBOOK
ADVANCED CREATIVE WRITING PROMPTS WORKBOOK
BEYOND CREATIVE WRITING PROMPTS

BRAIN POWER PUZZLES Volume 1
Stretch yourself by solving anagrams, word searches, cryptograms, mazes, math puzzles, Sudoku, crosswords, daisy puzzles, boggle boards, pictograms, riddles, and more in these entertaining puzzles books.

BRAIN POWER PUZZLES Volume 2
BRAIN POWER PUZZLES Volume 3
BRAIN POWER PUZZLES Volume 4
BRAIN POWER PUZZLES Volume 5 (Spanish Student Edition)
BRAIN POWER PUZZLES Volume 6 (Math Edition)
BRAIN POWER PUZZLES Volume 7
BRAIN POWER PUZZLES Volume 8 (Bible Theme)
BRAIN POWER PUZZLES Volume 9
BRAIN POWER PUZZLES Volume 10 (Christmas Edition)
BRAIN POWER PUZZLES Volume 11 (Word Search Challenge)

Children's books:

THE SECRET IN THE HIDDEN CAVE 12-year-old Missy Stark and her new friend Kevin Jackson discover dangerous secrets when they explore the old lodge, the woods, the cemetery, and the dark caves beneath the lake. They must solve the riddles and follow the clues to save the old lodge from destruction.

MYSTERY'S GRAVE After Missy and Kevin solved THE SECRET IN THE HIDDEN CAVE, they thought the rest of the summer at Big Pine Lodge would be normal. But there are plenty of surprises awaiting them in the woods, the caves, the stables, the attic and the cemetery. Two new families arrive and one family isn't human.

BULLIES AND BEARS In their latest adventure at Big Pine Lodge, Missy and Kevin discover more secrets in the caves, the attic, the cemetery and the settlers' ruins. They have to stay one step ahead of four teenage bullies, too, as well as three hungry bears. This summer's escapades become more and more challenging for these two twelve-year-olds. How will they make it through another week?

A TICK IN TIME 12-year-old Tommy MacArthur plunges into another dimension thanks to a magical grandfather clock. Now he must find his way through a strange land, avoid the danger lurking around every corner, and get back home. When he succeeds, he dares his new friend Noelle to return with him, but who and what follows them back means more trouble and more adventure.

BIGFOOT DAY, NINJA NIGHT When 12-year-old Anna skips the school fair to explore the woods with Callie, Sydney, Austin, and Natalie, they find evidence of Bigfoot. No way! It looks like his tracks are following them. But that's not the worst part. And neither is stumbling upon Bigfoot's shelter. The worst part is they get separated and now they can't find Callie or the path that leads back to the school.
In the second story Luke and his brother, Nick, go on a boys only camping trip, but things get weird and scary very quickly. Is there a ninja in the woods with them? Mysterious things happen as day turns into night.

THE TUNNEL SERIES 12-year-old Nick escapes from a reformatory but gets side-tracked traveling through multiple tunnels, each with a strange destination. He must find his way home despite barriers like invisibility. When he teams up with Samantha they begin to uncover the secret to all the tunnels. (6 books in series)

Printed in Great Britain
by Amazon

41196322R00109